Claws

Claws

a novel by

Ozzie Cheek

Premier Digital Publishing - Los Angeles

PREMIER
DIGITAL PUBLISHING

Published by Premier Digital Publishing

www.PremierDigitalPublishing.com

Follow us on Twitter @PDigitalPub

Follow us on Facebook: Premier Digital Publishing

A future becomes inevitable the moment it touches the present.

Robert Goddard
Borrowed Time

For Kimberly Myers

— who believed long before
there was reason for belief

ACKNOWLEDGEMENTS

Novels are long journeys, and many people make the journey possible. No doubt, there are some that I will overlook. To them, I apologize in advance for the slight.

First and foremost I owe a debt of gratitude to Judy Coppage, my agent when I wrote for television, and after that, my manager, as I entered the nebulous world of the free-lance writer. She has put up with me for years without much to show for it. Long ago I told her a story about lions, tigers, ligers, and other animals escaping from a ramshackle compound in Idaho in 1995. Judy thought it would make a great screenplay, but I never got around to writing it. When I told her in late 2008 that I wanted to write a novel, a thriller, she reminded me of the story.

Literary agent, Julia Lord, offered a critical and observant eye. Author and teacher, Keith Abbott, edited a manuscript in need of editing. Pamela Bothwell not only proofread the book, she read it twice. Kimberly Myers read each draft of the novel, and there have been many, and offered encouragement and a home in Los Angeles so that I could escape New England winters. Other people who aided my journey include Craig Feagins, Mary Salter, Amanda Russell, Nancy de los Santos, Neil Hassall, Jane Darling, Melinda Foley, Don Sprague in Pocatello, Jack Dudley, the Gun Library Manager at Cabela's in Portland, Maine, and Jeremy Hinkle, who helped educate me about ligers and let me roam his Wild Animal Safari at Stafford, Missouri. I especially want to thank researcher Glida Bothwell, my encyclopedia about all things Idaho. Any mistakes in describing Idaho are my responsibility, not hers.

Thanks to authors Alan Jacobson and Anne Kemp for responding to unsolicited e-mails and befriending me. You might not be reading this at all were it not for Joel Gotler and for everyone at Premier Digital Publishing.

PROLOGUE

The female liger was named Kali. In Kiswahili, an African language rooted in Arabic, Kali means fierce, while the Hindu goddess, Kali, is the lord of death. Of course, Kali was unaware of her name or even that she was special.

The offspring of a male lion and a female tiger, Kali's skin was tawny but overlaid with stripes. A tiger's stripes are usually black, but apart from the tip of her tail and an oval on each ear, Kali's stripes were orangey-brown. This same hue dotted her face, while her muzzle and underbelly were white and her legs two-toned: the inside white and the outside golden-tan. Even so, it was not her color that set Kali apart. It was her size.

A male lion mating with a female tiger creates a genetic abnormality – an exotic cat fifty percent larger than either parent. Instead of the usual length of six to eight feet, Kali was more than twelve feet long, and while a lion can top five hundred pounds and a tiger six, Kali weighed nine hundred pounds. Even without a mane, her head was much larger than a lion's. Huge incisors were deeply embedded and designed to crack bone, and her four inches of sharp, pointed fangs were perfect for ripping and tearing raw meat. Her diurnal claws, over five inches long when extended, were the envy of any German cutlery manufacturer.

In all, Kali was the most powerful and deadly feline ever to walk the planet. Fortunately for the creatures of eastern Idaho, Kali did not yet know how deadly she was. Like the few other ligers in the world, Kali had been born and bred in captivity. But unlike them, Kali was now free.

The Saturday morning in mid-September when Kali appeared at the Placett family's farm was only the second day of her three-year life that she had not been caged. It also was the second day she had to hunt and to kill in order to eat, and she was hungry. Kali reached the barnyard and was approaching a coop of fluttering chickens when the startling shriek of a smoke alarm in the farmhouse kitchen sent her bounding through the open door of a shed. Minutes later, Wade Placett came outside and called for his two black Labs, missing since dawn, walked past the old smokehouse, kicked the door shut, and latched it.

The barnyard remained quiet except for the chickens until mid-morning when Mandy Placett brought out the laundry. As she was pinning the last of four sets of sheets to the clothesline, her five-year-old daughter, Tammy, cried out. "Ouch!"

"What'd you do now?" Mandy asked.

Tammy pouted. "I didn't do nothing."

"Anything. And I saw you pestering Muggles."

Tammy was swinging a ball on a string, keeping it barely out of the reach of a tan-and-white tabby boxing at it with her paws. Muggles was a two-year-old barn cat, although not a good mouser yet.

"Look! See what she did." Tammy showed her mother a thin red claw-mark on the underside of her right forearm.

"Well, I think you'll live," Mandy said.

The screendoor banged and ten-year-old Josh hopped down the porch steps, saying, "My bike's broke again, Mom." Without saying more, he trotted across the backyard to the toolshed attached to the barn. Other buildings included the chicken coop, an old smokehouse used to store feed, a woodshed, and a long, open-faced building for machinery.

"Josh knows where daddy hid the firecrackers."

"And he knows better than to mess with them too," Mandy said, while on her way to the glassed-in porch where the washer, thumping away on the spin cycle, and the dryer, used only in the winter, squatted along the interior wall.

Outside, Muggles suddenly hissed and arched her back. Her hair shot up like she had been zapped by electricity. "Bad, bad kitty," Tammy said. She thumped the cat in the face with the swinging ball. Muggles leaped a foot in the air and the instant she landed darted across the dusty earth and spotty grass toward the old smokehouse.

"Don't let her in my chicken feed again," Mandy called from the porch. Although they piled rocks and firewood chunks to plug the holes where the gray planks had rotted away, the cat somehow managed to slip into the shed.

"Come back kitty," Tammy pleaded as Muggles squeezed through an impossibly small opening. "Stupid cat."

"Go get her, Tammy." A minute later when the washer stopped, Mandy heard the chickens flap and screech as Tammy ran past their coop, calling for Muggles. "Josh, come help your sister," Mandy shouted. "Cat's in the feedshed."

"Okay, Mom," he yelled back. Josh pulled a string of firecrackers out of a wooden box that set beside a wrench on the old plank workbench. "Cool," he said to himself.

"Here kitty, kitty," Tammy said when she reached a wooden shed that had been built for curing meats but now smelled like dry corn and manure. "Come're, kitty."

Even from the back porch, Mandy heard the sound - a loud and painful meow suddenly cut short by – by what?

"Mug-gles." Tammy tiptoed to reach the latch that secured the plank door and nudged it open. "Here kitty."

"Tammy, wait!" Mandy hollered as she slammed open the screendoor and in her hurry only toe-tapped the steps.

"I can do it, Momma. I'm a big girl now." Tammy peered inside the shed. "Here kitty, kitty." From out of the dark she heard a deep, guttural sound. "Kitty?"

"Tammy! No!" Mandy yelled, rushing to her daughter.

Josh opened the toolshed door and slid a wood match across the striker of the red matchbox.

"Kitty? Where are you?" Tammy said in a near-whisper, opening the smokehouse door wider. "C'mere, kitty."

Kali's head appeared out of shadows. The liger's head was a hundred times larger than the tabby's. Her huge amber eyes glowed. Her white muzzle and long whiskers were smeared with fresh blood. The giant cat flashed red-stained teeth and loosed a spine shivering sound. Tammy screamed and Josh, at the same moment, lit the fuse and tossed out the firecrackers.

"Tammy!" cried Mandy.

Tammy screamed again as a stream of urine ran down her legs. POW-POW-POW! The exploding firecrackers danced across the ground, while Kali sprang straight toward Tammy.

ONE

Jackson Hobbs was an inch taller than average and still fit at forty-two, although struggling to keep his waist within two inches of where it had been a dozen years ago. Dressed in worn black jeans, cobalt blue shirt, and black Blundstone boots, there was nothing about him that suggested the stereotype rural cop, not even with the scar. A burn scar began at his hairline and ran down his neck before turning onto his right shoulder. When it began to itch, Jackson shifted his head away from the sun. He resisted the urge to rub the scar. It never helped.

The 2008 black Grand Cherokee that Jackson drove as Chief of Police was parked by the east bleachers, near Ed Stevens' patrol car. Both men leaned against the Jeep while watching the Saturday football scrimmage. Beyond the Buckhorn High School playing field, dotted with red and white practice jerseys, eight girls in red skirts and sweaters, the word *Antlers* in white across the chest, practiced dance routines and cheers. A teacher in sweats prowled the sidelines shouting encouragement.

Jackson didn't care much for football and even less for cheerleading, but Jesse, his fifteen-year-old, needed to know that he supported her, especially since she had become a cheerleader mostly to appease her mother. Iris, Jackson's ex-wife, was Buckhorn town mayor and his boss.

On the field the huddle broke and the linemen dropped into formation, the quarterback barked signals, and the center delivered the ball. Shane Tapper, a tall and lithe receiver, jogged out of the backfield and then spun right and sprinted toward the sideline. The southpaw quarterback threw a perfect spiral. As Shane reached for the ball, Jesse, now only ten feet away, cartwheeled past him: red skirt flapping, white briefs shining, red and white sweater blurring, bare midriff and legs beckoning. The football skimmed through Shane's hands and hit him in the chest. A second later the defensive back knocked him to the ground.

Coach Pettigrew waddled up to Shane with surprising speed for a fat man. "Damn it, Shane," he said, helping the boy to his feet, "if you'd watch the ball instead of your girlfriend's butt, maybe we'd win a few more games." The coach gave three sharp whistles to end the practice.

Jackson gave in and rubbed the burn scar. "Guess we should go fight crime," he said absently. When Ed didn't respond, Jackson glanced over at him. Ed's head bobbed like an infant's, like it was too big to be supported by the body beneath it. Before radiation and chemotherapy, Ed Stevens had been a robust, short man. Now the blue uniform hung on him like he was playing dress-up. "Ed?"

"Short practice today."

"No reason for you to be out here. We'll cover it."

2

Ed pulled himself free of the Jeep. "Oh hell, I'm okay, just a little sleepy is all. Used to be, I slept like a baby, but now I wake up two, three times a night. Always dreaming too, the same damn thing over and over."

Although Jackson said nothing, he nodded his head to let Ed know that he was familiar with bad dreams.

"I dream something's chasing me. A monster with a man's body and a bird's head or a woman's head on a lion's body – crazy things." Ed reached into his shirt pocket. His hand came away empty. "Damn smokes are killing me, but I still miss them." He paused in thought. "I saw these pictures once, Jackson. Some guy painted the monsters I see in my dreams. What I keep asking myself is why me."

"We all dream, all the time. We just don't remember."

"Maybe so, but how come we mostly remember the bad ones? Why not dreams where we go fishing all day and your beer stays cold and elk walk right up to you and TV shows actually make you laugh? You know what my wife says? Eileen says the dreams are God writing me a warning ticket. What do you think about that?"

"Ed, I think you're about the best man I know."

The radio in Jackson's car crackled with static and then, "Chief Hobbs, what's your ten-twenty? Over."

"And I think Eileen spends too much time in church," Jackson said, moving toward the squawking radio.

Ed grinned. "Bosch. Like the spark plugs. That's the name. The guy that painted the creatures from hell."

Jackson removed the microphone from the holder in the Jeep. "Jackson here. What've you got, Sadie?"

"It's Mandy Placett. Said she found a monster cat in one of their sheds. Said it was long as a car. Over."

"Be a hell of a mountain lion half that size," Jackson said. "Anyway, she should call Fish and Game."

"The thing jumped right over little Tammy. She said her boy set off firecrackers to scare the tiger away. Over."

"Sadie, I know when you're done talking. What tiger?"

"Tiger, lion. She wasn't exactly sure. But you're their neighbor, Jackson, and the law. So she called you."

Jackson clicked the transmit button. "Who's free?"

"Angie responded to a four-fifteen-f, and Tucker, he's at the cafe trying to sweet-talk Suzy Beans into bed. He should be out with a radar gun at junction thirty-four."

Jackson looked at Ed to see if he had reacted to Sadie's commentary about officer Tucker Thule, his nephew. All Ed did was point to his own chest and grin.

"See if Angie needs backup on the domestic. And tell Tucker he's got ten minutes to get out to the highway. I'll take care of the monster cat. And Sadie, call Stilts or somebody else at Fish and Game, let them know."

"Roger that, Chief. Over and out."

Jackson replaced the microphone but stayed in the car. "If you won't go home, you may as well come with me."

"With you?" Ed tapped his watch. It hung loose on his wrist. "Don't you have a meeting to go to?"

"Damn!" Jackson stared into space, and then he said, "You go. You're better at dealing with them anyway."

"Probably true, but you're the chief now, not me."

Before the cancer Ed had been Chief of Police and Jackson Deputy Chief. A year later Jackson still wasn't comfortable with the role reversal. Neither was half the town. "They'll give me shit for not wearing my uniform."

"Just make sure you wear your gun. Town council, you never know if you'll need it," Ed said and chuckled.

Beyond Ed, Jackson noticed his daughter coming across the field. She had swapped her cheerleading outfit for jeans, boots, a t-shirt, and a fleece vest – an Idaho cowgirl uniform. Already five-eight, she was slender in that tight-skinny jeans-that-forgive-nothing-way only certain high school girls can be. While watching her approach, Jackson said, "So what do you think Mandy saw?"

"A big-ass mountain lion," Ed said.

"Except they don't look much like a tiger."

"Then there's only one thing it could be, but I sure hope she's wrong. We're cops, not big-game hunters."

"You know the Cheneys better than me. If one of their cats got out, would Ted come let us know?"

Ed shrugged. "They ain't lost one before."

Jackson turned from watching his daughter to looking at Ed again. "Not that we know of, you mean."

"I was there a while back," Ed said. "They're fixing it all up. Building a brand new, big cage. A real one."

"Huh! I thought they were poor as church mice."

"I asked Ted if they were finally gettin' all their permits. He told me to mind my own business."

Jackson knew the Cheneys discouraged visits until the safari park business was open, and they could sell tickets to view their exotic cats. "Maybe it is our business," he said and then added, "Jesse's coming. Right behind you."

Ed swiveled to look at her, and Jesse, some twenty feet away, waved and said, "Hi, mister Stevens. Daddy."

"Now how'd you get so pretty, Jesse?" Ed said. "Look at her, Jackson. She's just like her mother."

"I hope not," Jesse said softly but not soft enough.

"Jessica!"

"Sorry, Dad."

"One of us should go check it out," Jackson told Ed.

"Yep. Me."

"Check what out?" Jesse asked.

"Police business. You feel like doing it, Ed, then go on. Stop at Ted and Dolly's place too. Humor me."

"You got it, Chief." Ed moved as briskly as possible toward a black police cruiser with blue lettering. As he did, he grinned at Jesse. "So how's that gelding of yours?"

"Ready to beat them purebred Arabians."

"I bet he is." Ed laughed. "Got a real cowgirl here, Jackson. Must be doing something right." He was still grinning as he slid into the Ford Crown Vic and drove off.

"Who's Ted? You mean the lion guy?" Jesse asked.

"Don't be so nosy." Jackson kissed the top of his daughter's head. "You girls looked really good out there."

"Yeah right! Sis-boom-bah."

Jackson nodded, but even he wasn't sure why.

"Daddy, after work today I want to go on a nice long ride, a good three hours or more. Get Touie out there on some steep hills. Up and down. Work him hard. Get him used to being alone again after staying at the Double-D. Then I'll be at the farm."

"Well, in that case, I'll meet you there later and we can grill some hamburgers and –"

"I can't. It's Saturday night."

"Saturday night?"

"You understand, right? You were young once."

"Was I?" Jackson, already showing gray in his hair, wrapped his daughter in a hug. "Sometimes I wonder."

Jackson circled the little park and war memorial in the downtown square, turned onto Salmon Street, and a block later parked in front of the old Tapper Elementary School. A town of four thousand located in the northern part of rural Fremont County, Buckhorn was over an hour drive from St. Anthony, the county seat in the south. Whatever wasn't handled in St. Anthony or in Boise by the state was done here in the brick building, including town council meetings.

The Buckhorn Police Department was two blocks west on Red Hawk Road in the former home of an auto dealership. Instead of a showroom it now housed a 'bullpen', Jackson's office, a storage room, a tiny break room, and a large bathroom. There were no cells. Prisoners were escorted to St. Anthony or even Rexburg. On occasion someone was handcuffed briefly to a desk. Ed had tossed a few drunks in the storage room on a cot. Jackson had five *blue-pin* officers with full academy training and four reserve officers, people with other jobs and much less training. In Fremont County his officers were more likely to handle a car wreck than a shooting, more likely to bust beer-breath teenagers than they were burglars. There was an anti-government group rumored to exist in the area, but for the most part infidelity and not insurrection made up the bulk of town gossip. Of course everybody talked about money and jobs. Everybody felt the squeeze of The Great Recession.

Jackson notified Sadie that he was 10-7, but even after going out of service, he continued to sit and stare at the brick building. He had been in Idaho five years, having arrived with a wife, a gangly ten-year-old, and a new job as Ed's Deputy Chief. His wife was now his ex, his daughter training for the country's hardest endurance race, and he was Chief of Police. "Sis-boom-bah," he muttered.

TWO

Four miles north of Buckhorn on county road 34, Ed slowed to a crawl behind a green combine hogging the two-lane asphalt, even though Med Fedder steered far onto the shoulder. When the double-yellow line ended, the farmer signaled to Ed. He pulled out and, seeing no traffic, gunned the Ford. He beeped and waved as he passed.

A mile farther Ed met Idaho State Police trooper, Ronnie Greathouse, coming from Med's place. He knew Ronnie was seeing Maryann Fedder. Med's oldest girl had been in a wheelchair for the past three years, since a horse threw her and cracked her spine. Ed also knew that Ronnie and Tucker, his nephew, his sister Agnes' boy, both belonged to a white power, anti-government, militia group. If Med ever found out, Ronnie would not be welcome at the Fedder house, regardless of Maryann's wishes. All in all, Ed figured a crippled thirty-year-old country girl didn't have a line of men outside the door. Med would not find out from him.

While keeping his eyes on the road, Ed felt along the driver's seat for the Marlboro pack. He thumped the box and pulled a cigarette with his lips, leaned forward, and lit it with a match. He inhaled the smoke deeply and then, after lowering the window, slowly let it escape, the way he had learned to do it when he was young and invincible.

He always figured death would come as a surprise, not a trip he planned in advance, but once the doctors agreed not to tell Eileen how little time he had left, dying had become just another secret to keep. He had kept so many: hater's secrets, killer's secrets, and lover's secrets. A town has many secrets that only a cop knows, some that only the Chief of Police knows. For a while Ed wasn't sure if he would share his cache. He wasn't sure Jackson would stick around long enough, and town secrets shouldn't travel too far. Now, he felt relieved finally to shed them.

Ed finished his cigarette and started to toss it out before remembering the drought. The winter and spring had been wet and the spring growth lush. But it had been a hot, dry summer. Given a chance, the fields and forests would flame like a barn filled with straw. He dropped the butt on the floor mat and squished it with his shoe.

Before long Ed swapped the blacktop for a gravel road that snaked past Jackson's farm. The dust he kicked up forced him to close the car window. He had already written one letter to leave behind, revealing the secret Jackson most needed to know. Tonight, I'll write another, he thought, and tell him about Tucker and Ronnie and some other secrets too. Just one thing Jackson has wrong, Ed told himself as he turned onto the rutted dirt road to the Placett farm - it's him, not me, that's the better man.

* * *

When Jackson entered the meeting room, the talk died abruptly. Jackson nodded a greeting to the four council members seated around two folding tables set end-to-end: Fred Bulcher, owner of a gravel and sand business; Pamela Yow, head librarian and Buckhorn's self-appointed moral compass; Neil Fennis, owner of the Sportsman Motel; and Clancy Anderson, a retired railroad man. Iris, the town mayor, was at the head of the table. She once had been Iris Hobbs but returned to using Inslay – Iris Inslay.

At age forty-one Iris still turned heads. While other women might be pretty, Iris was exotic. Petite and Mediterranean dark, her lush brown hair almost black, she claimed to be Portuguese-American. In truth, she was part Mexican and part German-Mormon, but being Mexican didn't help the ambitious in Idaho, even if being Mormon did.

Jackson took the empty chair across from Dell Tapper. Besides owning the Bank of Buckhorn, a town institution since the 1930s, he was the father of Jesse's boyfriend. As far as Jackson was concerned, Dell also was the man responsible for ending his marriage, although Iris, seated between them, would certainly disagree.

"We all know how busy Chief Hobbs is," Iris said, her words conveying sarcasm without too much offense, "so let's move on to the police department's budget."

Due to the sparse population in northern Fremont County and the location of the county sheriff's office in the southernmost part, Buckhorn police officers held a cross-deputy commission that gave them full law enforcement powers outside city limits. In return, part of the department's operating budget came from the county, and Buckhorn currently had more officers than the county seat did. The town and the county were at odds about money.

"Well, to start with," Neil Fennis said, "none of us have a problem with the job you're doing as chief."

"Or with your officers," Pamela said.

"Who at least wear their uniforms," Clancy said.

"Tell me, Jackson," Dell said before Clancy could continue, "how many people did you arrest yesterday?"

"One. Billy Frasier. His third DUI."

"Any unsolved murders?"

"Not that I know of."

"How about car-jackings? Gangs? Drug cartels?"

"What's your point, Dell?"

"His point," Iris said, "is serious crime almost never happens here. But our budget doesn't reflect that."

Some of the council members muttered agreement or nodded their head. The town had money problems, and Jackson knew they wanted to cut his budget.

"You haven't been here as long as most of us," Dell told Jackson. A year older than Iris, Dell had been her high school sweetheart. He was a big man, fifteen pounds too heavy now, who wore western-cut suits and Paul Bond custom boots. He also wore contacts, but kept it a secret. Dell continued: "Used to be we had timber and farming and cattle. But now we live and die on tourism. Summertime we get fishermen and campers and hikers, and in the fall we get hunters. We count on them spending money. The State figures every deer shot is worth four thousand dollars; every elk, six thousand; a bear's worth five; and so on. But if hunters aren't hunting and fishermen don't fish, our cash flow dries up. We all know what this summer was like and the couple of years before this one. People are hurting and staying home. They're not coming here."

"Amen to that," said Neil, the motel owner. "I can tell you right now, my reservations for hunting season are half of what they were ten years ago. Half!"

"I'm a hunter. You all know that," Dell said. "Fact is the deer and elk and antelope aren't what they once were. Blame global warming or blame the feds for dumping gray wolves on us and them killing off our game or -"

Fred Bulcher, who resembled the wrestler that had been governor of Minnesota, piped up with a spew of complaints about the government. Iris finally shut him up just as he got to the Jews and homosexuals ruining the country.

"We've talked it over," Iris said, indicating the town council members, "and we want you to cut a position."

"You mean fire somebody," Jackson said. "Like who?"

For a second nobody spoke, and then Iris said, "How many days last month did Ed work?"

"More than he should have," Jackson said.

"I pray for him every day," Pamela offered.

Iris shuffled some papers until the one she wanted surfaced. "Paid full-time, worked half, that sound right?"

"Ed was Chief of Police here for twenty years."

"Nobody likes doing this, Jackson," Neil, the motel owner, said. His nose was etched with red lines from a lifetime of drinking. "But Ed can draw a pension now anyway, and he's the most expensive officer."

"Apart from you," Clancy added.

"There's got to be another way."

"There isn't," Dell said. "We've looked. And so has the county. We agree on this."

"Agreeing doesn't make it right," Jackson told them.

"Look at the bright side," Iris said, "if we make a mistake, you get to tell us about it. And you will."

Dell looked at Iris and Iris at Jackson. Jackson looked at the gray Riverton hat he had laid on the table when he sat down. Everybody in the room knew that Jackson and Iris were talking about mistakes already made.

A Kinder's Sav-On grocery bag set on the hood of Ed's cruiser. Mandy had provided the bag and the empty shoebox inside it to use for the remains of the cat. She hadn't actually seen Muggles' body, she admitted, but she still knew the cat was dead. Ed removed a Colt M4 tactical rifle from the trunk of the Ford. The M4 was a version of the M16 he had carried in Vietnam. He inserted a ten-round magazine of Remington .223 cartridges, although the M4 held up to 30 rounds, and went around the house.

It was not until he saw Josh waving to him from the back porch that Ed remembered the grocery bag on the hood. The M4 was in his left hand, so he flipped a wave at the boy with his right. He could go back for the shoebox if he needed it, Ed thought. The odds were he wouldn't need it. Mountain lions didn't usually leave much of a cat or dog behind. The Placett's dogs were missing too, and that bothered him. A pair of Labs weren't that easy to kill.

Ed stopped beside the remains of some firecrackers. From there he watched the door on the old smokehouse bang open and shut. Mandy had told him that a giant cat leaped out of the smokehouse and ran across the barnyard and into the barley field to his right. He scanned the tall, golden grains rippling in the wind but saw nothing else moving.

A moment later he caught the door of the smokehouse and pinned it open with a dusty shoe. With the stock of the M4 snug against his right shoulder and his finger on the trigger, he peered inside. Bags of feed were stacked thigh high, while empty bags littered the floor. The wind kited one of the empty bags, and as it danced away, he spotted the little brown-and-white head lying in a puddle of blood. "Mother-of-god!" Ed exclaimed. The tabby's head had been bitten clean off. The rest of the cat was gone.

When Ed was certain nothing was hiding in the shed, he latched the door until he could return with the shoebox. If he put a stick of wood with the head and wrapped it all in a towel inside the box, maybe the kids would never know.

Ed checked the toolshed and the woodshed, peering inside both, the rifle held ready. He also peeked in the chicken coop and an open shed that housed farm equipment. He saw nothing dangerous and moved on to the barn.

At first he searched the barn from the doorway, but his eyes kept bumping into shadows that took on whatever shape his imagination sculpted, while his ears worked overtime to sort the rustles and groans whipped up by the wind. When Ed finally entered, a charge of electricity combed the hair on his arms and neck. He squeezed the M4 and swiveled the short-barreled Colt from side to side.

As he moved slowly down the center, Ed felt himself stepping on a lush jungle path instead of barnwood, smelled pungent fish sauce instead of dry manure, felt the weight of a fully automatic M16 in his hands, his body young and strong and his senses as sharp as the knife in the sheath strapped to his leg. Left. Right. Slow and careful. In the jungle the survivors move silently. Left, right, left, right, left. He heard a crunch and stopped. If it was a Bouncing Betty beneath his foot, and he moved, the landmine would explode. He looked down, but he didn't see Army boots. Instead, he saw familiar black police brogues. For a moment there, my god, it had felt so real, thought Ed, that he had tasted the danger of Vietnam again.

Ed lifted his foot and stepped back to see what was beneath it. It looked like a rabbit's foot – small, furry, and – no, not rabbit. It was a cat's paw. The realization and the sound reached him at the same time.

The animal looking down at him from a twelve-foot high overhang was neither a monster nor a fantasy. It was Ted and Dolly Cheney's road to riches – one of the giant cats intended to be the feature attraction at a drive-through safari park that federal, state, and county officials had blocked from opening. Ed had seen the liger before, one of a pair held in a disgusting cage at Safari Land. He had seen their claws shred a metal barrel and seen them chomp through frozen chickens, bones and all, like they were potato chips. He knew the huge creature was dangerous.

Ed swung the Colt M4 around as Kali lunged. Her heavy body flattened him, and his breath was squeezed out with a whoosh. Then her claws clamped his head like a vice set with spikes. A tiger has the jaw power of one thousand pounds per square inch, and lions and tigers often kill their prey by severing the spinal cord. Kali's bite had far more power, enough to break open a bowling ball. When she bit Ed's neck, his bones snapped like dry twigs.

Ed's final thought was about the cigarette butt left on the mat of his police car. He had failed to pick it up and throw it out. That secret he had planned to keep.

THREE

Jackson heard Iris call to him as he neared the Jeep and turned to see her approaching. She wore suede boots, a khaki skirt that brushed their tops, and a thin, cream sweater that clung to her curves. He felt the same jumbled emotions he always felt when his eyes remembered her body.

"You didn't make any friends in there, you know," Iris said. She stopped two feet away from Jackson.

"Ed has a lot of friends in there."

"The town is broke, Jackson. We may have to borrow money just to make it through the fiscal year."

"Well, don't forget you sleep with the banker."

"And don't forget I'm your boss either." After Iris had said it, she looked away. She couldn't let him goad her. She couldn't afford a public fight, not in her town. Iris had come to Buckhorn when she was eight. That's when her father retired from the railroad in Pocatello and moved the family north. She had remained here until Dell broke her heart, and she begged her parents to send her away to college in Colorado. Fort Collins, Colorado is where her romance with Jackson began and for her where it had ended. "We need to talk about Jesse. You seen her today?"

Jackson nodded. "At the football field."

The purse strapped across Iris' left shoulder had somebody's initials artfully splashed across it. She reached inside the bag. When she brought her hand out, she showed Jackson the purple foil wrapper of a condom.

"Thanks, Iris, but I don't really need one."

She jiggled her hand. "This was in Jesse's dresser."

"You searched our daughter's room?"

"She's fifteen, Jackson."

"And what'd Jesse say about it?"

Iris shook her head and let her hand drop back to her side. "If I try to talk to her … you know what'll happen."

"Maybe she found it at school."

"There were a dozen more just like this one."

Jackson tried to think like a detective instead of a father but found that he could not do it. "Jesus!"

"I told you, she'll do anything to spite me."

"Even have sex? I kind of doubt that."

"Well, you were never a teenage girl, Jackson." Iris held out her hand again. "So you going to help or not?"

"I'll talk to her." He took the condom. Iris smiled, and Jackson thought about how even her smallest smile oozed sexuality, whether she wanted it to or not. "I'm not going to fire Ed," he told her.

Iris turned and walked away.

*   *   *

When Jackson entered the police station, Sadie Pope, the civilian secretary, dispatcher, and reporter of local police news for the county's weekly newspaper, was reading the final Harry Potter book. She had waited weeks to get it from the library. "Ed come back yet?" he asked her.

"Nope," Sadie said, putting down the book. "He called in his ten-twenty, oh, say thirty minutes ago. Last I heard from him." Although most law enforcement agencies were using plain language instead of codes now, Sadie was a holdout. She had spent too much time learning them, she said, to ignore them. "Want me to try his radio?"

"I'll call his cell phone. Ed never keeps the damn radio on. Not the one he wears anyway." Jackson picked up the closest office telephone. "So how's Harry doing?"

"The usual, saving the world."

He punched in the number. "Sounds like a tough job."

Sadie grinned. "Oh, you could do it, you had to."

Ed's cell phone rang until it went to voice mail. "Sadie, what's Wade and Mandy's number?" He lowered the phone and waited for Sadie to check the county phone book that was barely a half-inch thick and much of that due to advertisements. Fewer than twelve thousand people lived in Fremont County. Some people didn't have a landline; some didn't have a phone. Jackson called the number Sadie gave him. After two rings a boy answered. "This is Chief Hobbs," Jackson said. He tried to remember the name of the older Placett boy. He covered the phone with his hand and asked Sadie. She mouthed the name. "Josh, is that you?"

"Uh-huh," the boy said.

"You know Deputy-Chief Ed Stevens, Josh?"

"He's looking for Muggles. Our dogs are gone too."

"Is he there right now?"

"I guess."

Jackson didn't like the sound of it. "What about your mom? Could you ask her to come to the phone?"

Moments later, officer Angie Kuka, a Blackfoot from Browning, Montana, entered the station while Jackson was listening to Mandy tell him that Ed had gone out back to look for the monster cat, but she hadn't seen him since. Angie saw the frown wrinkling Jackson's face, and she quietly laid down the clipboard containing the Lead Sheet Report she had written after answering a family dispute call at the Slater doublewide.

"Stay inside," Jackson said. "I'm on my way."

"What's happening?" Angie asked when Jackson hung up.

"Some kind of big cat on the prowl. Ed went to check it out and he ... I need to see what's going on."

"Want me to ride along?"

"No," Jackson said, already moving toward the door. "Stay here. You can play chief."

Angie patted her mouth and gave a mock Indian war cry.

When Jackson arrived at the Placett house, the first thing he did was inspect Ed's patrol car: a grocery bag and a shoebox sat atop the cold hood, Ed's shotgun was secured between the seat and the dash, and a smashed cigarette butt littered the rubber mat. Jackson unlocked the trunk of the Ford and saw that the Colt M4 tactical rifle was gone. Then he went to the house and knocked on the door.

Mandy greeted him in the living room. A big, flat-screen television was on but barely audible. Sixteen-month-old Warren was asleep on the couch behind a wall of pillows, while Mandy cradled her five-year-old daughter in her lap, gently rocking back and forth. The girl was sucking her thumb. "That cat nearly scared her to death," Mandy said, explaining Tammy's regression.

"Heard anything from Ed?"

When Mandy shook her head, wisps of blond hair fell across her face. She brushed them aside. Tiny squint lines etched her eyes. Mandy was only twenty-eight, but three children and a hardscrabble country life can age a woman quickly, thought Jackson. "Maybe Josh's seen him," Mandy said. "His bedroom overlooks the back. He went up there to watch for Chief Stevens." She hesitated. "I'm sorry. I know you're Chief of Police now. It's just –"

"Hey, I still call him chief too," Jackson said and, despite being worried about Ed, he managed to grin.

"I'd yell for Josh to come down, but I don't want to wake the baby," she said. "Maybe you could –"

"Which bedroom?" Jackson asked.

Mandy told him, and Jackson climbed the stairs and knocked on the door of Josh's bedroom. When nobody responded, he knocked again. "Josh." He waited. "Josh, this is Chief Hobbs," he said in a calm voice. "Son, could I talk to you a minute?" He waited and listened.

When he didn't hear any sound in the bedroom, he tried the knob. The door opened, and Jackson stepped inside. The bedroom was empty. Jackson looked in the other two bedrooms off the hallway and then the bathroom, where he opened the shower curtain to see if Josh was hiding there, mistakenly playing hide-and-seek with him.

"Josh isn't upstairs," he told Mandy when he returned.

"Oh god no!" she said. "He's outside. What if that monster -" Her hand capped her mouth as she yelped.

* * *

Despite emergency lights mounted inside and computer equipment below the dash, Jackson wanted the Jeep to seem as much like a regular car as possible, so he did not have a security grill of any type. Because of that he did not keep his shotgun up front. The rear storage area held his M4 tactical carbine, a Stoeger P-350 shotgun, and a nylon bag with body armor, Taser, and other equipment. He selected the 12-gauge, a short-barreled pump action with a pistol grip. He filled the magazine with four slugs.

He pointed the shotgun at the ground as he skirted the house and circled around the sheets flapping in the wind. "Ed," he yelled. "Ed." He waited a few seconds and heard nothing and then shouted, "Josh? Josh, this is Chief Hobbs. Remember? We talked on the phone." When the boy didn't answer him either, Jackson knew nothing good was going to come of this. "Aw Christ," he muttered.

Jackson skipped the buildings with closed doors and instead headed toward the open barn. "Josh. Ed," he called as he neared it. He stopped outside the barn and listened. He heard noises inside, but he wasn't certain what he was hearing or what they meant. He set the rubber-padded gunstock against his shoulder. With his left hand on the grip and his right index finger on the trigger and the barrel of the shotgun leading him, he stepped inside.

He swept the gun left to right until he had covered the entire width and length of the barn. Then he reversed his movement until he returned to the starting point. The noises that Jackson began to recognize – the rustle of dry hay and some peeps – were coming from deeper inside the barn. He crept toward the

22

sounds, his eyes and the shotgun sweeping from side-to-side, passing stall after stall empty of horses and cows, until he ended up at a larger pen in the back of the barn. The noises were louder here.

Whatever it had been intended for, most likely sheep or goats, he imagined, the pen now was used for barley straw. Bales were stacked tall and deep, and the ground was carpeted with last year's straw. Some of the stalks had turned brown; most remained golden. Jackson moved his gaze up and down and left and right, but he didn't see any mountain lion or tiger. Then he realized how little he knew about how the animals would hide and hunt. The way the bales were stacked, there were dark crevices where anything smaller than a cow could hide out and attack.

As Jackson continued to examine the pen, he realized that the dark hole he saw along the floor where some straw mounded up was not a hole at all. It was a black shoe.

He inched forward until he could see dark blue cloth beneath gaps in the bales. He knew what it meant, but he didn't want to believe it. He felt his heart pound. His finger was damp against the trigger. The burn scar on his neck and shoulder itched from perspiration. He blinked rapidly. Then he saw a long, pink tail sticking out of the straw and followed it to the hairy body of a grey rat.

"Sonofabitch!" he said loudly and rushed ahead.

Without thinking about whether it was dumb or not, Jackson used the shotgun barrel to part the blanket of straw, for it was clear to him that someone or something had piled up the loose straw to cover a body. Once he removed the straw, he saw that Ed's neck was nearly severed, and then he saw the open stomach cavity where a dozen rats were feeding. His mind rapidly began shutting down to try to keep him from losing it. He heard a rustling noise behind him, and he swirled around and brought up the shotgun. Jackson was already fingering the trigger when he found himself looking down the shotgun barrel at Josh Placett squatting in a dark corner. The boy's mouth hung slack and his eyes were wild and wide and staring at the horror of the rats feeding on Ed. All the time the boy was rocking back and forth.

There was a pitchfork sticking in a pile of straw. Jackson set the shotgun aside, grabbed up the pitchfork, and swung it at the first rat he could reach. The one he hit shrieked. Half of the rats scurried off, but the other half was unwilling to leave. He raked the pitchfork over them, and one rat tumbled off and onto the floor by Jackson's foot. He stepped on its tail and raised the pitchfork. With all of his might he pinned the sonofabitch rat to the earth. The animal shrieked once and died.

When he turned back to Josh, Jackson saw that the boy hadn't moved anything but his eyes, which were now watching him. Tears ran down the boy's face and snot clotted below his nose on his lip. The peeps Jackson had heard were coming from Josh. It was all the sound he could muster.

FOUR

Officer Brian Patterson accompanied the gurney with the body bag to the ambulance. The vehicle was parked between Mandy's Chrysler minivan and Wade's ten-year-old Chevy Silverado. Jackson and Angie Kuka watched Patterson talk to the emergency medical team and then tack toward the Jeep. Jackson was sitting sideways in the drivers seat, feet resting on the sill, while Angie stood beside the open door of the black SUV. The small radios they both wore on their shirts crackled with law enforcement chatter.

Jackson's 10-74 call - officer needs assistance - to the county communication center in St. Anthony had brought all of the Buckhorn police, three Fremont County Sheriff vehicles, Ronnie Greathouse and one other State Police trooper, the ambulance, and the coroner. The area had been photographed, videotaped, sketched, secured, and processed for evidence by a county sheriff's detective.

"Where do you want them to ... where do they take Ed?" Brian asked Jackson in a calm voice. Brian had long lashes for a man and a soft, round face but was *semper fi* tough.

"The county prosecutor will want an autopsy," Jackson said. Eileen Stevens, he knew, wouldn't like that. He didn't relish trying to explain to her that under the circumstances it wouldn't much matter. "Take Ed to Madison Hospital, and we'll have Morris pick him up." Morris Mortuary had served Buckhorn for fifty years. Ed didn't deserve to be a toe-tag among strangers, Jackson thought.

While Brian Patterson returned to the ambulance, Angie said, "Tucker already went to tell his aunt Eileen so you don't have to ... I mean, Tucker's family and all."

The "and all" meant that Ed and Eileen Stevens had raised Tucker Thule after his father died in a roadhouse brawl and shootout, and his mother, a few months later, dropped the eight-year-old off for a visit while she spent the weekend with a rodeo clown and never returned.

"Christ! I almost shot that boy," Jackson said and then looked surprised to hear his thoughts spoken aloud.

"He's fine." Angie knew something but not everything about Colorado. She knew a little girl had been killed. She knew Jackson had left Fort Collins after it happened. She knew with that history, he was not just thinking about today. "Josh wasn't shot, and he didn't get eaten."

"That doesn't mean he's fine."

"Maybe not, but it means he's alive."

Jackson lapsed into another long silence before saying, "The gal from the county mental health office –"

"Becky Rebo."

"Yeah. Let's have her talk to Josh and Tammy."

"What about you, Chief? You gonna talk to her too?"

A door banged, and Wade Placett came out of his house carrying a hunting rifle. Jackson didn't bother to respond to Angie as he climbed out of the Jeep. He watched Wade approach them. At five-six, Wade was a few inches shorter than Jackson. He also was wider and more muscular. "How's your family doing?" Jackson asked once Wade drew closer.

"Tammy wet herself again," Wade told him. "And Josh, he won't talk about none of it. Not even to Mandy."

Jackson told Wade about his idea to involve Becky Rebo, and although Wade was skeptical, he didn't say no. "You going hunting?" Jackson then asked, nodding at the rifle held in the crook of Wade's arm. It was a Remington 770 Sporting Rifle with a black synthetic stock and a mounted scope. The 770 Sporting Rife was not fancy or glamorous, but slam in 7mm Remington Magnums 160 grain, and it could bring down any normal game in North America.

"Got a barley field to cut," Wade explained. "But after today, I ain't going nowhere without protection. That's for damn sure."

A few minutes later, Wade drove off. Once he was gone, Jackson said, "Officer Kuka, I'd like you to see what you can dig up on Ted and Dolly and Safari Land for us."

"So you don't think it's a mountain lion?" Angie said.

"I think we better find out what we're dealing with."

Sixteen-year-old Shane Tapper slid the black Tacoma 4X4 X-Runner to a dusty stop. The pickup truck had an extended cab, chrome exhaust tips and running boards, black overfenders, hood scoop and matching bumpers, roof-top spot lights, eighteen-inch alloy wheels, and the biggest V-6 with manual transmission the Toyota dealer could deliver. Jesse thought it was simply a Hot Wheels for teenage boys. While the dust swirled, Shane pulled Jesse toward him and nuzzled her neck. "Know what you smell like?"

"If you say horseshit, you're dead."

"Cotton candy. Remember? Pink and sticky and ...."

She felt his hand slide up her thigh. She was supposed to be excited. "Shane, don't," she said when his other hand brushed her breast. "Deborah might see us."

"So? Bunch of guys probably touched her boobs all at once." The joke was that the name Double-D Stables didn't come from Deborah Dawson's initials, but from her bra size.

It was probably funny to a ten-year-old, Jesse thought. "See you tonight, huh?" she said. She opened the door and scooted out. "I got this new shampoo from Missy. I bet that's why my neck smells like cotton candy."

"You use it anyplace else?"

"Is that all you ever think about?"

"Duh?" He smiled. He had sleepy gray eyes and an Elvis mouth. Being cute and popular and rich meant that a lot of girls were willing to do 'whatever' to be with him.

"Duh!" Jesse repeated. She shut the door, and Shane gunned the Tacoma. The rear end fishtailed. The dust it kicked up made Jesse cough. Shane always had to show off.

The Double-D Stables was known for its herd of small, sturdy pintos, a good trail horse, and Jesse stopped at a corral and gave each of the two pintos in there a carrot taken from her backpack. Afterwards, she went to the barn to begin mucking stalls. While she sat on the bench in the tack room and swapped out her riding boots for Wellingtons, she again read the notice on the wall. It offered three rules for how to train and care for horses:

- Have the right horse for what you intend to do.
- Establish a trusted relationship.
- Both the rider and the horse must be well trained.

It didn't seem that different from dating, thought Jesse.

She slipped on soft leather gloves before grabbing the wheelbarrow and wheeling it to the first stall. A single horse can drop up to forty pounds of excrement a day. As Jesse grabbed a shovel and started scooping manure, she heard the farrier working outside the barn. In addition to the Double D's herd of pintos, Touie, her dappled gray Arabian-Appaloosa gelding, was here getting shod.

Touie's name had started out as Two-A, for Arabian-Appaloosa, but it soon became the easier Touie. Horses are creatures of habit, and the gelding had been off his feed since they had brought him over in the trailer. When the shoeing was finished, Jesse would ride him home. Home?

Touie lived at the half-section farm her dad owned. Jesse had her bedroom there but spent most of her time in town with her mother. Touie had the better deal, she felt.

One pile of manure was wet and heavy, and Jesse bent at the waist to fill the shovel. As she did, a white I-Phone slid out of her pocket and plopped in the muck.

Jackson leaned against a locked metal gate that blocked the narrow dirt road to Ted and Dolly Cheney's house. To the left of the gate was a large and garishly painted sign advertising Safari Land. It featured lions and tigers and a giant cat that looked a little like both. Jackson had seen Ted's cats once or twice but didn't recall a monster cat. He always had figured the image was just an advertising gimmick. He dialed the phone number listed on the sign and got voice mail. He did not leave a message.

It occurred to Jackson that Ted and Dolly might be in town. A lot of country people did their grocery shopping, banking, and other errands on Saturday. He backed out of the turn off and pointed the Jeep toward Buckhorn.

Angie and Sadie were head-to-head when Jackson entered the station. Their conversation ended as soon as they saw him. He told Sadie to contact all the officers, including off-duty and reserve officers, and have everyone available report to his office. "Got anything yet?" he asked Angie.

"Working on it, Chief," she said.

"Brian out on patrol, Sadie?"

Sadie nodded. It was clear she had been crying.

"Have him drive around town, cruise the parking lots of the stores and the banks. Tell him to look for Ted Cheney's Dodge pickup and to call me if he sees it."

Without saying anything about Ed, Jackson went into the small office he occupied as Chief of Police. He sat down at his desk and stared at the computer on it. He had to write a report about what had happened today, and there were a thousand things that he would rather do than relive his actions of the past few hours. He could always relive his actions of a few years ago, he thought. So a thousand things better and one worse. He booted up the computer.

Angie opened the desk drawer with the file folder. A week ago she had found a provocative picture tucked in the drawer where she stored her gun while in the station. When she went home, the drawer was left empty and unlocked. The picture had been cut out of a magazine. It showed a large can of beans called Bush's Best, and above it were two girls kissing. Not exactly subtle, thought Angie.

She always explained her lack of a boyfriend by telling people that he had been killed in Iraq, but the picture in her desk was her second 'message' in a month. Who in the office knew the truth? And how? Who would enjoy harassing her: Brian, Tucker, Skip, John? The reserve officers were three men and one woman. Maybe one of them? Sadie? Jackson? Neither of them, she thought. Whoever it was, she was pissed at the picture and at herself. She had let it distract and upset her all week.

Eight people squeezed into Jackson's office while he went over the events of the day beginning with the phone call from Mandy Placett. He skipped the details of the gore he had found. He told himself he was doing it to spare Tucker, but he knew it was really to spare him. When he finished, he asked for Brian's report – nobody in town recalled having seen Ted or Dolly since Thursday – and after that he dismissed everyone except for Tucker Thule. "Close the door," he said. Tucker did. "You doing okay?"

"I still can't believe it, I guess."

"I didn't really plan for Sadie to drag you in for this, but I forgot to tell her." Ed's nephew didn't say anything. "How's Eileen doing?"

"About like you'd expect, I guess." Tucker pawed the worn carpet. Although twenty-eight and experienced, also having served as an MP in the Army, Tucker still looked like a big kid.

He had his father's East European features. "I know Uncle Ed's the one that hired me –"

"Ed hired me too."

"I guess what I'm asking is if you're gonna make any changes right off? I sort of heard you were."

For the first time in hours Jackson remembered the town council meeting. How did Tucker know what had been decided there? "No," Jackson said. "No changes."

Someone tapped softly on his door. Jackson said, "Take some time off, Tucker. Whatever you need."

Tucker thanked Jackson and opened the door and bumped chest to chest into Angie. She yelped and jumped back. Tucker laughed as he slipped past her.

Angie blushed and studied the papers on her clipboard for longer than necessary. She finally said, "I didn't find much on Safari Land or Dolly, but Ted's real interesting."

Jackson nodded and waited for her to continue.

"Safari Land's an Idaho LLC that was delinquent on fees until recently. Bank of Buckhorn holds the mortgage, and Ted and Dolly are still way behind on payments. I checked with Sharon Sheffield at Re-Max. She says they owe more than the place is worth unless they get their business going and make a profit. Electricity, phone, insurance, everything was overdue, but these all got paid up two months ago. The Cheneys found some money somewhere. Don't know where." She stopped and studied her notes.

"How much money we talking about?"

"I'd say a few thousand. Maybe as much as ten."

The amount surprised Jackson. "Tell me about Ted."

"Turns out he's not the backwoods crazy dreamer everybody thought. He has a degree in genetics and worked for

Monsanto. High earner, married, successful. Then the IRS got after him. He beat them twice, but the third time, they nailed him for tax fraud. Did a year in federal minimum security. Wife left him, took the money and kids, and he came out of prison a different man."

"Prison can do that," Jackson said. "And Dolly?"

"Squeaky clean except for some traffic violations. Ted's her third husband. She was a Grier until she married a man named Ryder, and then she married a Yow, and then Ted Cheney. No kids. That's about it except ... did you know Pamela Yow and Dolly, did you know they're cousins?"

"Seems like Sadie told me that once."

"But Pamela Yow, she's always going on about Safari Land being a godless abomination and stuff."

"You like all your relatives, Angie?"

Angie laughed.

"You say Dolly was married to a Yow?" asked Jackson.

Angie searched her notes. "Eddie Yow."

"What's the name of Pamela's ex-husband?"

"Got me," she said. "Want me to ask Sadie?"

"Naw. Forget it. We'll talk to Ted and Dolly."

Angie laid her report on the desk. "Anything else?"

Jackson leaned back in his chair and said, "Well, I'm going to need a new Deputy Chief of Police."

"You asking me if I'd want it?"

"Only if you don't let out a war cry."

FIVE

It was mid-afternoon when Jackson got to the Split-Rail Café. He had not eaten since breakfast. He was anticipating a cup of coffee, a turkey sandwich, and time to think. Once he saw Iris and Dell seated in a rear booth, and Iris motioning for him to join them, he knew that the coffee and sandwich were the most he would get. Jackson greeted a few unemployed or retired local men, nodded to a pair of tourists pouring over a map, and went to the counter. He gave Suzy Beans, a chubby Korean girl of nineteen, his order for the sandwich and coffee. He ordered turkey breast on dark rye toast, with mayonnaise, lettuce, tomato, and bread and butter pickles.

"You want espresso, cappuccino, latte, Americano ...?" Suzy asked with a bored voice. A year ago, Iris had convinced Jay and Janice Beans to add an espresso machine.

"Half-decaf, half-high octane. Black." Suzy, who had been adopted at birth by the café owners, went off to get his non-espresso machine coffee order, while Jackson moved to the booth and sat beside Iris. "Guess you've heard?"

They both said they had.

"I still don't believe it," Iris said. "It feels so, so creepy. What we were talking about this morning."

Jackson resisted any of a dozen comments that came instantly to mind. They weren't easy to resist.

"I know mountain lions have attacked kids and small women," Dell said, "but not a man with a gun."

"I can't say for sure what killed Ed." When Suzy Beans brought Jackson's coffee, he told her thanks.

"Sandwich'll be right up," Suzy said and then left.

"I hear it was one of Ted's big cats," Iris said.

Jackson didn't say anything.

"I've hunted lions before, real lions," Dell said. "When me and Dan went to Africa." Jackson had seen the trophy heads and heard the stories of the safari that Dell and his younger brother, Dan, had gone on six years ago. Dan Tapper was now the lieutenant governor of Idaho. After November, he would most likely be governor. "If a lion or a tiger got loose from the Cheney place, I can kill it," Dell added. "Go on safari right here in Idaho."

Jackson sipped his coffee and then said, "Let's hold off on a hunting party until I talk to Ted and Dolly."

"What if it kills somebody else first?" Dell asked.

Iris grabbed Jackson's hand, causing his coffee to slosh onto the table. "Jesse's out riding that damn horse today." Her voice was suddenly shrill. "We gotta find her. Stop her. She could be out in the woods with -"

Jackson was on his way out the door, cell phone in hand, before Iris could even finish saying, "- with that killer cat." His daughter was at the top of his speed dial list. Her cell phone rang, and then a message said the call could not be completed due to .... He hung up.

"You reach her?" Iris said, coming up behind him.

"Call Deborah. Have her go find Jesse, and tell her to stay put. Not go off riding. I'm on my way."

"I'm going with you."

"No," Jackson said. "I'll be faster by myself." He didn't stop to argue, hurrying to the Jeep.

"How could you let her do this?" Iris called out.

"Call Deborah now!" Jackson yelled. He jumped in, started the Jeep, eased into light traffic, and headed toward the Double-D Stables. On the edge of town he hit the lights and siren and floored the accelerator.

Jesse tugged at the Chukars' cap she usually wore while working at the stables. A thick ponytail dangled out of the back of the baseball cap. When she wore a riding helmet, her hair swung loose beneath it. Although her complexion was lighter than her mom's, her shoulder length hair was the same deep, dark brown. Today, in her hurry to get out of Shane's truck, she had forgotten the helmet. If her mom discovered her on horseback without it, she would ground her. Forever. She knew her mom would like that.

Forgetting the helmet was bad, but breaking her I-Phone was a zillion times worse, Jesse thought. If her cell phone hadn't fallen in wet horseshit and then been stomped on by a skittish pinto, she would call her mom now and delay her. Instead, she mapped a new route that went over evergreen and aspen hills, along the crop fields that lay beyond them, and then along the curling, willow-lined Big Tooth River. This route should assure her of reaching her dad's farm before her mom came to get her.

Jesse gently scratched Touie along the crest and wiggled in the saddle. She hadn't been riding enough since school started, and the specialized saddle felt unfamiliar. A variation of the English saddle, it was lightweight and designed so both horse and rider could endure long hours. The saddle even had metal rings for attaching the equipment she would need to compete in the Tevis Cup. The endurance race from the Lake Tahoe area across the Sierra Nevada range lasts a full day and covers one hundred miles of high, hot terrain. Her goal was to enter next year's race. No, she thought, correcting herself, her goal was to win it.

Although Arabian horses generally dominated the top endurance races, Jesse was sure her Arabian-Appaloosa mix would be better. Touie's Arabian bloodline gave him size and stamina; his Appaloosa genes meant good sprint speeds and agility. Appaloosas also were loyal and unafraid to tackle trails, cows, or whatever. Jesse had never encountered *whatever*. If she did, she would trust Touie.

Somewhere in the distance Jesse heard the whip-whip-whip of a siren. She turned the horse away from the sound and headed toward a timbered hill. On the other side of it the land would flatten out and skirt the Placett farm.

Jackson killed the siren when he turned off the blacktop. He barreled through the Double-D Stables archway and down a gravel road that crooked for a half-mile before reaching the ranch house. Deborah Dawson was on her front porch when he pulled up. He had slowed the SUV and eased it to a stop to keep from covering her in dust.

Deborah was a tall, raw-boned woman with a mass of red curls atop a high forehead. Jackson didn't know much about her other than she had moved from New York after a divorce and bought the riding stable. He knew Jesse liked her and trusted her and he suspected confided in her. As soon as he saw Deborah shaking her head, he knew Jesse was gone.

"Your wife called. I mean your ex," Deborah said, as Jackson hurried toward her. "I would have gone after Jesse, but Iris thought I should wait for you."

"How long ago did she leave?"

"Maybe thirty minutes."

"On Touie?" Jackson stopped at the porch steps.

Deborah nodded and said, "Uh-huh. Iris said there's a monster cat loose and that Ed Stevens was … is it true?"

Jackson hurriedly told her about Ed.

Deborah's tanned face turned ash-gray as she listened. "That poor man," she murmured.

"I need to find Jesse. Any idea where she went?"

Deborah shook her head. "Home is all she said."

"And there's no real trail she'll take?"

"No. Just through the hills and backroads."

"Damn!" Jackson looked off toward the hills. Finally, he said, "You any good at tracking?"

Deborah frowned. "I was raised to score cheap theater tickets and elbow my way to the counter at Zabar's. I can read a GPS and a compass. That's it. But Armando's not bad at tracking," she said, referring to her Mexican ranch hand. "I'll call him." Deborah picked up a Motorola portable two-way radio. "I got ATVs. Hate the things but guests love them. Or we can ride the pintos." Deborah spoke into the radio. "Armando, you read me?"

"If Jesse cuts through the woods, she'll come out at the Placett farm," Jackson said. "Close to it anyway."

Deborah nodded in agreement as her radio crackled and a man's voice said, "Deborah, I was jus' gonna call you."

She pushed the transmit button. "Where are you?"

"Where the sheeps are grazing. Deborah, one of the sheeps, I think a ewe, I found it in the bushes. *Muerto*."

"Somebody killed one of my ewes?"

"Some thing, not somebody," Armando told her. "Killed and ate her."

As Jesse came down off the last hill, she felt the gelding grow nervous and figured it was due to the hot dry wind that was blowing. Horses hate strong winds. Wind overloads their sense of smell. Ahead of her, a field of ripe barley slanted to the south, like thick golden hair combed to one side, while in a field farther away, someone was driving a combine. Suddenly, Touie balked.

"What's wrong boy?" Jesse rubbed his neck.

Touie's ears were pinned back flat. His nostrils flared, taking in scents. The horse backed up a couple of steps and gave a sharp snort. Jesse spoke softly, trying to reassure him, but the gelding snorted again and fought to turn around. It wasn't wind or farm machinery spooking him, she realized. It was the scent of something scary, and Touie didn't scare easily. Jesse attempted to look ahead, to search for the source, but Touie kept turning and backing up. Jesse considered wolves, bears, snakes, and mountain lions as a possible threat. Whatever it was, she didn't want to battle wills with a gelding standing sixteen hands and weighing over nine hundred pounds. Neither could she afford to waste time, not if she was going to reach the farm before her mom did. She had to convince Touie he was safe. But safe from what, Jesse wondered again?

Although Kali needed to consume twenty to thirty pounds of meat per day, and could gorge on twice that amount, she had not set out to hunt that afternoon. She had set out to search for her mate, a male liger, when she heard the prey approaching. Kali had heard the prey long before she saw them since a cat's hearing is five times greater than humans at the upper range. Now, as she lay in a thatch of common sagewort and cheatgrass beside the trail, Kali felt not only hunger but also the excitement of the chase and kill. In captivity she had eaten a variety of roadkill animals, as well as poached deer and elk and wolves, even cattle and hogs deemed unfit for human consumption, but horsemeat had been her favorite food. Kali licked her muzzle and watched the nervous prey.

A lion seldom begins a chase from more than fifty yards. A tiger, using stealth, often attacks from even closer. Despite not having hunted before yesterday, Kali had the instincts of both animals in her genes. These instincts informed her that the prey was aware of her presence and frightened and that she should retreat.

A moment later, Kali slipped off into a thick growth of yarrow. Once she was out of sight, she began to circle behind the prey, all the while keeping upwind.

Although he no longer smelled the cat, Touie backtracked a hundred feet before he finally stopped. Jesse dismounted and spent minutes rubbing his forehead while murmuring softly in his ear. She continued until Touie's ears were relaxed and slightly tipped to the side and his neck was in a soft, lowered position. Only then did she mount the gelding again. Only then, having assured Touie that they were safe, did she nudge him with her heels and say, "Walk on." Touie hesitantly headed toward home.

SIX

Kali watched the prey move farther away, but she still did not attack. Nor did she growl or flash her deadly teeth. A big cat's most ferocious face – snarling, teeth displayed – often is a warning shown to other predators. Since the horse and the human posed no threat, Kali simply remained crouched in tall, thick weeds, watching the neck of the larger prey. By locking her jaws on the horse's neck, while her front legs wrapped around it and her claws dug deeply into the flesh, she would make the kill.

When the prey was forty yards ahead, Kali leapt onto the narrow trail. Her lion father could reach thirty-five miles per hour in four seconds and sixty at top speed. Her tiger mother was nearly as fast and also adept at climbing trees and swimming rivers. Kali ran equally as swift as lions and tigers, and she had far more power in her stride, so much so that Touie heard Kali's paws thump the ground.

The gelding bolted, and Jesse nearly fell off. After she righted herself and glanced behind, she was stunned and horrified by what she saw. Jesse had seen a Bengal tiger in the San Francisco Zoo, while once vacationing with her parents, but the animal chasing them was far larger than a Bengal tiger, and it was less than a hundred feet behind.

Jesse faced forward again, settling more securely in the small saddle. She urged Touie to go even faster, and the gelding strained to respond. The ground was soft. Divots of grass and earth flew by. After a second peek back, Jesse realized the giant cat was gaining on them.

If they were going to escape, Jesse had to do something soon. Seconds later, she noticed the culvert ahead. On the far side was a dirt road used for moving farm machinery between fields. Jesse didn't know that big cats are soft-footed and prefer sandy trails or damp earth to rocky, hard ground, but she knew Touie had new shoes to protect her hooves. She knew that the gelding could run faster on firm ground. She turned Touie toward the culvert and did not slow him as they closed on it. Touie jumped the six-foot ditch and landed with a clatter of hooves.

Kali also easily cleared the ditch, stumbling when one paw landed hard on a rock, but she came out of the misstep with the nimbleness of an acrobat and continued the chase.

Wade Placett liked seeing the world from the seat of big farm machinery. The combine was like sitting on a moving hill or, according to Tammy, after seeing *Jurassic Park* for the umpteenth time, a dinosaur. Tammy? Wade was not overly worried about her despite the bout of wetting herself. Josh was another matter. Like his mother, Josh was highly sensitive. Nothing rolled easily off his son.

Wade was looking behind him while thinking about his family. When he turned back toward the blades and peered out of the cab, he said, "What the hell?" He knew Touie; he had seen the horse often enough on the dirt roads. He knew Jesse too, even without the usual black helmet, but he had never seen anything like the cat.

He shut down the operation and steered the lumbering combine toward his pickup, parked beneath a towering trash locust. While he was watching the monster cat chase Jesse and her horse, he ran into the old picnic table Mandy had placed in the shade of the tree. Wade cursed as he killed the engine, grabbed his rifle, climbed down, and ran.

The next time Jesse looked back, she expected to see the giant cat far behind. She was wrong. The hard ground had allowed Touie to put only another ten feet of distance between them. They would never outrun the predator.

Just ahead, Jesse spotted a trail that led to the willows, cottonwoods, and maples lining the Big Tooth River. The trail was rarely used and overgrown. Still, Jesse knew the riverbank was shallow here and the water deep, and she recalled reading or hearing somewhere that cats do not like water. She leaned forward and, using her knees and the reins, turned the gelding toward the river.

Kali was tiring rapidly but did not want to give up on the prey, not after expending so much energy. Even so, she was about to stop, for big cats do not have great running stamina, when the prey veered from the paw-pounding road onto softer ground. When the prey made a sharp ninety-degree turn, Kali did not follow. She used her leaping stride to thrash through some fireweed and musk thistle at an angle, shortening the distance to the prey.

Jesse heard the monster mauling the weeds and knew it might cut them off. She also knew the Big Tooth River was no more than a hundred feet ahead. She kicked Touie's flanks with her boot heels, something she seldom did. A sudden spurt by the horse in response to her nudge proved barely enough, for when Kali bounded out of the thistle and onto the river path, she was only twenty feet behind them.

Seconds later, Touie jumped the riverbank and landed on soft, moist ground. His front legs buckled slightly. Jesse fell forward across the horse's neck. At that same moment, Kali soared high over the horse's rear and swatted at Jesse with extended razor claws. Her right front claws raked the back of Jesse's vest and shredded it. Her left claws ripped through Touie's hide and snagged in his flesh, causing Kali to lose her balance for an instant. When one of Touie's rear hooves struck her chest, Kali was knocked off. The liger hit the ground with a thud.

Those few seconds allowed Touie to slog into the river, where he kept running until his four legs were churning nothing but water. Jesse slid out of the saddle and over the croup. She shoved against Touie's rear to get clear. She then held onto Touie's tail with both hands while she kicked her feet. The current pushed them downstream, but with Jesse's kicks and Touie's powerful legs, they still were able to swim toward the other shore.

Once they were in the middle of the river, Jesse dared to look behind. "No!" she cried out, taking in a mouthful of water. The giant cat was coming after them.

In fact, Kali hadn't even hesitated. Nobody had to teach her to swim. Instincts, tiger instincts mostly, told her what to do. After the minute it took her to feel assured of her movements, she began to close the distance.

Wade slid the pickup to a stop on the riverbank, jumped from the cab, planted his feet in soft ground, and slammed a 7mm Magnum in the chamber of the Remington. He took careful aim, aware that a wild shot could hit Jesse or her horse, and then fired. His bullet pinged the water. His second shot caused the big cat to list and flail. Wade took aim and fired again. He didn't know if the third shot hit the cat or not. What mattered was that the monster was drifting away from Jesse and her horse. Wade lowered the hunting rifle and watched until he felt certain Jesse was safe. Then he dug out his cell phone.

On the other side of the hills a dust cloud trailing the speeding Jeep soon obscured the Double-D ranch in Jackson's side view mirrors. He had spent nearly an hour on a Honda ATV following Armando, but the Mexican rancher had been unable to track Jesse's route. Jackson had his Nokia cell phone out to call Jesse again when it rang.

Touie clamored up the low bank on the far side and stood with his head low and dripping water, while Jesse stumbled out of the river and dropped to the ground. She had lost her ball cap, and her ponytail had come undone. Wet hair clung to her face like seaweed as she locked her hands around her knees and lowered her head and wept.

She had no idea how long she stayed there cradling her body, rocking back and forth, and weeping. She did not notice Touie graze on a patch of tender grass or hear him nicker. She remained unaware of time or place until a voice broke through the shock, and she heard her father saying, "Jesse, honey."

Jackson lifted his daughter off the ground and wrapped her in his arms. He felt her body heaving as her face pressed against his chest. "Jesse, honey," he said again. Then he shut up and held her and let her exhaust whatever it was inside her that had to come out in tears and gasps. When he felt Jesse's shredded vest and saw Wade staring at the damage in disbelief, Jackson held her even tighter.

After a while Jackson bundled Jesse into his Jeep and drove her home. Wade, who had removed the wet blanket and saddle from Touie and then dried him, remained behind with the gelding until Jackson could send a horse trailer.

Once he had Jesse soaking in a hot bath, Jackson called Iris, although Jesse asked him not to. They both knew that Iris would use the incident as another reason to oppose Jesse entering the endurance race. They also knew that Iris' dislike of riding wasn't because she feared Jesse would get hurt. Iris simply didn't want Jesse to be an Idaho cowgirl. She had higher aspirations for her.

While Jackson waited for Iris to arrive, he called Deborah Dawson and asked her to bring Touie home in a trailer. He then called the vet to tend to the horse's wounds. He made one other call as well. He called the library, where he reached Pamela Yow, and asked her to research lions and tigers and whatever kind of cat was even bigger. "Ligers," Pamela told him. "That's what Ted and Dolly are trying to raise. Devil cats. God didn't make them and man shouldn't." Jackson also asked Pamela to try to locate an expert on big cats, someone he could talk to.

Neither Deborah nor the large animal vet had arrived yet when Iris stormed inside, saying, "Where is she?"

"Upstairs in the tub. She's fine. Just calm down."

"Calm down my ass. Why didn't she answer her phone?"

"It broke. She dropped it in horse manure."

"Give me a gun."

"A gun?"

"I'm gonna shoot her goddamned horse." Iris never cursed unless she was on the verge of a meltdown.

"Touie saved her life," Jackson said, for Wade had told him the events, at least what he had seen of them, and Jesse, once she stopped crying, had filled in the rest.

"I don't give a damn. She'll never ride him again."

Jackson had seen it often during the last days of marriage. When Iris fell into a black hole of anger, she lost touch with anything good in others that might buffer her words and actions. She wasn't just mean; she was crazy at those moments. Was it going to happen now, he wondered?

"Mom," Jesse said softly from the top of the stairs. She was wrapped in a towel. "I'm okay. I'm not hurt."

"My god, Jesse," Iris said. "I've been so frantic. The thought of you being chased by some wild cat, I –"

"I'm cold, mom. I'm getting back in the tub. Come on up if you want." Jesse turned around and left.

"Maybe you can go easy on her," Jackson said.

"You have Dell kill that cat," Iris told Jackson as she started up the stairs. "He's the only one here who's ever hunted real lions or whatever this is. Promise me."

"If Dell can kill it –" He paused when his phone rang. "If Dell can kill the cat, I'm all for it," Jackson said, and then he answered his cell phone, saying, "Chief Hobbs." He listened to

Will Bailey describe how he found a tiger in his hog pen eating one of his sows.

SEVEN

Katy Osborne glanced at the man in the golf jacket. He had been fidgeting and scowling the entire time. She breathed deeply before returning to her book. This was the final page she would read. Afterwards, she would answer questions and then sign copies. The man would be trouble.

She read again, her voice strong but soothing, almost seductive. When she finished, she closed the book, titled *African Nights*, and listened to the applause. There were some seventy-five people in Tattered Cover, Denver's famed Cherry Creek bookstore, on a Saturday afternoon. Saturday night would have drawn a bigger crowd, but a reality TV star had nabbed the better slot. Katy's first book, three years earlier, had sold well enough to get her a second one in print, but not a Saturday night reading. "If anyone has questions," Katy said. Hands shot up. "Yes." She pointed to a college girl. Young women were often eager to please and lobbed soft questions at her, easy to begin with.

"How many other women are like you, you know, professional hunters and safari guides?"

"None. About two hundred licensed professional hunters work commercially in Africa. They're all men except for me," Katy said. "Now, I realize some people oppose hunting for any reason, but hunting clubs and safaris were preserving Africa's animals long before ecology groups even existed." Katy ignored the few protests and pointed to a thirty-something man in a suit.

"What's the most dangerous animal you've encountered?"

"Humans," Katy replied.

A mother-earth woman in her fifties was flapping her hands. "Next to the last row. Woman in the tunic." Katy listened to her defense of Elsa and the lion cubs made famous in the *Born Free* books and movies. Every audience included someone who thought lions were merely oversized house cats. "What the *Born Free* story fails to mention," Katy said, "is that one of Elsa's cubs later ate a camp cook and another mauled a little boy." There were gasps and moans. Katy waited before adding, "In truth, lions see people as only one thing - food. The question isn't why they kill us, it's why they don't kill more of us."

The man in the golf jacket raised his hand. Here it comes, Katy thought. All her life she had been tested: as a ten-year-old orphan sent to an American boarding school; on safari where men focused on her looks rather than her skills; in Botswana where she was a tiny snowflake in a huge, dark continent. Tested and survived. "You, sir."

"How big can a lion get?" the man asked.

It wasn't the question Katy expected. "Up to eight feet with the tail," she said. "Maybe three feet tall at the shoulders, and a male can weigh over five hundred pounds. A tiger can be a bit larger."

"So what kind of cat weighs a thousand pounds?"

"None that I've hunted." Katy smiled.

"Well, my wife's brother is an EMT in Idaho, and he says they have a cat that size running around. He says it killed a policeman there today, eviscerated him."

Katy sipped some water while looking at her literary agent, Janet Cook, standing in the back next to Stan Ely, head of ARK, an animal rescue organization. Janet shrugged, and Stan gave a wan smile. "When a lion or tiger charges you," Katy said, "they certainly appear that size. But then lions and tigers don't live in Idaho, do they?"

"They do at Safari Land," the man said smugly.

Will Bailey's rubber boots made a sucking sound in the muck. "Souie, souie," the farmer said, whacking a big boar with a stick to drive him away. "Souie." Jackson knew he wouldn't be eating bacon for a while, not after watching Bailey's hogs try to cannibalize the shredded carcass of the sow. "Pretty sure I hit it once, maybe twice," Will Bailey told Jackson. "And I'm talking a Remington seven hun'erd with thirty-ought-six Corelokts. The tiger went down, then got up and run off, over that way."

Jackson looked south in the direction Bailey was pointing, thinking about what Wade and Jesse had said. "This cat, was it really big? Like ten feet?"

"Naw. Half that size. Kind of skinny and starved. But that didn't stop it from guttin' a hog." Bailey herded the last of his hogs into another pen and closed the gate. They were still grunting, noses in the air, sniffing the blood scent. "Who's gonna pay for my sow, Chief Hobbs?"

* * *

"I sounded like a fool in there," Katy said as she got into the back of the rental car after signing books. The man in the golf jacket had not stayed for the signing. Most people did.

"Everybody gets tripped up doing Q and A," Janet said. Janet Cook was over fifty, but after two facelifts, you could bounce a ball off her cheeks. "Just forget it. Get ready for tomorrow. That man was a jerk."

"That doesn't mean he's wrong," argued Katy.

"I've heard of Safari Land," Stan said. "Some mom and pop operation in Idaho. Not sure it's still around."

Janet took out an IPad and tapped and touched the screen and a moment later said, "Here it is."

She passed the IPad back to Katy. "No mention of giant cats," Katy said after reading the few sentences.

"Told you. He's a jerk. Forget it." Janet then launched into Katy's itinerary for the following day.

By the time they reached the Oxford Hotel in downtown Denver, an older, European style hotel favored by Katy, Stan and Janet had forgotten about Safari Land. When they entered the lobby, Katy said, "What part of Idaho, Stan?"

"Ah, come on, Katy. Let's have a drink. Janet?"

"Not me. Gotta get in a workout before dinner. See you both in a while." Janet headed to the elevators.

Stan raised his eyebrows and flirted a smile. Katy had met him three years earlier. He was handsome and muscular, and she had come close to sleeping with him. Stan had since married, but he was still intent on getting her in bed. She shook her head no. "Where in Idaho?"

"East. Near Wyoming. Some dinky town."

* * *

Jackson sat with Will Bailey and his wife, Stella, at the kitchen table while he waited for Dell Tapper and two Buckhorn police officers to arrive. He asked for a coffee refill and was tempted by Stella's offer of a second piece of apple pie, still hot from the oven. The food and drink had helped, but tiredness kept a stranglehold. So much had happened since he climbed out of bed some ten hours ago.

He wanted to be with his daughter. He wanted to talk to Ted Cheney. He wanted to sit alone and grieve for Ed. He wanted to do many things, but hunting a wounded tiger was not one of them. Jackson looked at his watch; two hours of daylight were left. Lack of time was the reason he had invited Dell along. Despite his promise to Iris, he hated to involve Dell. "They should be here soon."

"I oughta go with you," Will Bailey said.

"Predators often return to their kill to finish feeding," Jackson said. "So you're as likely to find the cat by staying right here as we are out in the woods."

"What I told him," Stella said. "Take care of your own. We got no business having tigers in Idaho anyhow."

A moment later Jackson heard two cars drive up. He thanked Will and Stella for the pie and coffee. He promised them the tiger skin if at all possible and then went outside. He found Dell removing equipment from the back of his Cadillac Escalade. His son was helping him.

"What are you doing here, Shane?"

"Chief Hobbs," the boy said and looked to his dad.

"Shane knows how to shoot, Jackson. He didn't want to miss out on it. Hell, it's tiger hunting."

Jackson shook his head. "I can take you along, Dell. I can't allow a sixteen-year-old to go." He thought about his earlier conversation with Iris. The condom still was in his pocket. He said to Shane, "Have you talked to Jesse? I don't think she should go anywhere tonight."

"I was on my way to see her until Dad said –"

"It's a beauty, isn't it?" Dell said, stroking the walnut stock of a .375 Holland & Holland Magnum, a bolt-action rifle. "Load it with three-hundred grain Winchester Silvertips, it'll bring down anything short of an elephant or rhino." Dell returned the .375 to the padded case and picked up the second gun. "A two-seventy Weatherby. A fine all-around sporting rifle." He offered the rifle to Jackson. "If Shane's not going, why don't you use it?"

"You guys got your deer and elk rifles?" Jackson asked his officers. Both Skip Tibbits and John Plaides answered affirmatively. Skip was balding while John had thick brown hair. Apart from appearance they were much alike: about thirty, married, kids, ex-Army, skilled hunters, good cops. "Think I'll stick with the Stoeger twelve-gauge I got in my Jeep," Jackson said. "In case we need an up-close gun."

"We won't," Dell said, "not if I get a clean shot." Dell slid the Weatherby Vanguard into a soft case and zippered it and took up the .375 again. He handed Shane the keys to the Escalade. "You so much as scratch it, and you'll wish you were staring down a tiger instead of me."

Shane looked so eager to leave that Jackson doubted if coming on the hunt was his idea at all.

They started at the hog pens and crossed a long and wide potato field before climbing to a thicket of Big Tooth and

Mountain maple. A smattering of leaves already were turning red and yellow. They followed the blood trail through the maples and beyond them, always going higher. Thirty minutes later Dell held up his hand to halt them. They had reached a patch of snowberry and juniper. Dell pointed some sixty yards ahead to a grove of blue spruce. He motioned for them to go forward slowly.

Once they were hidden in the evergreens, Dell dialed in his scope for distance. During the walk he had told them all about the superior merits of his variable power scope over the usual 4X scope found on most rifles. While Skip and John sighted their inferior scopes, Jackson watched the thickly wooded area. Before long, he spotted four northern gray wolves, three adults and one adolescent, loping along.

"It's just wolves," Jackson said softly.

"You're wrong," Dell whispered. "See those young blue spruce about seventy-five yards up and to the right?" A second later, he said, "The tiger's laying flat behind one. I can just make out the head." Before anyone else could locate the tiger, if there was one, Dell's gun roared. Jackson hadn't put in his earplugs yet, and his ears rang.

Dell said something to Jackson and started forward. Jackson motioned for his two officers to follow. The four of them fanned out as they approached the small trees, although not so far as to create a potential crossfire situation.

Dell reached the area first. "Hell of a head shot," he said, looking down at the cat. The top of tiger's head was missing. His tongue stuck out and lay in the dirt. There were rips and bite marks in the dirty, loose skin. The tiger's belly had been torn open by something other than gunshot.

Jackson didn't see how anyone could think this tiger was longer than a car or how it could nearly bring down a horse or manage to kill the best man he had ever known.

John knelt. "This cat's been dead a while." He touched its belly. "Wolves were already feeding on it."

While the water warmed in the shower, Katy selected an outfit for dinner, undressed, and stood naked before the mirror: she was thirty-five, average height, her body firm from trekking and ranch work, mostly firm anyway, her fair skin prone to freckles, her eyes hazel, and her dark blond hair longer than she wore it when on safari. Many thought her beautiful. She scanned her face and her body. In most species it's the male that primps, she knew. She also knew that apart from looks, humans are like all other animals. All creatures are driven to survive and procreate. Africa taught her that.

Katy had spent the past hour on the Internet, but her search had yielded little information about Safari Land. She found nothing about a big cat attacking anyone in Idaho today or yesterday or on any other day. Still, the man in the golf jacket bothered her. She wondered why. Or maybe it was not the smug man from the reading that bothered her at all. Maybe it was Stan flirting with her.

Maybe Stan reminded her of how much she missed Jacques, the French photographer who had been her lover until a year ago, when Jacques had asked her to move in with him. As tempting as the offer was, for Paris was her favorite city, and she truly did care for Jacques, she knew that she would wither away if she gave up her life in Africa. Survival always trumps sex. Africa also had taught her that.

EIGHT

After stopping at Safari Land again and finding the entrance still padlocked and the phone unanswered, Jackson returned to Buckhorn. By the time he arrived, a crowd had gathered downtown to look at the dead tiger in the bed of Will Bailey's truck. Gary Chen, a reporter for the county newspaper, was photographing the animal. In the twilight he was using a flash. Between flashes Jackson saw Iris and Dell, him towering over her, standing shoulder to shoulder in the front. Jackson drove on to the police station.

Ed's Ford Crown Victoria now was parked next to a Dodge Charger. The cruisers were all black, with Buckhorn Police Department on the sides and the rear in light blue, but the cars remained a pack of mongrels. A second Dodge, out on patrol, had been confiscated from a drug bust. The Ford had been bought used from the Boise city police. The Jeep Grand Cherokee that Jackson drove had been donated by a car dealership that went broke. At home he had the same short-bed

Ford F-350 he had owned before his divorce. He seldom used it off the farm. He usually drove the Jeep. With such a small police force, he was never off duty.

Jackson checked in with Skip Tibbits, the duty officer, and then took a cup of coffee into his office and phoned around to locate the county prosecutor. When Jackson reached Bud Spiegel, he informed him of the latest events and the need to get onto the Cheney property.

"Could wind up a criminal prosecution," Bud Spiegel responded. Jackson already knew that or he would have cut the padlock and gone in. "Get a search warrant first."

"That'll mean tomorrow or maybe even Monday," Jackson said. He hated to wait that long to talk to the Cheneys.

"Try Judge Vetter. He'll be playing poker tonight."

"Need you to go to Saint Anthony," Jackson told Skip a few moments later. Skip was working the 4 P.M. to 2 A.M. shift. Regular officers worked four ten-hour days a week.

"When?"

"Soon as I can type up the search warrant."

"Who'll take my shift?" Skip was the lone officer on duty apart from a reserve officer working six to midnight.

"Me. I'll do it."

While Jackson was typing up the search warrant, Skip appeared in the doorway of his office. "It's Angie." He waggled the cordless. "She's in Idaho Falls right now. If you fax the warrant to the judge, she'll pick it up in Saint Anthony. That way you can go on home."

Angie often went to Idaho Falls on weekend nights when she was off duty. Jackson had never asked where she went.

* * *

Jackson parked in front of Benson's Sporting Goods store. The streetlights were throwing off a bluish glow, while a single streak of red on the horizon sought to keep night at bay. He had gone first to Iris's house but didn't find Jesse. Now he knew why. She was gathered with the others around the back of Bailey's flatbed truck.

"It don't look scary to me," said a man in the crowd.

"It might if it was chasing you," Iris snapped.

"That's not the same cat," Jesse said. She looked at Shane. "It was twice as big and -"

"This is the only tiger out there," Dell said.

Jackson heard the exchange as he walked up behind his daughter and said her name softly to avoid startling her.

"Daddy, this isn't the cat that chased me."

Jackson nodded. "Okay, Jesse. Then it's not."

"That's crazy," a woman shouted. "She don't know."

"I know," a male voice yelled. Everybody looked around to see who had spoken, but Wade Placett was too short to be easy to pick out in the crowd. Then Wade pushed his way to the truck and lifted the head of the tiger. "This thing's a pussy cat compared to the monster chasing Jesse."

An hour later Jackson was on his cell phone arguing with his daughter. Upon learning that the large animal vet had taken Touie back to his clinic, Jesse wanted to spend the night with her horse. Even a Saturday night date with Shane came second to Touie. Jackson finally talked her out of a sleepover in the barn at the veterinarian clinic. He was headed to his car when Pamela Yow caught him.

"I have the research for you," she said.

"That was fast."

She shrugged and handed over a large manila envelope that weighed a couple of pounds. Pamela had a thin, boyish body draped in shapeless dark clothes. Only thirty-nine, her hair was graying and cut severely. Rumor had it that she was once a singer in a country band fronted by her ex-husband, but Jackson had trouble imagining it. She told him she was sorry about Ed. Jackson thanked her and then waited for her to leave, but she didn't budge. "I warned all of you," she said. "I told the town, the county, all of you to take them cats away and shut the place down."

"The cats at Safari Land?"

"It's blasphemy, what they're doing."

"What exactly are they doing, Pamela?" he asked.

"Going straight to hell, that's what."

Once the librarian left, Jackson drove home. He ate dinner and read while seated on the couch in front of the unlit fireplace. Aspen logs filled the grate. The papers from Pamela filled the coffee table. A plate with the remains of a grilled ham and cheese sandwich and some sea salt and vinegar potato chips covered most of the pages. Next to it was a bottle of Sawtooth Ale. In Colorado he had developed a fondness for the Longmont brewery's beer. An Idaho Falls liquor store stocked it. He had forgotten to ask Pamela Yow the name of her former husband.

At first Jackson wasn't going to read Pamela's research. The tiger was dead. Most everyone believed the problem was fixed. But he couldn't stop thinking about what Jesse had said: "It's not the same cat." So he read.

Jackson had never imagined that lions and tigers killed so many people. In a mangrove forest in Bangladesh and India, home to the largest concentration of tigers in the world, the cats had killed some 1,500 people. A single tiger once killed 438 people in Nepal and northern India. In Kruger National Park, lions may have eaten up to 15,000 people, most of them refugees from Mozambique trying to cross the park at night to illegally enter South Africa to work in the fields and mines there. What chilled him the most, however, was reading about three generations of lions in Tanganyika, formerly Tanzania, that worked together to kill. The pride was so organized that after grabbing a person, they would race off into the bush, passing the body from mouth to mouth, like a baton in a relay race, until they were miles away and could devour their victim.

Jackson reviewed his notes. He always wrote notes. It's what policemen do. He read: *The lion is trained from birth to be aggressive, to fight and kill, to be a member of a hunting tribe. Tigers are solo hunters that use stealth more than aggression. Lions prefer open grassland; tigers like woods and trees.* Eastern Idaho offered both.

The last stack of papers he opened were interviews and book reviews and biographical information about a woman named Katherine Osborne. Katy, she was called. Jackson had asked Pamela to find an expert he could talk to about exotic cats. She had given him a writer who looked like a *Vogue* model. He needed a real hunter, not some poster girl. He looked again at the photographs of her and said, "Wow!" He stuffed the paperwork back in the envelope.

After her shower Katy decided to skip going out to dinner in favor of room service. She donned a thick, terrycloth hotel bathrobe and leaned against a mountain of fluffy pillows on the queen bed, surrounded by financial reports. She was examining the finances of Skorokoro, her ranch in Botswana, a ranch started by her Uncle Bucky. The hunting ranch was increasingly unable to compete with government-backed safari parks and to contend with increased costs and decreased clientele. She wanted to keep Skorokoro going, and not just for her. Families worked and lived there. It was their home too. But the money she made from books and safaris and the special jobs to kill a man-eater or track down an injured animal left to suffer or to cull a herd to allow the strongest to survive simply weren't enough anymore. She needed more money.

Katy tossed down the paperwork and absently stared at the television where a Denver news program droned softly in the background, the modern way of combating loneliness. Suddenly, the image switched from a pair of doll-people behind a desk to a dead tiger with people gathered around it. A scroll along the bottom read *Buckhorn, Idaho.* Katy grabbed the remote and hurriedly increased the sound. According to a female reporter at the site, an escaped tiger had been shot and killed by local policemen and a man identified as a bank president. The bank president, even in a brief soundbite, came off as a blow-hard.

Another man, dressed more like a rancher than a policeman, thought Katy, was identified as the Chief of Police. He answered the reporter's questions but used few words to do so. When he was asked if the dead tiger had escaped from Safari Land, the police chief admitted that he didn't know where the animal came from. In answer to the reporter's next question, the policeman said, "No, I can't say for certain that it's the only big cat out there."

"What?" Katy said aloud, her eyes glued to the screen.

"So there might be another tiger?" the reporter asked.

"I don't know," the policeman said.

"Chief Hobbs, if we're not talking about a tiger, then what? Do we have a lion running loose here too?" The reporter managed to sound genuinely concerned.

"Well, what's the biggest cat in the world?" the Buckhorn police chief said. "That's what might be out there still yet."

A while later Katy was about to drift off to sleep when she sat up and turned on the light. She was wide-awake now. No way, she told herself. A liger? No way.

NINE

Angie Kuka awakened at dawn and for a moment thought she was home. But the sounds and smells were different: a leaky toilet, the scent of incense burned. In slow motion she rolled out of bed and tiptoed to where her uniform hung on the back of the door. Underwear, gun, handcuffs, makeup bag, nightstick, bra, equipment belt, all were stuffed in a duffle bag that said Bank of Buckhorn. Dell Tapper's bank had given them as Christmas gifts one year.

"Hey you," Sharon said, while gazing at Angie's soft curves. Angie's skin was naturally tan. Her eyes were dark brown and long-lashed and her black hair cut short to frame high cheekbones and full lips. But despite Angie's feminine looks, Sharon knew she was capable of wrestling most males to the ground. She even had seen her do it once. Sharon was getting aroused watching her, but Angie wasn't much for morning romance. "I'll get up," Sharon said feebly. She loved to sleep in. Weekdays, she had to be dressed and at school teaching history before her body was even fully awake. "I can make some coffee."

"Stay in bed. I gotta go meet the boss."

Sharon rolled over to face the wall where her Shambhala meditation banner hung. "You coming back anytime soon?"

Twenty minutes later Angie tossed her gym bag, now filled with last night's clothing, in the trunk of her Subaru Outback. Her car was parked two blocks from Sharon's bungalow outside a male teacher's house. He was a friend of Sharon's. Even so, staying overnight was dangerous. Angie knew that she might survive as a lesbian cop in Idaho, if she could handle the abuse, but Sharon, a high school teacher and sponsor of the cheerleading squad of teenage girls, would be out of a job. Sharon's name made her life hard enough. What parent with the last name *Tate* would name their baby girl Sharon? Sharon had told her that even kids who thought 1776 was the Civil War era knew about Charles Manson and *Helter Skelter*.

Jackson was nursing his coffee and re-reading Pamela's research when Angie reached the Split-Rail Cafe. "Thanks for coming in so early," Jackson said as she slid into the booth opposite him. Angie wore a blue uniform; Jackson had on black jeans and a blue-black plaid shirt. "You get it?"

"If I did, do I get breakfast?" Angie gave Jackson a tri-folded piece of paper without waiting for an answer.

He read the signed search warrant. "My treat," Jackson said, offering the slightest hint of a smile.

Angie ordered a full farmer's breakfast. Jackson ordered light and nibbled. When they had finished they dropped Angie's car at the station and, after she retrieved her M4 and body armor, rode together in the Jeep. Neither of them said much during the trip to the Cheney house.

The gate at Safari Land remained locked. Jackson took a large bolt cutter from the back floorboard and snapped the chain. Then he drove on to the house, where he pulled up beside the Cheney's battered Dodge pickup. He tapped the Jeep's horn a few times, but nobody responded.

At an altitude of over 5,000 feet, the September morning carried a chill, and neither of them had the windows open, so the stench didn't hit them until they got out. "Oh Christ," Jackson said. "You smell that?" Anyone who lived on a farm knew the odor. Most cops knew it too. Death stinks. "Vest and rifle." Jackson called in their location, donned his Kevlar vest, and removed his shotgun. He said, "We walk together. You watch our back."

They moved away from the SUV toward a two-storied farmhouse with rotting wood siding and peeling paint. The smell led them to the rear where they disturbed a flock of scavenger crows that nosily flew off. They found a human head behind some neglected evergreen shrubs that had been planted years earlier. A ball cap with an American flag decal lay inches away from gray hair. The head belonged to a man, but the face was too chewed up to be identifiable. Except for some scattered pieces of flesh and cloth, the rest of the man appeared to have been eaten. A wallet covered in blood and other fluids that Jackson didn't want to think about lay on top of a larger piece of flesh.

"I'm gonna be sick," Angie said right before she turned away and emptied her stomach.

Jackson had thought that a bran muffin and oatmeal had a better chance of staying down if things turned nasty. So far he was right. While he waited for Angie to finish, his eyes swept the yard and beyond. A .458 Winchester lay on the ground some twenty feet away. "You gonna be okay?"

"Yeah. Except my mouth tastes like shit now."

Jackson poked at the wallet with the tip of a ballpoint pen. The Idaho driver's license he nudged out of it confirmed what he already suspected. "Theodore Cheney." He used the pen to slide the license back into the wallet. They would need photographs before anything was removed.

"Want me to call it in?" Angie asked.

"Let's see what we've got here first. Get yourself some water. Then clear the house. Maybe Dolly's in there hiding in a closet. We need to find her if she's here. Dead or alive. Then get the camera out of the Jeep and start photographing everything. I'm going to look out back, check the animal cages. We may not be alone."

A hundred feet behind the house Jackson found an old school bus faded pale yellow. The bus windows had been replaced by barbwire, crisscrossed to form a net. Next to the bus was the trailer part of a semi. One wall of the trailer was missing. Pieces of rebar had been used to create cells for animals. Both rigs were empty except for feces-infested water troughs thick with Blue Bottle flies. There were a few smaller cages too. Beside them was a partially constructed cage with twelve-foot metal poles set in cement and strung with nine-gauge wire. It was the start of a real animal compound, a replacement for the shabby prisons. The makeshift cages all had hasps and hoods for a padlock. None of them had a lock in place.

While Jackson checked the cages, Angie drank from a hose in the side yard and then wet her face. She used her shirtsleeve to dry her face as she reached the front of the house. "Police," she called. When nobody responded, she knocked and then opened the unlocked door. "Anybody here? Hello. Dolly Cheney? Police." Angie stood still and listened - no radio or TV, no footsteps, no – and then she heard something. She waited but didn't hear anything more.

Angie entered the house slowly, glad that she had worn her shoes with the soft rubber soles, even if they were too butch for her taste. She shouldered the M4 tactical rifle.

The living room was furnished with flea market junk, but the house was clean. A newspaper lay open on the couch - last Thursday's edition of the *Fremont County Journal*.

A doorway led into the kitchen and another to a hallway. A third one seemed to lead to a room that wrapped around to join the kitchen. Dining room, she figured.

Outside, Jackson searched each outbuilding he saw, those standing and those nearly falling down. He found nothing more except for pieces of a dog or a few dogs or maybe even wolves, and then he returned to the cages. He remembered once seeing about a dozen big cats caged up here. He felt certain the lions and tigers hadn't gotten together and hatched an escape plan. Somebody had freed them. That made it a crime scene. He called the communication center in St. Anthony and requested a State Police Crime Scene Response Unit, ISP troopers, Sheriff Midden and some deputies, the coroner, an ambulance, and his own people. When he finished, he headed to the house.

In the kitchen Angie examined a skillet congealed with grease and a sink with a few dirty dishes. Other dishes were scattered on the floor, most of them broken. An unbroken plate looked clean. She dropped down and ran a finger over it. Not washed clean, licked clean. That's when she heard it again, that sound.

"Dolly?"

Nothing. Slowly, Angie skirted the broken crockery and crossed the kitchen and entered a small dining room set up as an office. She saw Dolly Cheney on the floor in a pool of blood. Angie knelt beside the woman and felt for a pulse in her neck. Faint. Skin warm to the touch. She radioed Jackson and told him Dolly was alive, but barely.

"I'm on my way now," he said. "And I'll call for another ambulance. Do what you can for her."

While she waited for Jackson, Angie examined Dolly's injuries. Her face was clawed. One arm looked like it had been run through a meat grinder. The hand was intact but bloody and holding something shiny. Angie removed a silver cross and chain from Dolly's fist. She was examining it when she heard a noise behind her - a hacking or a low guttural growling, a big cat sound. The M4 lay on the floor beside her. She slowly reached for it.

Jackson had climbed the broken concrete steps and looked through the glass panels of the antique side door. He saw Angie squatting beside Dolly, and behind her, he saw a tiger, a Bengal tiger, he thought. The tiger was ten feet away and crouched to leap. Jackson stepped back from the door far enough that he could raise the shotgun and aim it at the tiger, but he didn't shoot. He wanted to but -

Then the tiger leaped. Jackson's shot hit mid-body and kicked the cat sideways. It still slammed into Angie, knocking her forward. She screamed. He shot again. The second deer slug took off part of the tiger's rear leg. The tiger yelped or cried or made whatever sound a tiger makes with a leg shot off and dragged himself or herself through a doorway that – Jackson would learn – led to the kitchen and then to the back porch and then outside.

Angie rolled over and sat up. Her hair and her face were covered with bits of blood and flesh and tiger skin. When she looked at Jackson through the blown out glass panes of the door, she saw that he was trembling.

An hour later Angie sat in the back of the same ambulance that had been at the Placett's farm a day earlier. Cars were scattered everywhere: county sheriff cars and state police cruisers, a crime scene van, every patrol car in Buckhorn, Tucker's pickup, the coroner's minivan, plus a few personal vehicles. The area had taken on the appearance of a reservation roadhouse on Saturday night. Some of the vehicles had their emergency lights silently flashing. The ambulance that rushed Dolly to a hospital in Rexburg had left using lights and siren. A flashing and screeching black and white state police car led the way. More troopers were busy keeping the news people out on the county blacktop and away from the scene.

Once the medical staff cleared her, Angie returned to the house and located Jackson sitting on the front porch staring at a spreadsheet. Inside the house radios crackled and cell phones rang and voices, some loud, gave orders. The county sheriff and the state police were gathering evidence. "Chief," she said, "you saved my life in there."

Jackson looked at Angie like he hadn't heard her. "This chart is how they keep track of the cats: ten tigers, eleven lions, and two ligers. Twenty-three big cats."

"Maybe they sold them all?"

Jackson shook his head. "This chart was updated on Friday, two days ago. I think Ted's been dead since then."

Angie slowly absorbed his meaning. "So what are you saying, that we've got twenty-three wild cats loose?"

"Twenty-two," Jackson said. "One tiger is dead. One hurt and maybe dying. But all the rest of them ...."

They both looked out at the fields and woodlands.

TEN

A door opened upstairs, and Iris heard the girls whispering. They barely had left Jesse's room since Missy arrived today after attending church. Today there was none of the jarring music and teenage giggling that she often found annoying. In a few days Iris knew the boom-boom and the oh-my-gods would return. Teenagers somehow retain a sense of invincibility despite encountering the contrary.

Iris returned to the budget paperwork on the dining table. Usually, she worked in her law office on Sunday afternoon. Her two-room office was connected to the house by a breezeway, although it also had a separate entrance.

She did not like Sundays: mornings of guilt and repentance, afternoons of lethargy and dullness, and a night that was time's purgatory. This Sunday was worse than usual. Today was the Sunday Dell and Shane visited the cemetery. Today was the sixth anniversary of Tilda's suicide. Even now she could not escape the woman.

When Iris was in high school, Dell's parents had pressured him into dating Tilda Flemming instead of her. Eventually, Dell gave in. Eventually, Dell always did.

Upstairs, the bedroom door closed. What was Jesse doing? Why hadn't they come down? Were they waiting for her to leave? Earlier, she had tried to talk to Jesse about the animal attack but received monosyllabic replies. All Jesse had said was that she wanted to go to the movies with Shane. Iris had told her "maybe," but she would let them go. Normalcy would be good for Jesse. Anyway, she had her own plans tonight, plans that didn't include the kids. She would cook Dell's favorite meal. She would dress to entice him. She would help him forget the past.

Dell was hesitant to commit to the relationship because their kids were dating, but Iris wasn't concerned. If the teen romance didn't fizzle out, she would end it. Despite what Jackson thought, Iris knew the truth. Jesse had never forgiven her for divorcing her father. Messing with her mother's romance was Jesse's revenge.

The cell phone startled Iris. By the third chirp she found it beneath the budget file. Buckhorn badly needed money. Everybody had an idea for how to get it. They were dull ideas and doomed to fail. She answered the phone.

Iris greeted Sheriff Midden and Stilts Venable, head of the regional Idaho Fish and Game Department, and then Jackson introduced her to a tall, handsome black man with a pencil mustache and a tailored uniform. "Major Jessup is from Meridian. He's in charge of region six, Captain Bundy's boss. Major, our town mayor, Iris ... Inslay."

After Iris shook hands with the Idaho State Police major, the group sat in folding chairs fanning Jackson's desk. Mark Venable was six-six and barely weighed two hundred pounds. He had been called 'Stilts' since junior high basketball. Beside him, Sheriff Midden sported a fringe of white hair and a mouthful of teeth stained from chewing tobacco. Major Jessup, next to Iris, sat ramrod straight, legs apart, hands on his thighs, the crease in his dark blue trousers sharp enough to cut.

"So where's Captain Bundy?" Iris asked. Bundy was head of the ISP office in Idaho Falls that covered Fremont County. Everyone in the room had worked with him.

"The captain's in Quantico training with the Feds," Jessup said. "Something like this, I'd be here anyway."

"Then let's get started," Jackson said. He had outlined the situation for Iris on the phone while the others either had appeared at the Cheney farm or had been briefed earlier. He began by reviewing what little they knew. Afterwards, they spent an hour discussing how to eliminate the lions, tigers, and ligers loose in Idaho. Poisoning, trapping, and hunting were all considered. Shooting the dangerous cats won out. Less discussion was required to realize that only the Idaho State Police could mount an immediate operation to locate and kill the cats.

"We can set up by nightfall," Major Jessup said. "A few hunters, a helicopter, ATVs, and support personnel. We'll need a place to park everything and motel rooms. Shouldn't take more than a few days to do the job."

"Let's hope not," Stilts said. "With deer and elk season around the corner, we need to take care of this fast. Last thing we want are lions attacking hunters."

Paul Midden was frowning. After eighteen years as sheriff he was as much politician as lawman. "Choppers, motels, hunters, ATVs? Sounds like a lot of money."

"Yes, it does," Iris said. "So who pays for it?"

Jessup raised his eyebrows, and Iris noted that half of his right eyebrow was gray, while the other brow and the mustache were dark. "You do," replied Major Jessup. "The town of Buckhorn and the county of Fremont."

"Us?" Iris spat out the word like a hiss.

"Now, just hold on a minute," the county sheriff said and threw up his hands in a defensive gesture. "I got me an election next month. People want drug busts and sex perverts jailed. That's where county money has to go."

Jessup was from Meridian, but the rest of them were aware that Midden's reelection as sheriff in the strongly Republican Fremont County was more secure than the buttons on the blue uniform shirt trying to hold back his belly.

"The ISP is a state-funded agency," Stilts said to Jessup. "Why does anyone have to pay you to do your job?"

"Because this action falls outside our budget."

"So ask the governor for extra money," Iris said.

"Colonel Rudolph did that already," Jessup told her. "Governor Hale's people said they'll see what they can do."

Iris shook her head. "That's not good enough. I'll have Dell get his brother to talk to the governor."

"Good luck with that." The state police major smiled at Iris. "Governor Hale's on his way to China."

Stilts Venable, an avid Democrat, moaned. Like many others, he believed Governor Hale, a two-term Republican, was on a taxpayer-supported vacation before leaving office.

"But our town has no money," Iris said emphatically.

"And we have no choice either," countered Jackson.

Iris knew that Jackson was right, but there was something besides the cost of the operation making her resist. Something about the plan to use the ISP to kill the cats struck her as ... dull and doomed to fail.

Ten minutes later Stilts left to attend a baseball game, Sheriff Midden to campaign, and Iris to pour over town finances again. This time she would go to her office.

Meanwhile, Jackson and Major Jessup worked out the logistics: the ISP would arrive Sunday night and begin the hunt Monday morning; their equipment would be parked at the Elk's Club; and Jackson's officers would provide support.

"That seems to cover it," Jessup said, "unless ... now my men are crack shots and game hunters, but we don't know this area. Having a local guide could help."

"So could someone who's hunted lions."

"You mean the banker? I heard about him." Jessup smiled. "No thanks." He put on his Mounties' hat and added, "Find me a real lion hunter, I'd welcome that."

Jackson had a bad feeling about sending police officers into the woods to hunt lions and tigers. Deer and elk didn't attack the hunter; big cats did. As soon as Jessup left, he got a cup of coffee, returned to his desk, and opened the file on Katy Osborne. This time he looked beyond the photographs. He read the interviews and the biographical information. This time he realized that beautiful or not, she was a professional hunter and experienced guide, someone who had tracked and killed lions. In India she had hunted down a Bengal tiger that escaped a reserve and terrorized a remote area. Her achievements were impressive. He also learned that tragedies marked Katy's life as often as achievements. Her parents had died when she was young, leaving an uncle in Botswana as her guardian. A professional safari guide and hunter, the uncle had disappeared two years ago. There was no mention of Katy Osborne having a husband or children.

Jackson spotted a note that Pamela had stuck to the file folder. It said that Katy Osborne currently was in the United States on a book tour. He saw the dates of her tour and was surprised to learn that she was in Colorado right now. Pamela even had the name of a hotel in Denver.

Maybe Katy being so close to Idaho was nothing or maybe it was what one Buddhist philosopher he had read called 'auspicious coincidence'. Jackson phoned the hotel and asked for her. Then he waited, and a moment later, he heard a telephone ring. It rang for a long time, and then a woman said hello, and he asked if she was Katy Osborne.

She answered by saying, "Who're you?"

"Jackson Hobbs."

"Well, I don't know you, and I'm just leaving so -"

He quickly said, "I'm a policeman."

"Sure you are. How'd you get my number?"

"We have over twenty big cats loose in Idaho," Jackson said, ignoring her question. "Yesterday, one of them killed the best man I ever knew." There was silence on Katy's end of the phone. "Another one almost killed my daughter."

"My god! Tell me your name again."

He did and also told her he was from Buckhorn, Idaho.

This time Katy made the connection. "I saw you on the news last night. You shot a tiger in Idaho yesterday."

"And today I found a man's head but not his body and a woman so chewed up she'll likely die," Jackson said.

This news shook Katy. Even in Africa where lions and leopards and crocodiles kill humans with regularity, where elephants stomp people and Cape Buffalos chase you down and spear you, even where death by nature is no surprise, and even though she in fact had been the bringer of death to those same animals, Katy still felt each death, human or animal, with a sense of despair. She said in a quieter voice, "You said twenty cats. How's that possible?"

"Twenty-two to be exact. Mostly lions and tiger."

"Mostly?"

"Two of them are some monster cat called a liger."

ELEVEN

Despite her hunger, after failing to kill the prey she had chased, Kali returned to searching for her mate. She heard his territorial roar, common in male lions around sundown, from four miles away and found him prowling the same hills Jesse had ridden Touie across earlier.

Ted Cheney had named the male Shaka after a Zulu warrior king. Shaka was a year older than Kali. Thicker and taller, he weighed over a thousand pounds. While he lacked a full mane, he had a slight, white ruff at his throat. His skin was tawny, like Kali's, and also overlaid with orangey-brown stripes, but the markings on Shaka's face were black. There had been two male ligers at Safari Land. When Kali first came into estrus, the males fought to mate with her. Shaka killed the competing male.

After a reunion of cuffing, rolling, and nipping, Shaka licked the blood that oozed from Kali's ear where Wade Placett's bullet had removed a thumb-sized piece. Big cats have been known to carry half-a-dozen bullets in them, so the wound, while an irritant, was nothing more. A while later, Kali followed Shaka out of the wooded hills to the pastures below in search of food. When they reached the Double-D sheep pastures, not only were all the sheep gone, the remains of Shaka's earlier kill also had disappeared.

The ligers sniffed around, but large cats rely on sound more than smell. Today, the wind was blowing the wrong direction for them to hear the bleating sheep in Deborah's barnyard pens. So when they heard a wolf pack in the forest nearby, the ligers abandoned the sheep pasture and pursued the wolves. If they failed to kill a wolf or two, they at least would be headed back to where Kali had found food before, to the farm where she killed Ed Stevens.

By the time Jackson returned to his coffee, an oil slick with rainbow colors was floating on top, reminding him of a rain puddle on tarmac. He set aside the cold coffee and replayed the phone conversation. Katy had asked him to describe Ed's body. After he had done so, from the gnawed neck to the gutting, she said that it certainly sounded like an African lion or Asian tiger had killed him.

"Lions consume the viscera first, probably for the fat," Katy had said. "Then move on to the denser muscles. If left alone, they'll eat most every part, even bones."

Another time, she said, "Cats mostly hunt at dawn and dusk, and that's the best time to track them, when they're moving around. Other times, they like to lay up and hide. Last thing you want is to stumble unaware on a lion or tiger. Before you can get off a shot, you're dead."

He found her friendly enough after the beginning, but she had abruptly ended the call ten minutes later, saying that she had to leave. She gave him a cell phone number and told him to call again if he had more questions. Questions were all he did have. It's answers he needed.

While Janet Cook maneuvered the rental car toward the Boulder Turnpike, Katy glanced at her notes or stared out the window at the land. She paid little attention to either.

"I'd say 'a penny for your thoughts'," Janet told her, "but given how weak the dollar is, it'd be an insult."

Katy grinned and said, "I got a phone call right before we left." She then told her book agent about the phone conversation with Jackson Hobbs in Idaho.

When Katy mentioned the number and kind of big cats that had escaped, Janet tried to furrow her brow. "Ligers? You mean those cute things in the *Napoleon Dynamite* movie?"

"I mean a cat big enough to bite you in half."

"Oh! So not that cute." A second later, Janet said, "Funny, I don't remember ligers in either of your books."

"Because they're not. Ligers don't exist in Africa or anywhere else in the natural wild. For one thing, lions and tigers don't usually share an area. And even if they did, they wouldn't mate. They're enemies. They're not in the book because I've never hunted ligers. Nobody has."

"Nobody?" Janet said. "Really?"

Stan Ely was waiting for Katy and Janet outside a small theater on 13th Street opposite Boulder's downtown park, home to an antique train. Katy's talk and book signing were taking place in an old brick building. The event was co-sponsored by a local bookstore and Stan's group, Animal Rescue Kingdom. ARK's headquarters was in Boulder although their land base, one hundred and eighty acres, was in south-central Colorado near Pagosa Springs.

Katy did not think about Idaho again until the talk and book signing were over, when she was sitting with Janet and Stan in the ornate Dushanbe Teahouse a few doors north of the theater. Despite the tempting array of teas, Katy ordered red wine. While they waited for the appetizers to arrive, Katy said, "I got an interesting call from an Idaho policeman today, Stan. About Safari Land."

Stan surprised her, saying, "I know."

"About my phone call?"

"Un-uh. About the missing cats. The killings."

"I didn't hear anything on the news," Janet said.

"Me either," Stan said. "But the animal rescue grapevine is all over this story." The appetizers were delivered, and Stan waited until the waiter had fussed over them and left before saying, "So what'd the Idaho cop want?"

"Advice. Information."

"Hmmm. Well, if I can scrounge up enough money, we'll go up there and rescue these cats."

Katy eyed him curiously. The police chief had told her the Idaho State Police were mounting a search and kill operation tomorrow. "Idaho officials agreed to this?"

"Not yet." Stan dipped a vegetarian samosa in a black sauce. "But why wouldn't they?"

"You're right," Katy said. "Why wouldn't they?" They talked for a while longer about Idaho before the conversation drifted into other areas. Thirty minutes later, Katy and Janet said goodbye to Stan and returned to the rental car. Janet started the engine, but didn't drive away. "Janet?"

"I think YOU should go to Idaho."

"Uh, Janet, I'm on a book tour. Two more weeks."

"You know I can cancel the remaining tour."

"I know if I suggested it, you'd go ballistic."

Janet laughed and drummed her perfect red nails on the steering wheel. "Just think about it a minute - giant cats stalking people in America. Not India or Africa. America! This thing could go viral, and if it does, oh god, the publicity would be great for sales. Besides, nobody has ever hunted ligers before. You'd be the first." She paused and smiled at Katy. "I smell a new book in this."

Janet didn't usually attend book tour events outside the east coast, and Katy knew Janet was doing her a big favor by being here. "Well, let me think about it, okay."

Janet spent another ten minutes convincing Katy that she should go to Idaho immediately. Katy did not tell her that she had booked a flight before even leaving the hotel.

Jackson was still in his office Sunday evening when he got the phone call. He had intended to contact Katy again, but her offer to come to Idaho surprised him, and he hesitated. When he did, Katy said, "I'm sorry. Maybe I misunderstood. I thought you'd want my help."

"Want it and need it," he said. "But without talking to the town mayor, I'm not sure how much we can pay."

"In Africa if a village has a man-eating lion or rogue elephant or some other dangerous animal terrorizing them, and if you're the closest professional hunter, you have to drop everything and go kill it. It's your duty."

"But Idaho's a long way from Africa."

"Not if you have lions and tigers killing people. Anyway, the point is you don't have to pay me." Katy then told Jackson her flight schedule and that she had failed to get a connecting flight from Utah to either eastern Idaho airport late on a Sunday night. "I'll rent a car and -"

"Don't. I'll pick you up at the airport."

"In Salt Lake City? Isn't that kind of far?"

A drive to Salt Lake City and back would take most of the night. "It'll give us a chance to talk. Give me a chance to learn as much as I can about lions and tigers."

"Learn about me, you mean," Katy said.

"That too," Jackson said with a chuckle. After they ended the phone call, he thought about the drive to Utah for a few minutes, and then he called out, "Brian."

"He's gone," Tucker said, appearing in the doorway.

"Tucker? What are you doing here?"

"Brian's little girl, she's sick. So I came in to give him a break. We were going to tell you, but you've been on the phone. Brian's afraid it's swine flu."

"Swine flu? What's next, plague of locusts? A burning bush?"

"You shouldn't blaspheme," Tucker said. "Chief, sir."

"Probably not. Anyway, thanks for helping out." Tucker nodded as Jackson asked, "Eileen managing okay without you?"

"She's at the funeral home now," Tucker said. "She said Uncle Ed, he left something for you."

"She say what?"

"No. Just that his funeral is gonna be Tuesday."

"I'll let everyone know."

Once Tucker left, Jackson phoned Angie Kuka. Ten minutes later, she entered his office.

"What's up, Chief?" Angie asked.

"You," Jackson said. He handed her a memo that he had written while waiting. "You're now the Deputy Chief. I'm going to Salt Lake, so you're in charge until I return."

"What's in Salt Lake City?"

"A woman who's a lion hunter."

Angie's mouth hung open in surprise.

"An ISP major named Jessup will be arriving with some hunters tonight. He'll be in touch with you.

Angie glanced behind her at Tucker. "You know, not everybody's going to like me being promoted."

"Everybody doesn't have to. Just you and me."

TWELVE

As for as anyone knew, including wives, the men at Jerry and Marcy Umfleet's log-kit house were playing cards Sunday night, although no cards were out on the kitchen table. Marcy, a stout woman in a short skirt, the lone female present, was handing out cold Budweiser when Ronnie Greathouse said, "Let's get started." Ronnie had swapped his state trooper uniform for jeans and a t-shirt with Jesse James' image on it. Ronnie had both a swagger and a voice that commanded attention, and the others had ceded the leadership role to him after Ted Cheney quit.

"What about Tucker?" Jerry asked.

"Running late. He had to work," Ronnie said. "Probably just as well given what happened to his uncle."

Apart from Ronnie and Jerry, a non-union plumber, only Fred Bulcher, owner of a sand and gravel business, and Joe Kennet, a truck driver from Rexburg, had shown up for the meeting of the Knights of the Golden Circle.

"I wanna know who let them goddamn cats out," Ronnie said. Everybody looked at everybody else but nobody spoke up. "Goddamnit, we said we'd send Ted a warning!" bellowed Ronnie. "We said we'd let ONE of his cats out to show him we mean business. A warning to keep his trap shut. But we didn't say do it right now." A month earlier Ted ridiculed the small group – they never had more then eight members - and then resigned. "So who screwed it up? Who opened the goddamn zoo doors and killed Ted? I know one of you did."

The three men claimed innocence and tossed out wild theories about how Ted's cats got free. When Ronnie tired of listening to them, he described the plan to bring in the state police hunters. He advised everyone to lay low until the ISP had left. Eventually, they discussed other topics, including a plan to replace Chief Hobbs with Tucker Thule. Jerry reported that the Aryan Brotherhood would back their efforts to defeat the Jew county prosecutor in the upcoming election. Fred was dismissive of Jerry's plan. He believed change came through violence. Burning out the baby killers in Rexburg had been their biggest moment so far, although among friends they also had taken credit for a murder there. "Revolution spills blood," Fred argued.

By the time Tucker arrived, the meeting was nearly over. As soon as the men began popping fresh beers and telling jokes about mud people, dykes, beaners, and ragheads, Ronnie left. Usually he would have joined in, but tonight he had better things to do.

The night was cool so he zipped his leather jacket before firing up the 2006 Custom Fat Boy. He decided not to wear a helmet. He had photochromic sunglasses for riding at night. He had bought the bike in Pensacola, Florida and ridden it across country. That had been the best week of his life. Pearl black with chrome wheels, the Harley-Davidson had been a pussy magnet from day one, which he knew made it even stranger that he was on his way to see a woman who rode a wheelchair instead of a motorcycle.

After Maryann Fedder's accident, her dad had installed a separate door with a ramp that led directly into her ground floor bedroom. The door would be unlocked now and Maryann in bed watching television or reading. At first Ronnie was simply curious about sleeping with a crippled woman. Then he discovered that he truly liked Maryann, and he kept returning to see her. Now he was the backdoor man. The thought made Ronnie laugh. Backdoor man! He wondered if Maryann had done it that way before? Maybe tonight!

Jackson studied a photo of Katy while he waited in the baggage claim area. This late at night there were few other people. After a while he laid the photo on the seat beside him. He stretched his legs, clasped his hands behind his head, and stared up at the ceiling.

To be a policeman, he thought, was to spend each day pushing a boulder up hill knowing that it will naturally roll down again. Although his job was to maintain order, disorder was inherent in life. It simply was a matter of whether we created it or whether disorder found us. There was both rape and Katrina. There was murder, and there was 9/11. There was assault with intent, and there was whatever you call a monster cat that kills a dying man looking to fly-fish his way into that gentle night. His real job, Jackson decided, was to maintain a myth of order.

When he heard the announcement for the arrival of the flight from Denver, Jackson got up and went to the men's room. As he came out he nearly ran over a young woman pushing a wobbly baby stroller. A wheel was bad, and he offered to look at it. The woman wore the old-fashioned long dress of the conservative Mormon sects clustered in southern Utah. She stammered a shy "thank you" but declined his help. He watched her leave, struggling with the stroller. She reminded him of the few traditional Muslim women he had seen in Colorado, the invisibly caged.

Jackson took out Katy's photograph again, but he didn't need it to recognize her. Katy was smaller than he expected and thin too but without looking starved. She moved with the grace of someone who had learned posture by walking with a book on her head. Although most of the other women wore clothes designed for a gym instead of an airport, Katy was dressed in a loose pants and jacket outfit and nice shoes suitable for traveling. She wheeled a sage green carry-on with a computer bag riding piggyback. The strap of a small purse angled across her body, emphasizing her breasts. She spotted him now and smiled.

"Miss Osborne," he said, going up to her.

"Katy," she told him and smiled again.

They shook hands. "I'm Jackson Hobbs."

"I know," she said. "From the TV, remember?" Jackson forgot that he was still holding Katy's photograph until she took it out of his left hand. In the photograph she was on safari and carrying a large caliber rifle. "I tend not to travel with my elephant culling gun," she said. "I hope you're not disappointed."

"Not too much," he said. "We waiting for luggage?"

"I'm afraid so. I've been on the road over a month."

They continued to make small talk while they waited for Katy's luggage to arrive, and when it did Jackson lifted a large Briggs & Riley roller bag off the conveyor.

Twenty minutes later they were in the Jeep and leaving the Salt Lake City airport. They drove north on Interstate 15 toward Pocatello, some two and a half hours away.

As soon as they settled into the drive, Katy asked Jackson questions about Safari Land. He told her some of what Angie had dug up on Ted and Dolly Cheney and then said, "They were living in Buckhorn when I arrived, five years ago. It wasn't called Safari Land then. It wasn't called anything. Just another abandoned farm going to seed. At the time I think they had a couple of lions and tigers and some Great Northern wolves too. Not sure what else they were keeping there. I heard they were trying to breed the wolves with Huskies. Anyway, about four years ago they got rid of the wolves and started bringing in more and more big cats. I'm not sure where they got them."

"A failed circus, overcrowded zoo, dumb people trying to raise a lion or tiger in their yards," Katy said.

"So not that hard to come by?"

Katy nodded.

"I was out there maybe three years ago with my daughter, Jesse, and then again about a year or so back. The Cheneys wanted to open a safari park. Take you on a protected drive while the animals roamed free. But they could never get all of the permits they needed and then —" Jackson glanced over at Katy. She had been quiet for the last few minutes. She was asleep. "Oh hell," he said.

* * *

Kali and Shaka heard the motorcycle when it was two miles away, but they paid little attention to it. Raised in captivity, the ligers were familiar with machine noises. Anyway, they were too hungry to concern themselves with the noise. They had followed the wolves into the hills, but with Kali moving slower than usual, failed to catch them. Now, Kali was leading them toward a distant chicken coop.

The ligers crossed a creek where the water was lowest and climbed up a steep bank. At the top of the bank was a paved road, hard beneath their paws. They were halfway across the road when they saw the bright headlight.

Ronnie still was thinking about the meeting at the Umfleet house as he rounded the bend before the bridge over Brown's Creek. Fred had been the instigator in turning the guys against Ted Cheney. He had told them that somebody in town was talking to the law about the militia group. Fred wouldn't reveal how he knew this. He claimed that there was somebody high up that backed the KGC but couldn't be seen as part of it. Fred cast suspicion on Ted. Ronnie doubted if any part of Fred's tale was true, but he was glad to be rid of Ted Cheney. Ted was difficult; Fred, he could handle.

As soon as Ronnie crossed the bridge, his light beam illuminated the animals. He couldn't believe his own eyes. Two monster cats stood as still as statues in the middle of the road. Ronnie slammed the brakes and swerved to miss the animals. The Harley-Davidson went into a slide. He rode the slide off the asphalt and clung to the handlebar when the bike caught air. The Fat Boy flew over a steep bank and came down front-wheel-first on a bushy hillside. Ronnie catapulted over the handlebar and turned a perfect somersault before landing on his back. The motorcycle bounced and banged its way into dense weeds.

When Maryann Fedder woke up, the television was on. It took a moment for her to remember what she had been watching before crying herself to sleep. A woman on the Shopping Network had been selling the identical nightgown she was wearing. She rubbed the satiny fabric and felt the lace edges. She was certain Ronnie would like it. She imagined him fondling it and slipping it off her and ....

Maryann made herself stop. She didn't want to cry again so she focused on the television, flipping channels. Three years earlier her parents had upgraded the satellite service to receive over two hundred channels. She paused for a moment when she saw a guy on a motorcycle. Ronnie had never made a date and failed to show up before. She guessed this was how he planned to dump her.

She switched channels. Usually, she watched cooking shows. New dishes were appearing regularly on the family dinner table now. She paused. Africa. The channel had to be National Geographic or Discovery. What she saw reminded her of something her dad had said earlier about lions and tigers loose in Idaho. She gasped when she saw a leopard bring down a helpless baby wildebeest. At least she hadn't bought the crotchless panties Ronnie wanted her to wear.

By the time Jackson stopped at a service station and Katy awakened, it was after midnight. They both got a coffee-to-go, and then Katy offered to drive.

"I'm fine," Jackson said, "but unless you want to sleep, you could tell me about hunting lions and tigers."

"As I understand it, I'll be briefing the State Police hunters in –" she looked at her watch "– something like six hours, so you'll hear most of it again."

Jackson cracked a grin. "Hearing it twice probably won't hurt me."

For the next thirty minutes Katy told him about tracking and hunting big cats. Jackson interrupted her often to ask questions, and when they finally fell silent, she said, "So what do you think?"

"I think finding and killing the lions and tigers won't be as easy as people imagine."

"It never is." Katy looked out the window and saw the green and white sign that indicated they were twenty miles from Pocatello. "I need to stop in Pocatello."

"Stop? Where? Kind of late to pay a visit."

"Not to this guy." Katy turned on the map light and read off an address and asked if Jackson knew it.

"The university district," he said. "I can find it."

"It's a house. Belongs to a gun dealer."

Jackson glanced at her curiously.

"I can't go lion hunting without rifles. This gun dealer said he'd provide what I need if I stopped by tonight. He's actually a friend of someone I know in Colorado, a man who runs an animal rescue operation."

"An animal rescue guy that's friends with a gun dealer that's helping a safari guide. Did hell freeze over?"

"Maybe. Or maybe it's an American luxury, seeing the world as left or right, good or bad, hunters or preservers," Katy said. "In Africa the lines are fuzzier." She watched him as she spoke. "Take you for instance. You're a policeman. But does that mean you never do harm?"

Jackson kept his eyes on the road. Katy didn't see the sadness deep inside them. "Aren't you half-American?"

"American mother, British father. I was born in England, but I lived a lot of places growing up, including Africa and the States. My dad worked for the World Bank."

"Guess that explains the tiny accent."

"What accent?" she said with a laugh as she watched his profile in the dashboard lights. Jackson's face was not classically handsome, but she liked the combination of rugged and sensitive. He had a burn scar on the side of his neck. It didn't look to be more than a few years old.

"House fire," Jackson said once he noticed her looking at the scar.

Katy waited for him to say more. Most people felt a need to annotate, to explain, as if they owed the world a reason for their imperfections. Jackson silently returned to watching the road ahead. Katy repeated the question from before that remained unanswered. "So do you?" Katy asked. "As a policeman, do you ever cause harm?"

Jackson knew Iris would say yes. Eileen Stevens too. Nancy Larson certainly would say yes, if she weren't dead. "Nobody walks through life without leaving a footprint," Jackson said. "Not even if we want to."

THIRTEEN

"This is it," Jackson said as he stopped behind a white Mercedes SUV parked outside an immaculate 1930s' Craftsman bungalow. Katy knocked, and a man wearing pajamas under a bathrobe made from loud beach towels opened the door. Ollie Hamm was six-two and twice as wide as a normal man. When Katy shook hands, it felt like she was gripping sausages. Hamm was cordial despite the hour, but after Jackson answered his questions about the escaped cats without adding commentary, Hamm soon got down to business.

Ten minutes later, in the glow of bright outside lights, Jackson and Katy loaded two gun cases into Jackson's Grand Cherokee. One rifle Katy identified as a .375. "It's the one I use in Africa unless I'm culling elephants," she explained. "My Weatherby has a few custom modifications, but even without them, it's the single best big-game rifle for a safari."

"So I've heard," Jackson said, recalling Dell's lecture. The second gun case was hard and shaped differently, like a bow-hunting case or a case for some musical instrument. "And this one?"

"A Remington model three-eighty-nine pneumatic dart gun. And a variety of darts with gel collars."

"A dart gun?"

"Killing an animal isn't the only way to stop it." Katy didn't say anything about the animal rescue group coming to Idaho. Stan had asked her not to mention it.

They continued north on Interstate 15 to Idaho Falls, picked up U.S. Highway 20 through Rexburg and Saint Anthony, and then turned east on ID47. Some two and a half hours after visiting Ollie Hamm, they reached Buckhorn in the middle of the night. Jackson's first stop was the Sportsman Motel. They found three black, unmarked Chevy Suburbans, each a few years old, parked in a row. Jessup and his hunters had arrived. Jackson rang the night buzzer for a long time before the sleepy clerk responded.

After Jackson helped Katy unload her gear and made plans to return for her in a few hours, he drove out to the western edge of town and turned into the Elk's Club. He didn't belong to the Elk's, although Iris did, but he had been there for meals and other events. A National Guard Black Hawk helicopter sat on the grassy playground. In the parking lot there was a trailer with two ATVs. Everything was just like Jessup had said. Jessup intrigued him. For an African-American man to be a major in the Idaho State Police, Jackson knew he either had to be so good that he would be a colonel if he were white or so incompetent that he was a safe token to equality. He suspected that Jessup was very good.

A state trooper car was parked alongside the building. Unlike the SWAT team's plain Suburbans, the black cruiser had a white diagonal band across the front doors with the words: Idaho State Police. The trooper guarding the equipment was asleep behind the wheel. Jackson left him alone and drove home to doze for a couple of hours.

The State Police team sent to Buckhorn to shoot the big cats consisted of two detectives and six troopers under the command of Major Jessup. They wore camouflage on Monday morning, giving them the look and feel of a military instead of a police operation and distinguishing them from everyone else gathered at the Elk's Club. Club members had cooked breakfast, and the men were eating as dawn broke. Major Jessup sat with Stilts Venable from Fish and Game and two troopers in regular dark blue ISP uniforms. Jessup had little appetite for his eggs, even before the phone call.

"Listen up!" Jessup yelled after dumping his Blackberry on the tabletop with a bang. He stood and addressed his men. "Any of you men here buddies with trooper Ronald Greathouse?" He waited. "Anybody?"

His question was met with silence until trooper Bill Roberts said, "Not exactly buddies, Major, but I know him. We worked a Boise State football game last year."

"Well, trooper Greathouse is MIA," Jessup said. "He was scheduled for guard duty at two A.M. last night and didn't show." Jessup sent one of the uniformed troopers at his table to Ronnie's house and then checked his watch. "Soon as Chief Hobbs and his lion expert get here, we'll be runnin' and gunnin', so you men chow down."

Iris stepped out of the shower and onto the scales. Two extra pounds. Damn! Why is it that a single pound above starvation on a woman with a drop of Mexican blood always sticks to her ass, tummy, or hips, she thought? But even the unwanted weight didn't stop Iris from feeling happy as she dried her body with a plush Turkish towel. Last night had been a success. By the end of the meal, Dell, who had arrived in a grim mood, had forgotten about his cemetery visit. With Jesse and Shane in Rexburg at the movies, the evening flowed naturally from dining room to bedroom. Her body still tingled when she thought about it.

Iris was brushing her teeth when the idea that had flittered just out of reach yesterday suddenly landed. It was so obvious, like hiding something in plain sight. She spit out the toothpaste and rinsed her mouth. They were going about it all wrong. Faced with two problems, you use one to solve the other. Her plan was bold and brilliant.

She hurriedly dressed and grabbed her car keys and rushed out. Instead of going to the Elk's Club to greet the State Police hunters, she drove to Dell's house.

Major Jessup did a poor job of hiding his surprise when Jackson introduced Katy. Asked to 'look authentic' for a couple of television interviews, she had been carting around the boots, cargo pants, Solumbra shirt, and cotton fishing vest she often wore on safari. She never imagined that she would use her gear on an actual hunt. Since September mornings can be chilly in Buckhorn, Katy also wore a nylon windbreaker.

After a few minutes of conversation designed to both charm and grill Katy, Jessup gathered his men in a semi-circle and introduced Jackson who then introduced Katy.

At first Katy simply looked at the hunters. "I was nineteen when I shot my first lion," she said a moment later, "a man-eater that'd killed thirty-two people." She watched as the men's eyes crawled off her body and up to her face. "My uncle had a game farm in Botswana and was a well-known hunter and guide. I was on Christmas break from the university when he was asked to kill the lion. Now some people say only an old or injured lion will attack human beings. Don't believe it. This lion was young and healthy when he developed a taste for human flesh.

"Uncle Bucky was just starting to have problems with his eyes about then, so I talked him into letting me go along on the hunt. My job was to provide fresh meat for the camp. My uncle was particularly fond of eland."

Katy paused and sipped some bottled water. "A week into the hunt Uncle Bucky broke his ankle. And it's only because of his accident that I was following Ezekiel, our incredible, ageless tracker, through seven-foot-tall yellow thatching grass when the man-eater attacked us.

"If a lion charges you, don't try for a head shot. Above the eyes a lion is all muscle. A central shoulder shot is the safest and easiest. Aim for the middle part of the chest region, and you have a chance of hitting lungs, heart, major veins and arteries, important bones." Katy paused again and looked from man to man. "The average shot will be long, but some may be as close as fifty feet. A lion can cover that distance in a second. I had my uncle's three-seventy-five Ruger loaded with three-hundred-grain soft-points. It still took two shots to drop the lion. Even then I put a third bullet in him. And I'm talking about a single lion. Lions mostly hunt in prides. Had there been more than one lion, I wouldn't be here now."

She watched the hunters shift in their chairs. She had them listening and alert, the way she wanted. "Now, let's talk about tigers," she said. "Our solo assassins."

"It was something you said in the café on Saturday," Iris told Dell. They were in his kitchen where Iris was making coffee while Dell fixed toast. "You said you could go on safari right here. So I started thinking, if you'd go on a lion safari in Idaho, how many others would too?"

"A hell of lot of people."

"Then why should we pay anyone to kill these cats if we can get people to pay us? The town can make money, and we get rid of the animal problem too. What we should do is hold the first lion safari in America."

"I can't believe I didn't think of it. Hell, it's a great idea, Iris," Dell said. "But we'll have to make it affordable, you know that. We can't charge safari prices."

"We'll do better than that. We'll offer prizes. Each hunter buys a license to shoot lions and tigers and maybe goes home with a big check as well as a trophy."

"Then the only thing I see standing in our way is politics. The State Police hunters are already here."

Iris opened the refrigerator door and looked inside. "That's where you come in. Crap. You're out of fat-free half-and-half." She shut the door, saying, "You need to call your brother, our acting-governor, right now."

When Katy finished answering their questions, the men applauded loudly. Major Jessup then reviewed the plan, and afterward the hunters gathered their equipment. They were more familiar with a Colt M4 or the Blaser .308 and R93 sniper rifles than they were a Weatherby Mark 5, Winchester .458, or a .375. None of them even had seen a Churchill Double 470. Some of the sharpshooters had no special training. Others were trained to handle raids and hostage rescue. None of them were trained for lion hunting. Even so, they were confident they would find and kill the big cats, despite the scare that Katy had thrown at them.

Troopers Dwight and Bill Roberts were especially eager to get started. The twins had served together in Iraq and trained as snipers. Afterward, they both joined the State Police. The Roberts twins were the two shooters that would hunt from the helicopter using borrowed big-game rifles.

Two other hunters would travel by ATVs, while the rest of them - two troopers and two detectives and Major Jessup - would follow Katy on foot. The starting point of the hunt for everyone would be the Placett's farm unless the helicopter spotted a tiger or a lion pride elsewhere.

The helicopter took off and the noise nearly kept Major Jessup from hearing his phone. He covered one ear with his hand when he answered it and sought the shelter of the Elk's Club. The other hunters got ready to pull out.

Jackson was showing Katy how to use the police radio he had given her when they saw the helicopter turn around. They were watching it land when Major Jessup returned.

"What's going on?" Jackson shouted to him as soon as Jessup was close enough to hear.

"New orders. We're to pack up and leave town."

"Leave?" Jackson said in disbelief. "Whose orders?"

Jessup didn't answer until he was standing three feet away. "Colonel Rudolph, my superior. And his orders came from Lieutenant Governor Dan Tapper. The acting-governor."

Katy walked up and joined them. "What's going on?"

"That answer's above my pay grade, Miss Osborne," Major Jessup said. He looked back at Jackson. "I'm told your town mayor can explain everything."

FOURTEEN

Jackson found Iris and Dell in the Split-Rail Café and headed toward them. Katy hurried to keep up.

"I knew it wouldn't take you long," Iris told Jackson a second later, while her eyes fixed on Katy. "And you must be the lion hunter I heard about," Iris said to her.

Jackson introduced everyone, providing names and roles. No mention was made of Iris being his ex-wife. "Now that we've all made nice," Jackson said, "one of you mind telling me what just happened with the State Police?"

"We don't need them here," Iris said.

"We don't?" Jackson said. "Last I heard we have twenty-two big cats running around killing people."

"And we'll get rid of the lions and make money for the town too," Iris said. "We're going to have a public hunt."

Katy's mouth opened in amazement, and Jackson muttered, "Are you out of your mind?"

"Coffee?" Suzy Beans asked. Nobody had paid attention to the waitress standing beside the booth. "And menus?"

Jackson and Katy didn't want coffee or food.

"I know who you are," Dell said to Katy as Suzy shrugged and indifferently sauntered off. "I heard about you when I was on safari. Read your books too. Tell Jackson how much it costs for an African safari."

"It all depends on the length and the services."

"My brother and me, we spent over twenty-five grand for ten days in Kenya and a short stay in South Africa."

"Well, it's expensive to run a good safari."

Iris sipped her latte and then said, "A thousand dollars. That's what we'll charge each hunter for a license. And they can get it back and a lot more money to boot. We'll offer prizes for the biggest cat killed."

"You won't get ten people," Jackson argued.

"Oh we will, and not just from around here either," Dell said. "California, Texas, New York. People will flock here from all over. A once in a lifetime adventure and you won't need a passport or twenty grand to have it."

"We'll be on the national news by noontime today," Iris said. "It'll put Buckhorn, Idaho on the map."

"But maybe not for the reasons you want," Katy said. She turned to look at Jackson. "Can they do this?"

Iris laughed. "We already did it."

"So when is this hunt going to happen?" Jackson asked.

"As soon as my brother gets here," Dell replied. He then said to Katy, "Dan's the lieutenant governor."

"The acting-governor," Iris added with emphasis.

Jackson looked skeptical. "Dan agreed to this?"

"Hell yes. He's flying in tomorrow to kick it off," Dell said. "And I bet we have two, three hundred hunters by then, with another three hundred or more on the way."

"Every one of them buying a license and paying for food and drinks and motel rooms and gas," Iris said.

"And caskets," Katy said. "Don't forget about caskets. You'll sell some of them too."

A short time later Jackson eased the Grand Cherokee into the motel parking lot and stopped outside Katy's door. He left the engine running but shifted into park.

"You know what's going to happen here, don't you?" Katy asked.

"Nothing good. I'm pretty sure of that."

"These lions and tigers, they're not going to call a time out until the town's ready," Katy said. "Big cats eat ten to twenty pounds of meat a day just to survive. That means they have to kill something and keep on killing. Today, tomorrow. Animals or people, whatever they can."

"I can talk to Iris again, but ...." Jackson shook his head. "She's blinded by the upside and can't see the down."

Katy thought about her own money problems. How far would she go to save Skorokoro? Pretty damn far! "You and the mayor don't appear to see eye-to-eye about much."

Jackson shut off the engine. "She's my ex-wife."

Katy bobbed her head. "I didn't catch that part."

"We have a daughter, Jesse, a fifteen year old."

"The girl the tiger chased."

"My guess is it was one of the ligers chasing her." Jackson then told Katy the story of Jesse's escape.

When he finished, Katy said, "I hope I can meet her."

"Me too. But after what just happened this morning, I figured you'd be on the first plane out of here."

"But then you don't know me yet, Chief Hobbs." She opened the door and slid out. "I'll be waiting for you."

"To do what?"

"To come pick me up."

Jackson said, "And where exactly are we going?"

"To Safari Land. To go liger hunting."

Jackson barely had settled behind his desk at the police station when Sadie announced that Major Jessup wanted to see him. Jackson followed her to the bullpen and greeted the state cop and asked him if he wanted coffee.

"I'm a tea drinker myself," Jessup said.

"So is Sadie." Jackson nodded toward her. "She's very picky." Jackson led them to the breakroom where he poured coffee while Major Jessup made a cup of Assam tea heavy with cream and sugar. "So what can I do for you?"

"Trooper Ronnie Greathouse is missing." Jessup explained about Ronnie's schedule and his failure to show. "Nobody's seen him all day." Jessup sipped his tea. "If it's okay with you, I'm going to have two of my men look for him. The Roberts twins. You met them earlier today."

The police department should run a missing-person search in town. Jackson knew it, and the ISP major knew it too, but with everything else going on, Jackson was not going to get territorial. "Two of the hunters, right?"

"Uh-huh. And that's really why they volunteered. I know they'll find a way to get out in the woods today."

A moment later they headed to Jackson's office, mugs in hand. "Don't let the mayor know they're hunting," Jackson said, "or she'll want them to buy a safari license."

Jessup sneered. "A public hunt is crazy and dangerous. Whoever thought this up -"

"Will regret it. I know it and you know it, and they'll learn soon enough," Jackson told Major Jessup. "Tell your troopers to let me know if they need our help."

Jessup nodded and sat in a chair in front of Jackson's desk while Jackson eased into the gray Aeron chair behind it. "You know trooper Greathouse very well?" Jessup asked.

"Ronnie? Not all that well. One of my officers hangs out with him. Tucker Thule. You're welcome to talk to him, but we'll have to call him in. It's his uncle that was killed on Saturday. I gave Tucker some time off."

"If my troopers don't find Greathouse," Jessup said, "I'll turn it over to a detective in Meridian. He can talk to your officer later if he needs to." Meridian, Idaho's third largest city, with a population nearing 75,000, was the location of the Idaho State Police headquarters and training facility. "This is damn good tea," Jessup added.

After Katy talked to Janet Cook, who claimed the public lion hunt would provide her with a can't-miss best-seller, Katy turned on the motel television and watched the news. She was amazed at how quickly the story of the escaped cats and proposed safari was spreading. It was the top story on CNN, Fox, MSNBC, and most other news channels.

She had just switched off the television when Stan Ely phoned. Stan also had heard about the public lion hunt and spent the first few minutes railing against the plan. For that matter, he had not been thrilled when Katy first had told him she was going to Idaho to hunt lions, but he still had helped her connect with the rotund gun dealer.

When Stan paused for breath, Katy said, "A public hunt's not what I expected. It's not what I came here to do. You know that, Stan."

"I know ARK's going to file an injunction."

"An injunction?" Katy said.

"To stop the public lion hunt."

"Wow! You can do that?"

"Maybe, maybe not," Stan admitted. "But even filing the injunction gets us press and leverage. Maybe it'll encourage people to donate money. It's been a rough couple of years. When people lose their jobs, we lose their support."

"If you stop the public hunt and bring your rescue people up here, won't there be trouble?"

Stan laughed. "Katy, trouble is what I live for."

Late Monday morning the Roberts twins parked the black Chevy Suburban Jessup had left for them outside a modest ranch house. They knocked on doors, peered through windows, and called Ronnie's cell phone. The knocks went unanswered, and the cell phone did not ring inside the house. A search of a Dodge Ram pickup parked in the driveway yielded no clues either. Then they split up and talked to the neighbors. Nobody reported having seen Ronnie since Sunday night, but more than one person told them that Ronnie owned a bike as well as the truck. The Dodge Ram in the driveway could mean anything or nothing. The motorcycle might be missing or in the garage.

"We have to get inside," Bill said once they returned to Ronnie's house and compared interview notes. "I'm going around back again, and when I'm ready, you bang on the front door real loud. Give me two minutes."

"Copy that," Dwight said.

Bill then hurried to the back, and a moment later Dwight pounded on the front door. Even so, he still heard glass breaking. Before long, the front door swung open.

The twins searched each room of the three-bedroom house but found nothing of interest except a pornography collection, mostly girl-on-girl, a wrapped gift addressed to someone named Maryann, and a box of papers pertaining to something called The Knights Of The Golden Circle. The papers included a notebook filled with writing that they couldn't decipher.

"It looks like a goddamn code book," Bill Roberts said, thinking back to his days in the military. "What the hell's this guy up to anyway?"

FIFTEEN

For the next hour Jackson dealt with routine matters - there was a DUI, a family fight, and some petty thievery to handle - but when he tried to update the duty roster, he couldn't bring himself to simply replace Ed's name on it. In the end he put the old roster sheet aside and started a new one. He then briefed two reserve officers on the route the funeral procession would follow from the church to the cemetery on Tuesday. He reminded himself to dig out his police blues and make sure his uniform was clean and pressed. He also told Sadie to find the black armbands they would all wear to Ed's service.

Next, he called Angie into his office and gave her a small, plastic evidence bag containing the necklace taken from Dolly. "See if you can find out where it came from," he said. "May belong to whoever let the cats out."

"So you're thinking a woman let them out?"

Jackson said, "Could be."

"Or it could be Dolly's necklace?"

"That too."

"Not much for me to go on."

Jackson said, "Enough for a deputy-chief." He said it dryly, but his lips twitched a grin and his eyes crinkled. He got out his car keys and put on his gray hat. "Not sure exactly when I'll be back. You're in charge."

"Should I ask where you're going, just in case?"

"Liger hunting," he said. "What I heard anyway."

When Jackson pulled into the Sportsman Motel parking lot, he noticed more cars than he had seen there earlier, including cars with Montana and Utah tags. He figured someone's hunting buddies had been tipped off and were now first in line for the safari. He knocked on Katy's door.

Some twenty minutes later, Jackson rolled to a stop outside the decrepit farmhouse at Safari Land. When she saw the place, Katy asked if he was playing a joke on her.

"Oh, it gets worse," said Jackson. "Wait to you see the animal cages." He parked the Jeep in the same place he had parked two days ago – or was it yesterday? He had to stop and think. So much had happened so quickly.

Jackson removed the Stoeger P-350 from the back of the Jeep and loaded it with slugs. His officers carried a Remington 870 12-guage pump, but he had brought his own shotgun from Colorado. While Katy retrieved the .375 from its padded carrying case, Jackson examined the land and the buildings, turning in a full circle.

"They won't attack us here," Katy said. "Too open. But you're right to be careful. The cats associate this place with food, so they'll return here if they're hungry."

"May not be all that hungry. We've already had five reports today, everything from a missing Irish Setter to a pet llama to a pair of gray wolves found near a chicken house. The farmer said there wasn't much left but the heads and some skin. I doubt if the chickens killed them."

"Sounds about right," Katy said. "For whatever reason, big cats don't always eat the head and the groin." She couldn't hide her tiny smile. "Ready?"

Dix Wagner had lost money on cattle. When he tried raising sheep, wolves and mountain lions decimated his herd. He considered raising ostrich until buying one of the birds. The beast had nipped him. After he shot it, both Dix and his wife, Anita, discovered they did not like ostrich meat anyway. As a last resort, Dix tried goats. He soon discovered a thriving market for goat milk, yogurt, and meat, especially in Asia, and he now had a growing herd of Spanish, South African Boer, Nubian, Myotonic, and pygmy goats. There were over one hundred goat breeds that he knew of. Dix was experimenting to see which ones survived best in the rugged eastern Idaho climate.

In midmorning a flurry of barks and yelps from Rufus, his border collie, and the howling and crying of his goat menagerie caused Dix to grab his rifle, an old Remington .30-30, and rush to the pens to see which of Idaho's predators he would have to contend with now.

When he got there, two female lions were gutting his Nubians; a large male lion was dragging away a live pygmy goat; and a fourth cat, another lioness, had Rufus by the throat. Dix shot the dog-killing lioness first. He hit her high in the head above the eyes, but she didn't fall over like he expected. She did drop Rufus, but Dix knew his dog already was dead. Dix kept shooting even as the pride scattered, and the male lion carried off the pygmy goat in his mouth. The tiny goat was crying and screaming.

Dix ran after them. That pygmy goat was his wife's favorite of the herd. Fortunately for Dix, none of the lions turned back and attacked him. Unfortunately, Dix was sixty pounds overweight, smoked two packs of Camels a day, and took sixteen different pills for various ailments. After running a hundred feet he slowed; after another fifty feet he stumbled; after two hundred feet Dix fell over.

Anita Wagner's 911 call went to the County Communication Center in St. Anthony and was rerouted to the Buckhorn Police Station where Angie responded. The Roberts twins picked up the call on their police radio while on their way to talk to Maryann Fedder, the woman they had identified as the intended recipient of Ronnie's gift.

"Lions!" Bill said. "Hot damn! Let's go!"

"What about this?" Dwight indicated the gift.

"Hell, leave it." They were stopped at the road leading to the Fedder house. Bill nodded toward the mailbox. They had opened the gift to see what it was. Bill grinned and said, "We wouldn't want to deprive her."

After showing Katy the ramshackle cages and then admiring her ability to curse in three languages, Jackson cut the yellow and black crime scene tape across the back door. County sheriff detectives had processed the house, but he wanted Katy to look through the files and charts. He hoped he was wrong about the number of freed cats.

When they reached the office, Katy immediately was drawn to a framed diploma from the California Institute of Technology, a small college that is home to many Nobel Prize winners. "Cheney went to Cal Tech? Really?"

Jackson nodded. "Ted was a scientist. Genetics."

She said, "Impressive," and replaced the diploma. After that, Katy began sifting through file cabinets.

When Jackson's cell phone rang, he left Katy in the dining room, walked outside, and listened to Angie tell him about the attack at the Wagner goat farm. Jackson resisted the urge to rush to the Wagner place. Instead, he said, "Let me know what you find over there."

"Did you see this?" Katy asked the moment Jackson returned. Her voice had an urgency that was lacking before.

"See what?"

"You remember me telling you about ligers?"

"Enough to know they sound like sharks with claws."

"That's not a bad description," she said. "I don't really know all that much about them, but I do know the difficulty in raising ligers is getting them to breed. The male is usually sterile. Some people claim they're always sterile. Female ligers have reproduced, but only with a lion or tiger, never with a male liger." Katy waved the file in her hand. "Safari Land has two ligers, and according to this paperwork, the female is pregnant and due anytime."

"And that changes things how?"

"It says that Kali, the female, is pregnant by the male liger named Shaka." Katy paused like she was waiting for the drum roll and said, "If two ligers have bred for the first time in history, it means we have to save them."

* * *

After spending the night and Monday morning near Brown's Creek, Kali and Shaka reached Jackson's farm at mid-morning. At first the ligers were cautious and stayed out of sight, but before long, they explored the corral, the barn, and the outside of the house and the few sheds.

Their exploration complete, they hid in a patch of Great Basin Wild Rye grass that was six feet high. The rye grass was part of a two-acre prairie south of the house. No grasses, bushes, flowers, or trees existed here that were not native to the Idaho prairie in the early 1800s. The prairie was a restoration project for Jackson and his daughter. Jesse had done all of the research herself. The prairie was never cut, although Touie and Boots and Blaze, Jackson's two quarter-horses, were turned out to graze on the land and to fertilize it with what they left behind.

In hot climates big cats lay up during the day, but after Kali rolled around to flatten a small patch of dry grass and the ligers had rested, they went off in search of food. They soon smelled water and, knowing that all animals eventually end up at water, headed east toward it.

On the drive to the Wagner farm Angie used the flashing lights in the Dodge cruiser but not the siren. Still, she went as fast as the two-lane road with an abundance of curves and dips safely allowed, especially knowing that she was pissed off and distracted again.

Before leaving the station, Angie had gone to her locker in the big bathroom. There was a stack of half-lockers there, six up and down. Not all of them were in use. Her locker was up top and on one end. The moment she gripped her combination lock, it fell open. It had been cut. Stuck to the inside of her locker door was a pinkish, rubber dildo that looked like Pinocchio's nose. When she tried to remove it, the dildo wouldn't budge. Super Glue, she thought instantly. She had wasted valuable time getting rid of the thing. If she found the person who put it there, she might cut off more than a rubber dick.

At the goat farm Angie encountered a pair of troopers that looked like clones and the same two emergency medical technicians she had seen at the Placett farm on Saturday. The EMTs were struggling to get Dix Wagner off the ground and onto the gurney. A woman stood nearby watching. Angie tried to remember her name. Dix had an oxygen mask over his nose and mouth. At least he's still alive, Angie thought. Anita, that's the wife's name, Angie recalled.

On her way to the field Angie walked past the goat pens. Splotches of dirt were stained reddish brown from dried blood. A dog and a couple of goats lay on the ground, all dead. The wetter blood spots and a pile of entrails still attached to one of the goats were covered with blue flies. The gore in the pens reminded her of the 'slasher' movies Sharon liked to watch. She hated them.

As she strode across the mowed hay field, Angie felt the small, plastic evidence bag in her shirt pocket bounce with her breasts. Why was Dolly clutching the necklace, she wondered? Was it a plea to God to help her? Did she rip it off someone's neck? Was she trying to tell them something, like a murder victim writing the killer's name in his own blood? A moment later Angie stopped, nodded to the twin troopers, and then greeted the emergency medical techs before asking them about Dix Wagner's status.

"Looks like a heart attack," the youngest of the EMTs told her. "But I'm not a doctor, so we'll have to see."

"I'm Deputy Police Chief Angie Kuka," Angie said to Anita Wagner. "Can you tell me happened here?"

SIXTEEN

Dell's bank office was spacious and festooned with trophies. Trophy heads were not unusual in the west, although some people preferred antlers only to the glassy-eyed stare of a deer or elk head. But no other room in Idaho, Dell informed Katy, also had a grizzly bear, moose, gray wolf – legally shot, he insisted, mountain lion, bighorn sheep, a number of birds in flight, and the *coup de grace* of a Cape buffalo, a kudu, and an African lion.

"I still want to complete the big five," Dell added. He was shy an elephant and a leopard kill. "Maybe I'll return to Africa and go on safari with you, Katy."

Katy answered with a tight smile. Jackson and Katy were seated opposite Dell's desk in a pair of leather chairs with brass studs, like any other bank customer.

"Check this out," Dell said, as he went to a closet and removed a large caliber rifle. "A Weatherby Mark Five elephant and hippo gun." He pointed the gun at the head of the Cape buffalo. "One of my customers wanted to see it so I brought it from home. You ever hunt with one of these?" he asked Katy as he handed her the gun to admire.

"I never use four-sixty-magnums or five hundreds," she said. Jackson was lost and looked it, so Katy explained, "This gun is bored to shoot the most powerful sporting cartridge you can buy without a special permit."

"These babies right here," Dell said, producing a rack of cartridges. They were over three inches long and fat. "Just one of them can bring down a grown elephant."

"Any big game rifle can if you're good," Katy said.

"Now that sounds like a challenge to me," Dell said with a laugh. "Wouldn't you say so, Jackson?"

Katy sniffed the barrel. "Well-cleaned or unused?"

"Not many elephants around here." Dell took the gun from her and put it away. "Well, since you're not here to admire my trophies, what can I do for you folks?"

"You can help me save Kali and Shaka," Katy said.

"Who?"

"The two ligers." She told him what she had discovered at Safari Land and the importance of the ligers surviving. She finished by saying, "These two ligers are like the Adam and Eve of a new sub-species of big cats."

"Adam and Eve were created and man was given dominion over the animals," Dell said, "including life and death."

"Dominion also means protecting what's special," Katy said. "We can do that if I capture them. I've done it before, brought down large animals with a tranquilizer gun. I just need a chance to find them."

"Then find them. Nobody's stopping you."

Katy glanced at Jackson, but he just tipped his head to tell her to keep going. "I'd like you to exclude the ligers from this public hunt that's starting."

Dell laughed and shook his head. "Everybody coming here wants to shoot the monster cats." He picked up a stack of paper a quarter-inch thick. "These are inquiries and deposits. And we've got a web site up and running now. Already sold two hundred licenses at a thousand dollars each, and we'll sell even more tomorrow. So what do we tell people? Huh? If a big, dangerous cat is charging you, hold your fire until you're sure it's not a liger? Hell, half these people can't tell a lion from a tiger. We'll get sued from California to Connecticut." Dell looked to Jackson. "You know I'm right about this."

"I just want the cats gone," Jackson replied.

"So do I," Dell said. He paused and then said to Katy, "Look, you're a professional hunter. Surely you're not worried a few ranchers and bankers and weekend hunters can beat you to these ligers? You want to save them, go find them. Blow them away or dart them, your choice." Dell smiled at her. "Think of it as a challenge."

Upon leaving the bank Jackson and Katy drove to Jackson's farm so Katy could pick up the Ford 350. For a while Katy was silent as she looked out at the parched, dusty land. Halfway there, she suddenly said, "On safari Dell is the kind of customer I worry about. He'll take chances, unnecessary risks. It's why I have strict rules and follow them. It keeps me alive." She looked at Jackson. "Funny how his type attracts so many women."

Yeah, funny, thought Jackson. "But not you?"

"Against my rules," she said without humor.

When they arrived, Jackson took a county map out of the truck, and they went inside. He briefly showed Katy the house, but they didn't spend much time on a tour. In the kitchen Jackson spread the county map on the table and pointed out the major roads. "There aren't that many roads to show you," he said. "Lots of logging roads and private roads, but they're not on the map."

"I'll manage," Katy told him. "Show me where the cat attacks and sightings have been?" Jackson indicated the Placett farm, the Bailey place, Wagner's goat farm, and his own farm. "All of them are bunched near you," Katy noted. "It could mean you're simply convenient. Or it could mean the cats are drawn here for food or shelter."

"I got two quarter-horses out to pasture," Jackson said. "And my daughter's gelding, but he's with the vet. Couple dozen head of Angus. But everybody has animals."

"Well, the good news is the cats won't likely roam very far. Not if there's food and shelter right here."

"I hadn't thought about that," Jackson said.

"I can help you bring your horses in. Your cattle probably should be penned and guarded or put in the barn."

"My barn's not big enough, and I can't guard them."

"I'd hate to see your horses get hurt."

Jackson nodded. "Me too, and I'll go find them as soon as I can, just not today. My job is to protect people. Right now, my animals are on their own."

He started to fold up the map, but Katy stopped him. She tapped a finger on a darker green area. "What's this?"

She was pointing to the westernmost sliver of Yellowstone National Park to the northeast. He told her about the west entrance and said, "I don't even want to think about the mess if these cats got loose in the park."

"Then I should get started."

"Where?"

"This goat farm. Last place we know cats were seen. Can you come up with somebody to go hunting with me?"

Jackson recalled what Major Jessup had said about the two troopers he had left in town. "I think I might."

The Roberts twins were waiting for Katy when she arrived at the Wagner goat farm. She had met both men on Monday morning while briefing the State Police hunters, but she had met many other people too, so she hadn't really talked to them. Now, she asked them about their hunting background and heard about their military experience. They had never hunted big cats, but nobody she was likely to meet in Buckhorn had, except for Dell, and she guessed Dell's brother, whom she was likely to meet on Tuesday.

When Katy asked to see their guns, they showed her sniper rifles and Glock handguns. Neither weapon was suitable for hunting lions, as the twins well knew. Dwight still was laughing at their joke as he produced a Remington 770. His cartridges were lighter than Katy liked, but it was a good rifle and could bring down a lion if the shots were well place. Bill had borrowed a .458 Lott and loaded it with 500-grain cartridges. It was overkill, but Katy preferred for them to have too much firepower than not enough. The Roberts twins will do fine, she thought.

The twins were both skilled hunters and adept at tracking. Even so, Katy led the way, and the men fell in step behind her. Between the scat and the blood, none of them had a problem following the trail. After crossing half-a-mile of fields, they reached a hill spiked with black limbless trees that looked like candles on a witch's cake. Cheatgrass covered the ground, choking out most native plants. Sumac and rabbit brush and a few flowers sprouted up here and there. It was unusual territory for lions, which prefer open, grassy plains, but Katy looked for signs anyway. She found fresh blood clinging to the cheatgrass and pointed it out. "They went up hill."

"Shit!" Dwight said. "I was afraid of that."

They climbed the hill single file. Katy took the point and Bill the rear. All three hunters were in good shape for walking, but they went slowly and stopped often to examine the trail and to scout for lions.

After slogging through grass and brush for an hour, they came to a valley between two hills where the land flattened. Water from an underground source trickled through irrigation ditches. The land was being farmed.

"I'll be a sonofabitch," Dwight said, eyeing the remains of a marijuana field harvested a week or two ago.

"We're on public land here," Bill added.

"You get a lot of pot farms?" Katy asked.

"Our fair share," Bill said. "Meth labs too."

For a moment they all stood and eyed the half-acre. There was little left except for a few wilted plants.

"Let's keep going," Katy said. They did, walking rapidly through the pot farm. Despite the drought, the ground beneath them was soft, even squishy. Once they crossed the marijuana farm, they waded into yarrow, rabbit brush, silver sagebrush, and a clumped, tall grass that Katy didn't recognize. They slowed the pace and moved eyes-alert and body-tense without speaking. Halfway through the valley, Katy signaled to stop.

She squatted and took out a hunting knife and speared a piece of goat hide. Flesh still was attached to the underside of the hide. The flesh was bloody and wet. Wet meant recent.

Katy raised her gaze and looked into a pair of amber eyes. The male lion was forty feet away and low to the ground. He was crouched and locked in on her. Before Katy could say anything to alert the twins, the grass and brush parted revealing a golden-brown blur. Katy swung around the .375 and fired. She only got off a single shot. By the time the lion fell over, his tongue was licking her boot.

SEVENTEEN

By Monday evening the streets were jammed with SUVs, pickups, campers, vans, and rental cars. Five media trucks emblazoned with initials also rolled into town. To handle the traffic Jackson called in half his reserve officers and John Plaides as well. His budget was being beat to hell. In addition to traffic snarls they dealt with two fights and three fender benders early that evening. The last fight resulted in an arrest. Jackson and officer Plaides cuffed the drunks to desks in the station until a deputy sheriff could pick them up. Jackson was getting coffee when Bill Kenny, a reserve officer, informed him that Iris was on television. The Idaho Lion Hunt was national news.

After watching Iris' interview, Jackson worked out a schedule to have two reserve officers cruise the town at dawn and at sundown, when big cats were most on the move. The last thing he wanted was lions and tigers in Buckhorn.

He had not talked to Katy since she called to tell him about killing the lion near the Wagner goat farm, so after cruising the downtown area and surrounding streets one more time, he drove to the Sportsman Motel. The lights were off in Katy's room. Jackson didn't see his truck in the parking lot, and he was about to drive away when Missy Yow stumbled out of a nearby motel room and vomited. In the seconds the motel door was open, Jackson heard loud hip-hop music and saw a few teenagers inside the room.

He got a bottle of water out of the Jeep and crossed to where Missy was retching. He waited for her to finish and then gave her the water. "You gonna be okay?"

"Oh god!" she said when she recognized who had asked the question. "I'm so sick. Uh, stomach flu I guess."

"Nasty stuff, stomach flu." Jackson went to the door. "Take some aspirin. Might help the hangover." He opened the motel door and found a dozen teenagers gathered in the room. He spotted Shane, Buzz Phelps, Grace Lake, and two other kids he recognized as Jesse's friends, as well as some kids he didn't know well or at all. He smelled pot and saw two cases of beer. Grace turned off the boombox and the room got quiet. Then the bathroom door opened.

Jesse came out smiling and talking. "What'd everyone get so –" She stopped when she saw her father.

Christ! Jackson thought. "Whose room is this?"

After a long silence a tall curly-headed boy who looked about seventeen spoke up. "Mine, sir."

Jackson didn't know him. "What's your name, son?"

"Justin Sable. I'm ... I'm his cousin." He pointed to Buzz Phelps. A junior at Buckhorn high, Buzz was Missy's boyfriend. "My dad, he's coming from Utah tomorrow for the hunt but he had to rent the room today or lose it so ..."

"We got two people dead and one missing and others in the hospital, people some of you kids have known all your life. I should bust you just for being callous." Jackson paused. "So listen up, all of you. I'm going to look the other way. When I turn back around, I expect to see any dope you got tossed on the bed." There were two queen beds in the room. "The dope and the beer stay here. You don't. You got thirty minutes to get home." Jackson turned away as small amounts of loose pot, some joints, and tabs of Ecstasy were dropped on the bed before the kids scampered out. When Shane tried to leave, Jackson said, "Not you."

"Daddy," Jesse said. She hadn't moved.

"You stay, Jesse. And you, Justin." Jackson gathered up the drugs and told Shane to follow him. "I'm going to ask you something," Jackson said when they were standing in front of the motel room. "And I want you to tell me the truth." Jackson waited until Shane had nodded. "You and Jesse getting high in there like the others?"

Shane shuffled his feet before saying, "Well, I, uh, I smoked a little weed, but not Jesse. She never has, I don't think. And she doesn't like beer."

"Jesse's been through a lot these past few days, so I want you to cool it with her for a while."

"You mean like break up? Stop seeing her?"

Jackson shook his head. "Shane, I know what'd happen if I said that. I'm just saying, might be good to cancel your social plans until … until things are normal."

Minutes later, he let Shane leave. Then he talked to Justin Sable. He told the boy he was under house arrest and wasn't to leave the motel room unless it was on fire. Jackson stuck crime scene tape across the door to further impress Justin and told Jesse he would take her home.

"Can't I just go to the farm with you?"

"Not without telling your mom."

Her face dropped. "Everything?"

Jackson didn't answer, and when they reached Jesse's home in town, she started to bail out before the Jeep rolled to a stop. "Hang on a minute," Jackson said.

"Dad, Mom will kill me if -"

"Close the door," Jackson told her. Jesse shut it softly. He opened the glove box and took out the condom Iris had given him. "Your mom found this in your dresser."

"She searched my room? God!"

"Fifteen is kind of young, Jesse."

"This is like so creepy."

"Are you and Shane -?"

"NO! We're not ... I mean, I'm still ... I'm not. God!"

Jackson indicated the condom in his hand. "Then what're you doing with this condom and a dozen more?"

Jesse hesitated. "Do you have to tell Mom?"

"You're really not in a position to bargain, Jesse."

Jesse waited and Jackson waited and then she said, "I'm hiding them." Jackson waited longer. "For Missy and Buzz. They used to keep them at school, but the principal started doing locker checks, even in the gym and stuff. And Missy's mom, she's like really strict, and so are Buzz's parents. They all go to the same church."

"Give the condoms back to them."

"Please don't tell Mom."

"No promises," Jackson said and then smiled. "But I think it can wait a few days."

As Jackson returned to the police station he thought about how easy it was for kids to get liquor and drugs even in rural Idaho. The pot he knew about already. Rob Piccard, a young man who had returned badly messed up from Afghanistan, was the local supplier. Jackson figured that as long as amounts were small, it was safer for the kids to buy pot from Piccard than to go out of town where they might encounter more serious criminals.

When Jackson reached Justin Sable's father in Utah, the man raised all kinds of hell. He didn't want Jackson talking to his son, a minor, without him being present. Reed Sable said he'd be in Buckhorn the following morning.

Katy returned to her motel room after having dinner at Palomino's Bar & Grill and called Stan Ely. She asked him about the status of the injunction.

"We hit a snag," Stan said. "Our paperwork won't get filed 'til tomorrow. But I still hope we'll get to argue it on Wednesday and get the judge to rule."

"Look, I think it's great you're doing this."

"Then go public with your support. It would help."

"With the injunction? I don't see how."

"With me trying to raise money."

If Stan arrived before she could capture Kali or any cubs Kali might have had already, Katy was certain he would want the rare liger cubs for his animal rescue ranch in Colorado. He would be a competitor. An injunction to end the hunt would help her, while Stan raising money to rush to Idaho would not. "Let me think about it," Katy said.

* * *

Jackson slept fitfully on Monday night, his sleep dream-filled. He was up and in town early on Tuesday. He didn't wear his uniform but took the dark blues and some black dress shoes to change into later that morning.

The day didn't start well. Within two minutes of meeting Reed Sable, Jackson disliked him. Maybe it was because Sable tried to blame the local kids for the booze and drugs? Maybe it was because Sable asked Jackson if he was Mormon? Maybe it was because Sable was an investment banker? Or maybe Sable was simply easy to dislike?

Still, there was no reason to drag it out. Jackson had gotten the information he wanted from Justin Sable: the pot was local, the "X" came from Seattle, and the beer was purchased by Grace Lake, a senior, using a fake ID. It had come from a store in Idaho Falls. Grace already had turned in her fake ID and agreed to do community service.

"Justin won't be charged with anything, Mr. Sable. I'll leave any punishment up to you." Before Sable could say anything more to irritate him, Jackson stood, shook hands, and wished Sable and his son good luck on the hunt.

Iris showed up at his door not long after Sable left. She wore a black dress with black pumps and had toned down her usual bright lipstick for something barely noticeable.

"Why is Annie Oakley shooting lions before the hunt even begins?" she asked.

"Annie Oakley? Where'd that come from?"

"She didn't buy a license."

"And Katy's not going to. She's helping me."

"I bet she is."

"She helped Dix and Anita Wagner too. Dix will be fine, in case you didn't know."

Iris shifted to a friendlier tone. "Dan Tapper wants to meet her, so make sure she comes to the lunch."

Jackson nodded. "I'll pass the invitation along."

Iris hesitated. "You talk to Jesse yet?"

"Not yet," he said, lying. "But I will. Soon."

"The lion hunt is going to work," Iris said as she walked off. "Don't be late for lunch. And bring Annie Oakley."

The door had barely closed on Iris when Jackson heard the helicopter. Last night, news helicopters had buzzed the area so often that he had contacted Boise and the FAA. Once he did, the flight path had been restricted. Nobody wanted to risk the choppers scaring the cats and causing them to scatter. The no-fly-rule over the town, thought Jackson, must not apply to the lieutenant governor.

EIGHTEEN

Dan Tapper knew the governor would give him hell for borrowing the Black Hawk from the Idaho National Guard. He also knew that stepping out of a military chopper dressed in hunting gear made a bolder statement than arriving by car. Besides, as acting-governor, it was Dan's job to deal with emergencies, and he figured lions and tigers terrorizing Idaho qualified. While Dan waited for the blades to cease their thwap-thwap-thwap, he watched Dell and Iris, heads lowered, come forward to greet him. Iris' hair whipped around wildly. She wore a black dress and held the bottom of it with one hand while she waved with the other. Her dress still ballooned up, showing Dan a lot of thigh.

A moment later Dan stood in the doorway, waved, and smiled at the reporters his campaign manager had alerted. Then he stepped down and hugged Iris, who said, "Welcome to the Idaho Lion Hunt, Mr. Acting-Governor."

"Quite an entrance," Dell said without smiling. Dell had swapped his western suit for a sober blue pinstripe.

"I'll need to change for the funeral," Dan said.

"I like your outfit," Iris told him. "Very bold."

"And I like your dress," Dan said with a smile before looking past them. "I see Fox News here so I should say a few words. A good Republican network, they like me."

When Jackson got to the Methodist church late Tuesday morning, he was wearing his blue uniform, a black armband, and an ankle holster with a .38 revolver. His cell phone was set to vibrate. Half the town was there already and more were arriving as he parked in a spot Brian Patterson was guarding for him. Other drivers weren't as lucky.

On his way into the church Jackson greeted Dan Tapper, spoke to Iris and Dell, and hugged his daughter, who then split off to be with her friends, including kids from the motel room party. The nature of Ed's death, coupled with the public hunt, had attracted the media; the media and Dan Tapper's presence had brought out a number of State Police troopers. All Buckhorn officers were present except for Angie Kuka. After the service Brian would relieve her so that Angie could attend the burial at the cemetery.

Jackson endured the hymns and the sermon, but when Becky Rebo, the psychologist sent to visit the Placett children, and also the best singer in the county, warbled Merle Haggard's *Sing Me Back Home*, and sang it as slowly and soulfully as possible, Jackson felt the weight of regret dragging him under and struggled to stay afloat.

Jackson had recovered by the time he served as a pallbearer. Then he drove alone to the cemetery west of town. As soon as the burial ceremony was over, he left like everyone else so that the family could have the final moment alone to say goodbye to Ed. He leaned against his car and except for nodding to people and muttering a few soft hellos, he spent his time thinking about how lucky he was to have known Ed Stevens. He was so lost in thought that he at first did not hear Eileen Stevens say his name.

"Jackson," she said again. The group that accompanied Eileen, including Tucker and his wife, waited in a tight cluster a short distance away. "Thank you so much. It'd mean a lot to Ed, knowing you and the others are all here."

Jackson hugged Eileen. "I don't know what to say, Eileen. If I hadn't sent Ed out there –"

"He'd have gone anyway," she said. "Ed did exactly what he thought a good lawman should do. He always told me you're just like him."

Oh damn, thought Jackson.

"Ed left a letter. He said I was to give it to you once ...." Her voice finally cracked. "I meant to bring it today, but I plumb forgot. Maybe you can stop by and get it. Ed told me not to read the letter, ever."

"Don't worry about it. I'll stop by."

"Ed, he didn't think I knew," Eileen said.

"Knew?"

"That his days were numbered."

Jackson said, "From the cancer, you mean?"

"Ed liked his little secrets."

Jackson nodded and kept quiet.

The moment the service ended, Angie hurried away from the cemetery. She had until the big lunch event before she had to be at the Elk's Club. At least I don't have to work with Tucker, she thought, then chided herself for having such a thought on the day his uncle was buried. Still, she didn't like the way Tucker ogled her crotch or the smirk he often wore or how careless he was as a cop. Angie should have gone home and done laundry or bought groceries or done a number of other things. Instead, the moment she left the cemetery, she made a beeline to Divine Jewelry Store.

The jewelry store had changed owners a few times since the Divine family sold it, but the name and location on the town square had remained the same for seventy years. Sean and Maggie Curly, the current owners, were cleaning and stocking the jewelry cases when Angie entered. She placed a silver necklace on a black mat on top of a long glass case.

"You carry anything like this?" Angie asked.

Angie was wearing a pressed blue uniform, necktie, hat, black armband, and equipment belt. The couple stared at her for a moment before Sean picked up the necklace and examined it. "It's silver plate, not sterling," he said. "We can sell you a nicer one. For a good price too."

"I'm not shopping. I'm investigating a crime."

"Oh!" Maggie said. She stopped dusting a display of watches and came over to examine the silver cross.

"So did this come from here?" Angie said.

"Not our style." Maggie returned the necklace to the mat. "I hope some poor girl wasn't mugged for this?"

Angie shook her head. "Any idea who might sell it?"

"Maybe the Walmart in Rexburg," said Sean, looking at his wife for confirmation. When she shrugged, her whole body giggled. Both Maggie and Sean hit the buffet lines too often. "It could've come from anywhere," Sean added. "Shopping Network, on-line stores, no way to know."

It was common for people to share food and drink and memories following a funeral. Jackson had attended these gatherings a few times before, but he had never been to a funeral that was followed by anything like the welcoming luncheon for Dan Tapper to kick off the Idaho Lion Hunt.

The event was held at the Elk's Club. At first the atmosphere was subdued, but before long conversations became louder and laughter more common. Though Katy had not attended Ed's funeral, she had accepted the lunch invitation. Jackson finally spotted her in a corner with Dell. He had started toward them when Major Jessup walked up to him. "I didn't know you were coming," Jackson said.

"Didn't plan to," Jessup said. "But the LG invited me. In my world that's the same as a subpoena."

Jackson chuckled. "Ronnie Greathouse turn up?"

Jessup hesitated a second. "Not yet."

"So your troopers are still looking for him?"

"No. A detective took it over." Jessup scoffed. "Anyway, the Roberts boys are too busy strutting around like roosters in a hen house. Big shot lion hunters now."

Before Jackson could comment, an announcement was made asking everyone to be seated. During lunch Jackson paid little attention to the speeches or chatter. Although Katy and he sat at the head table along with Dan Tapper and his chief of staff, Iris and Dell, members of the town council, Sheriff Midden, and Major Jessup, the first time Jackson spoke to the lieutenant governor that day was after the meal. Dan approached him while he was talking to Katy and said, "Chief Hobbs, I hear you don't like the public hunt."

"The cats have to be found, Mr. Lieutenant Gov –"

"Let's stick with Dan until after November. It's easier to say." Dan Tapper smiled and touched Jackson's elbow. His smile was practiced, his touch perfected.

"Okay then, Dan," Jackson said. "Let's just say I have concerns about the safety of people."

"And you should," Dan said. "That's your job." He turned to Katy, having met her earlier. "Maybe Chief Hobbs is right, Miss Osborne. I'd certainly feel safer if you go with us. Show us how lion hunting should be done."

"I doubt if we have the same objective, sir."

Dan Tapper chuckled. "Don't be so sure about that."

"Dan," Iris said, coming up to him from behind, "we need to go or we'll be late for the opening assembly."

The moment Iris was alongside Dan Tapper, he laid his hand on her back. "Your town may need a new mayor soon. I can see Iris over in Boise on my gubernatorial staff next year." Iris beamed, and Dan did not remove his hand.

"You're that sure you'll win?" Jackson asked.

"Of course. Aren't you?" Not waiting for an answer, Dan turned to Iris. "Chief Hobbs and Miss Osborne tell me I made a mistake in supporting this public lion hunt idea."

"Well, you're a politician," Iris said. "I'm sure you can tell when people are giving you bad advice."

Dan Tapper laughed and rubbed Iris's back. "Boise."

More than three hundred people crowded into the Buckhorn High School gym. While the audience was settling in, Jackson spotted Pamela Yow, told Katy he would catch up with her, and dodged people until he reached the librarian. He drew her away from the crowd and found a private spot.

"Don't tell me you need more research?" she said.

"Nope, but I do appreciate your help."

"I bet you do," Pamela said and looked disapprovingly over at Katy who was talking to reporter Gary Chen.

Jackson laughed softly. "You didn't mention that you and Dolly Cheney are cousins."

"Didn't I? Well, we were never close. Guess she never seemed like a cousin. And certainly not a friend."

"I get it. I have cousins I wouldn't even recognize." He paused, like he was trying to think of something to say. "I was wondering, what's your former husband's name?"

Pamela was clearly surprised and without moving seemed to withdraw. "Why do you want to know that?"

"Just official paperwork."

"I haven't seen him in ten years."

Jackson waited.

"King Yow," she told him.

"King's his legal name?"

"It's what everybody calls him." After a moment Pamela added, "Edward King Yow."

"Eddie? The same man Dolly married?"

The microphone shrieked, and then Iris appeared at the podium and motioned for people to be seated and silent.

"By the way," Jackson said, "you going to the hospital to see your cousin?"

"Didn't you hear? She died this morning."

Iris welcomed everyone and introduced the city council. Then Dell introduced his brother. After that, Dan Tapper delivered a short, rousing campaign speech in front of a mysterious backdrop, a six-by-eight foot sign covered by a cloth. Nobody had mentioned it yet.

Once Dan finished, Iris explained the details of the Idaho Lion Hunt: it would end when all the animals were accounted for or after ten days. That's the way she said it – 'accounted for' rather than 'killed'. She explained the procedure for purchasing a license - $1,000 for each person carrying a hunting rifle, for verifying the kill — an official weight and measurement station was set up in Reynolds's Auction Barn just outside town, and she laid out the rules for collecting the prize money. "The hunters who bring in the biggest lion AND the biggest tiger will each receive ten thousand dollars," she announced.

The hunters clapped, cheered, and whistled.

"Wait, wait." Iris tried to silence the crowd. "There's a grand prize too." At that moment Dell and Fred removed the cloth covering the large sign, revealing a painting with two lions, a male and a female, a tiger, and, dwarfing the other animals in size and placement, a giant liger. "We've got two monster cats," Iris said, while presenting the painting with a flourish worthy of a TV host. "We're offering a twenty thousand dollar grand prize for the first liger killed."

"What about the second one?" someone yelled.

"Five thousand, and we'll pay to have it mounted for you. You can take it home and use it for a picnic table."

The audience jumped up and applauded.

NINETEEN

Kali and Shaka watched patiently from behind some antelope bitterbrush two hundred feet below the clearing where the doe was tethered. The ligers had barely twitched a muscle, other than in their tails and ears, since Eagle Cassel, a Fish and Game Department employee, had arrived on a Yamaha Grizzly 700. To the ligers the ATV was simply noisy and inedible. Cassel had removed an injured six-month-old whitetail deer from its carrying rack and staked and trussed the doe with heavy rope before riding away.

The ligers did not know that Wade was waiting in a service station tow truck at a barley field two miles away. They did not know that Dell, Dan, and Stilts Venable had arrived and were spilling out of Dell's Cadillac SUV and Shane out of his Toyota pickup. A State Police cruiser attached to Dan Tapper's security detail also pulled in behind them. Kali and Shaka did not know that the armed trooper would remain with the vehicles or that additional troopers were stationed on the county road to keep other hunters out of the area. Neither did they know that the injured doe was bait and that Dan's hunting party would soon be trying to use her to kill them. The ligers did not know these things, but they were suspicious of easy prey, so they watched and licked their muzzles and waited.

The ligers waited while the hunters gathered their weapons: Dell carrying his .375 Holland & Holland Magnum; Shane the .270 Weatherby; Dan a powerful short-barreled .500 Jeffrey; Wade his Remington 770 Sporting Rifle; and Stilts, who preferred bow hunting, had a Mossberg pump shotgun loaded with deer slugs. Shane, Wade, and Stilts toted backpacks with water, food, first aid kit, cameras and such. Most of the hunters had binoculars. Everyone except Shane wore hunting knives. Shane had forgotten his.

When the hunters reached the fawn, she was still unable to move or make a sound. After checking the rope and the stake, Stilts untied her legs and muzzle. The doe sprang up and bolted. The rope around her neck jerked her down, and she grunted a frightened contact call. The men walked on another hundred and fifty feet and climbed a ladder to a platform built in a large Douglas fir. Hot, dry weather had dulled the usually vibrant color, but the fir was thick with branches and needles and was good cover.

After the assembly, Katy quickly changed clothes and then followed Jackson home. She waited while he changed. With her help, Jackson planned to check on his cattle and bring his two quarter-horses to the barn. Deborah had lost another sheep, so Jackson knew the big cats were close.

"What gun are you taking?" Katy asked when he came downstairs. She was examining his gun cabinet. Katy wore the safari outfit she had worn Monday morning, minus the windbreaker, while Jackson had on jeans, a plaid flannel shirt, fishing vest, and well-worn Red Wing boots.

"Thought I'd take the Stoeger shotgun."

"Dear slugs?"

"Uh-huh. I have my Glock 21 and the M4 tactical rifle." He unlocked the gun case. "And these, my .22, this old Benelli 12-guage, and my thirty-ought-six."

"I'd take the thirty-ought-six. And let's see what ammo you have that'll stop a big cat."

As Jackson removed the Remington 700 from the gun cabinet, his cell phone rang. He answered it but barely spoke, mostly saying, "Uh-huh" or "When?" or "Why didn't you call me earlier?" When he ended the call, he looked at Katy and said, "The ligers are back."

"Bored?" Dan quietly asked Shane upon seeing his 'anywhere but here' expression after an hour of waiting.

Shane shrugged and glanced at his father.

"Well, I could tell you a story," Dan said.

"Uncle Dan, I'm not a kid anymore."

"I know. It's a grown-up story." Dan flashed his practiced smile. He spoke softly, barely loud enough to be heard. "There are these two guys in Africa, you see. And they're out walking one day when they realize a lion is stalking them. Now unlike us, they don't have a gun or anyplace to hide. So the one guy, he kicks off his boots and takes some running shoes out of his backpack and starts lacing them up. 'What are you doing?' the other guy says. 'Man, you can't outrun a lion.' 'But I don't have to,' the guy in the Nikes explains. 'I only have to outrun you.' "

Everyone laughed, even Shane. Kali and Shaka heard the noise. They were watching the human prey up in the tree.

"Ssshhh!" Dell hissed, cutting off the laughter. He was scanning the area with his binoculars. "About nine o'clock," he said. "It's some goddamn wolves."

Everyone who had binoculars looked through them. "I see them," Stilts added. "Six big northern grays."

"Shit, they're coming for the doe," Dan whispered.

"Don't shoot or we'll scare off any cats," Dell said.

Wade moved to the edge of the hunting platform. "I'll climb down and scatter them."

"Let Shane do it."

"Me?" Shane said to his father.

"Sure. Since you're bored. Nothing like a little excitement to take care of that."

"You're sure this was the animal you saw?" Katy asked, showing ten-year-old Josh a color photo of a liger with its front paws high up on an extension ladder. The man beside the liger was half the height of the giant cat.

"Uh-huh." Josh indicated the liger. "Two of them."

"Two of them?" Katy looked over at Jackson. "And did you see where they went?"

Josh nodded and said, "Want me to show you?"

"Right, that's even better." They got up from the couch, and Josh took her hand. On their way out of the room Katy looked back at Jackson and Mandy and said, "The girls in Buckhorn better watch out in a few years."

As they left, Mandy said, "Some more coffee?"

"Not me," Jackson said. "I'm about to float."

Jackson was seated on a sectional rust-colored couch, while Mandy occupied a rocker, her five-year-old daughter in her lap, just like the last time he was there. Tammy was sucking her thumb, and Mandy removed it from her mouth.

"Oh Tammy, Tammy. What am I going to do with you?" she said and then looked over at Jackson. "I bet they'll just keep coming back here, won't they?"

He remembered Katy saying the cats would return to where they found food, but he didn't want to think of Ed in that way. "Maybe not. Did they get your chickens?"

"Nope. Wade put a wire top on the coop." Mandy smoothed her daughter's hair. It was the color of corn silk. "I know you're scared, honey. And I am too."

"Nothing's bad's going to happen."

"I wish I could believe that."

"You can," Jackson said.

"Did you tell Ed Stevens the same thing?"

Jackson left his coffee and stood up.

"I'm sorry," Mandy said. "That was really mean."

"Mean or not, you're right," he said. "Nobody's truly safe with these cats running free."

A second later, Katy and Josh returned. "The ligers went north toward a hunting blind," she told Jackson.

As the sun hugged the horizon, the doe stopped trying to pull free of the rope and froze. Dan peered through powerful Ricoh binoculars, scanning the area the doe was fixated on, and spotted the liger first.

"Holy shit," he murmured. His hushed voice still revealed the excitement he felt. "About seventy-five, eighty yards southwest ... in some chokecherry bushes." Dan softened his voice to a whisper. "The size of that thing. It's a fucking monster."

"I see him," Dell said softly. He watched the liger slink along the ground toward the deer. Come on baby, right to us." Dell removed his binoculars and peered through the scope atop the .375. He adjusted the range until he could clearly see the liger again. "Got him. About sixty-five yards and still coming."

Everyone else in the blind except for Stilts, who had a shotgun, dialed in their riflescopes.

"Dell, remember my first time elk hunting?" Dan said, his voice barely audible. "You let me take the shot. A rite of passage you said. Let's give Shane that chance."

"But I knew you wouldn't miss," Dell said softly.

"Thanks, Dad."

"Besides, that Weatherby won't stop a cat this big."

"I said the first shot, not the last," Dan whispered.

Dell hesitated and then said, "Oh hell! Why not?"

"So what should I do?" Shane said too loudly.

"Ssshhh!" Dell warned. "Don't piss yourself. Just crawl around and get on your belly. Use this tripod right behind me. And when you shoot, don't jerk the trigger. Squeeze it gently like it's your girlfriend's nipple."

Somebody tittered, but not Shane. His heart was beating too fast and loud. He wiggled into place and laid the barrel of the .270 across the tripod. After that, nobody spoke or moved. A couple of times the sweat on Shane's forehead reached his eyes, and he wiped it away.

"Get ready, Shane," Dell whispered. "Ready ... wait ... wait ... wait ... hold it ... hold it ... wait—"

Shane twitched and squeezed the trigger. The doe fell over so quickly that the sound of the rifle shot, echoing off the hills, seemed to come afterward.

"Oh shit," Dan said.

"Shot the fucking deer!" Dell said.

"The liger is running away!" Wade shouted.

"Get down! Hurry!" Dell ordered. "Follow it!"

The men scampered down the rough, homemade ladder nailed to the fir. Shane was the last one to the ground. His ears were ringing from the shot, but he still heard his father say, "Shot the fucking doe; I can't believe it."

TWENTY

Jackson and Katy were crossing a barley field when they heard the shot. They stopped and waited, expecting more shots. When none came, Katy said, "On safari I know where the guns are. Out here, I don't. That worries me."

Jackson, who thought about being shot each time he rushed through a door or got between an angry husband and wife or pulled over a car on a dark road, said, "I know the feeling. Comes with the job, I guess."

"I've been lucky." While she spoke, Katy scanned the land, looking for movement. "But my uncle was shot once."

Jackson remembered reading about her uncle in Botswana. "Your uncle that's missing?"

Katy nodded. "Two years ago Christmas morning. When Uncle Bucky went blind, he took it hard. Working the ranch, safari life, he missed them so much. I got up to exchange gifts, and he was gone. We looked for him but ...."

"I'm sorry," Jackson told her.

She nodded. "That's how he wanted it," she said softly. "To walk off onto the land and just disappear."

Jackson couldn't think of anything meaningful to say, so he remained silent. He turned away and eyed the horizon, and when he looked back, Katy was examining the ground.

Her sadness, her memories had been put aside. "You ever shoot anyone?" she asked. "I mean, as a policeman."

"Probably."

"Don't you know?"

"More or less," Jackson said. "So what now?"

It was obvious that Jackson did not want to discuss it further, so Katy moved on ahead, looking for signs of the ligers. A moment later she squatted and pushed aside the golden barley. There were two main ways to identify the kind and number of animals that passed over a land and the direction they went in: their droppings and their tracks. The tracks Katy found in the barley field were unmistakable. "Both ligers went north," she said.

"Goddamn cat's toying with us," Dell said. He was looking three hundred feet north at the liger. The cat and the hunters had been playing hide-and-seek since the men left the hunting blind. They hunters had stopped in an aspen grove. A few leaves had turned gold. The ground was thick with last year's leaves. "Let's get closer," Dell said.

"Wait a sec," Shane said. "I can't. I mean, my stomach feels bad. I gotta go before -"

Dell had not spoken to his son since Shane shot the doe. Now he interrupted him to say, "We don't need the details. Just get downwind of us. And hurry it up."

Shane went behind a thick clump of aspens sixty feet away. His stomach was churning. As he unbuckled and unzipped, he could hear bits of conversation: " ... goddamn cat ... risky to go off alone ... just watching us ... shot the fucking deer ...." He was about to drop his jeans when he saw the liger. No fucking way! The big cat's out front; it can't be back here too, he told himself. But it was.

Shane stepped back and bumped into a tree. Without taking his eyes off the liger, he reached down, found the Weatherby leaning against the aspen trunk, and lifted the gun by its barrel. He tried to say, "Dad, Dad, Dad," but only croaked. What happened next happened so fast that it did not feel sequential. It felt like time collapsed.

The liger charged, and Shane, his rifle halfway up, fired a wild shot. The cat kept coming. Then there was a loud boom from behind Shane, and the animal jerked. There was a second loud boom, with the cat in the air now, and Shane slid down the white tree and landed on his tailbone. He fought against releasing his bowels. Then there was a third even louder boom, and the liger seemed to stop dead still in the air. Then it crashed to the ground.

Dell and Dan reached the liger first. Wade and Stilts were right behind them. Stilts stuck his Mossberg shotgun in the cat's ear, but Dell said, "Don't! You'll destroy the head." Dell placed the Weatherby .375 over the lungs and shot the animal. The big cat jerked and then lay still.

After that, everybody talked all at once except for Shane, who sat on the ground and stared blankly ahead.

"Take a drink of this." Dan held out a leather-covered flask until Shane focused on him and took the cognac. "It'll put bristles on your balls."

"I don't get it," Wade said, amazed. "The cat was way out in front of us. I was watching him the whole time."

"He's still out there too," Stilts Venable said, for he was not looking at the dead liger but was watching a second liger, some two hundred feet away from them.

"Not he, she," Dell said, while checking the genitals of the dead liger. "It was a goddamn trap. The female's out front, and the male here was sneaking up behind us."

"Damn!" said Wade. "Cat's really do that?"

"Feeling better?" Dan asked Shane.

"Go easy on that stuff," Dell told his son.

"So they're not just big, they're smart," Stilts said.

"Not smart enough," Dell said. "This one's dead."

It took an hour for the hunters to hike back to the vehicles. Everyone but Wade and Shane got into the Escalade and, with the State Police trooper leading the way, drove off. Wade and Shane stayed behind to transport the dead liger.

They set off in the Shetland Service Station wrecker. Wade first eased it down a rutted logging road, then maneuvered the truck through a rocky field, and eventually had to thread it through the forest to reach the kill site. Neither Wade nor Shane said much during the drive or when they got there, and when they did talk, they did not talk about what had happened earlier in the aspen trees.

As they worked to load Shaka, from time to time they would stop and search for Kali or some other danger lurking in the woods. Even so, neither of them saw the liger, although Kali watched them struggle to get the sling beneath the giant cat before lifting him off the ground and depositing him on the bed of the wrecker. They also did not see her keep pace with the truck once Wade drove off.

The return trip went faster, and when they reached the barley field, Wade said, "Listen, I'm going to stop and show the cat to my wife and kids, so you go on to town." Shane mumbled "okay" and started to leave. Wade put his hand on the boy's shoulder and said, "Anybody can miss a shot. I've missed my share. I bet your dad has too."

Shane bobbed his head, and his eyes teared as he got out. Wade waited for Shane to safely reach his Toyota and drive off before he phoned Mandy and told her about the liger. He was still talking to her when he started home.

Two miles later Wade stopped beneath a trio of sugar maples. They were near where the dirt road intersected with the blacktop. He put the truck in neutral, set the parking brake, and climbed out. At the rear of the wrecker he tugged on the ties that secured the big male liger. He would be driving faster on the paved road, and he wanted to make certain that the animal would not slide off.

Just as Wade climbed back into the cab, he heard a thump overhead and felt the cab rock. A second later, a giant cathead appeared in the windshield upside down. Wade yelped! Kali then thudded off the roof and onto the hood and with a whack of her giant paw cracked the windshield.

Wade fought the manual shift, grinding the gears in his haste to escape. He felt as much as saw Kali jump off the hood. Once the truck was in gear, Wade stomped the gas pedal. The truck lurched but didn't go anywhere. The emergency brake! He released it and was reaching to close the driver's door when Kali sprang into the cab.

* * *

Neither big cats nor hunters appeared after the flurry of shots, so Jackson and Katy returned to the Placett house. Mandy met them with the news that Wade was on his way home with a monster cat they had shot.

"Male or female?" Katy asked sharply. Mandy did not know the answer to Katy's question. After a tense thirty minutes of waiting, with no sign of Wade and the dead liger, and no answer to their many calls to Wade's cell phone, Jackson and Katy left Mandy and her children at home and went to look for him.

By the time they found the wrecker, a moonless night blanketed the land. Jackson stopped fifty feet away and pointed the Jeep headlights at the truck. When the light hit it, Katy cried out and Jackson said, "Christ Almighty!" The cracked windshield was splattered with red and the driver's door hung askew, torn half-off the wrecker.

"Stay here," Jackson said as he got out.

Katy thought about some of the awful things she had seen in Africa, the mauled and chewed up bodies, things she never talked about. "No," she told him. "I'm coming too."

After a second, he nodded, and they slowly got out, one of them watching while the other retrieved the rifles. They each had a flashlight, and they approached with the guns and the lights pointed at the truck. Even at night, when red appears black, they knew it was a bloodbath.

They circled and came from the rear so that the headlights did not blind them. They stopped fifty feet away. "Watch my back while I get closer," Jackson said. Katy nodded, and he crept to the driver's side. When his flashlight beam shone on the driver's seat, the seatbelt was pinning a man's shoulder and arm against the seat back. The bodypart was all that remained. Jackson fought against the bile that climbed up his throat but lost the fight.

An hour later, Mike Hawn, a portrait photographer who worked for the police when needed, finished photographing the dead liger on the wrecker and the cab and what was inside it. Powerful lights driven by a small generator had been set up to light the truck and the area around it. "Looks like I'm done here," Hawn told Jackson. "Anyway, I should get home. My wife and kids ...." His voice trailed off, and his eyes darted around. Hawn was scared.

"How soon can I get the pictures?" Jackson asked. Hawn used both film and digital cameras but liked to print his shots since they might be used in court.

"They'll be waiting for you at the station," the photographer answered. "I sure don't want 'em around."

Mike Hawn left without asking how soon he would get paid, something he always did. Still, he had stayed longer than some of the others, thought Jackson. Dustin Falmouth, a young doctor elected county coroner, left shortly after stating that he could not pronounce Wade Placett dead without a DNA analysis, since that was the only way he could identify the remains as Wade. "I can barely identify them as human," he said.

Sheriff Midden left after Falmouth allowed the EMTs to remove 'the parts.' Some State Police troopers had come and gone without doing much more than gawking. Jackson's own officers searched for Wade's body, but they did not venture far away from the lights or look all that hard.

Katy was one of the first to leave. She had not wanted to go, despite having turned ashen, but once Angie arrived, Jackson had her take Katy to town. Now, the crime scene processing was complete, and Jackson sat alone in his Jeep in silence looking out at the yellow and black tape illuminated by his headlights. The tape looked foolish surrounding the truck out here in the open. He drove off.

A short time later, Jackson pulled up outside the Placett house. Mandy rushed outside onto the porch as he exited the Jeep. Jackson looked at her and shook his head, and she dropped like a boxer hit with a knockout punch.

TWENTY-ONE

Katy preferred her outdoor shower in Botswana to the motel bathtub. Even so, she was on her second tub of hot water. She had cried and cried during the first bath. Now, she simply lay in the too-short bathtub, a rolled towel pillowing her head, her legs up and resting on the ridge, while she drank wine and tried to forget. Her phone rang again, and she looked at the number, hoping it was Jackson and not more reporters calling. It was neither.

"Some good news and some not so good news," Stan Ely said by way of hello.

"Good news first."

"Good news is we filed the injunction, and we drew a great judge. A ruling might even come tomorrow."

Katy felt her mouth move, but no sound came out.

"Katy? Hey, what's wrong?"

It took a while. There were stops and starts and sobs, but she eventually told Stan about finding the – she wasn't sure what to call it – the torso of Wade Placett.

"F-me! No wonder you're freaked out," Stan said.

Katy wiped her eyes with a corner of the bath towel. The minimum makeup she sometimes wore was rubbed off long ago. "You said there's some 'not so good news'."

"Oh man. People are guarding their checkbooks like a Jewish mother guards her daughter's virginity."

Katy groaned and said, "So what will you do?"

"I need something to entice the donors. Something special to tell them or somebody like you to make the public take notice. What do you say?"

Although Katy often supported animal rescue groups, she didn't want Stan and ARK in Idaho, not yet anyway, and she didn't want Stan knowing about Kali or her baby ligers. "If you get funding, how soon would you come?" she asked.

"An operation takes planning. Maybe a day or two."

A day or two? A lot could happen by then, Katy thought. "See how your injunction goes, Stan. If there's a problem, I'll get on board publicly, okay? Or maybe I can come up with something even better for you." After the conversation ended, Katy remained in the bathtub although the water was cool now. Deception made her feel dirty.

When Jackson returned to town, Bobby Grunfield, a reserve officer, was manning the station, while Brian Patterson and another reserve officer were on patrol. Grunfield, retired from the Air Force, was watching a TV interview of Iris. "She's good," Grunfield said.

Jackson watched long enough to learn that Iris remained in favor of the public lion hunt despite the attack on Wade. "Anything I should know about?" he asked.

Grunfield ticked off the incident reports with trained precision: a camper had been broken into and some money stolen from a Nebraska family; a minor traffic accident had sent a local man who was too old to drive to the clinic; two citations were handed out for public intoxication and one for indecency; and last night's fighters had made bail. When Grunfield asked about Wade Placett, Jackson begged off from talking about it and went to his office.

A large manila envelope lay on Jackson's desk, and he opened it. After looking at a few photos he leaned back in the expensive desk chair he bought after hurting his back in an arrest scuffle and thought about Mandy Placett.

Once he got her up and into the house, she had sent Josh and Tammy upstairs where the baby was asleep. She told them to stay there. She ignored their repeated questions of "What's wrong, Mommy?" and "Where's Daddy?". After that, he followed Mandy into the kitchen where she poured two shots of bourbon. Seated beside a refrigerator covered with yellow duck magnets and kid's artwork, he told her what little he knew for certain and some of what he suspected. She listened to it all with dry eyes and a blank face. When he finished, he removed the untouched glass of Wild Turkey she had been squeezing the whole time and said he would call someone to come over.

"Rhonda Fedder," Mandy said before she got up and walked out.

Jackson listened to her climb the stairs, each step as heavy as if her ankles were weighted, and then he heard a door close. He phoned Rhonda Fedder, told her what had happened, and sat in the kitchen to wait for her to arrive. A few minutes later, the wailing began. Even muted by a closed door, it was as piercing a sound as anything Jackson ever had heard. He had not been the one who told Nancy Larson's mother the girl was dead. He knew that it was cowardly, but he was grateful when Med Fedder's wife arrived and, after talking to her, he could leave.

"Chief?" Bobby tapped on the open door, and Jackson covered up the photos. "Chief, there's a woman here to see you. The gal that does the local evening news on ABC. She says you know her. Says you're friends. She's not the first reporter to come here tonight. I told her that."

Karen Cormac was waiting by the entrance. She was a small and shapely brunette who wasn't pretty enough to get a national news desk. Jackson had met her three years earlier while helping to search for two missing girls near Rexburg. Cormac had shown more sensitivity and dignity than most other reporters when the girls' bodies were found. They shook hands, and he said, "Friends, Karen?"

She smiled sheepishly and told Jackson she wanted to interview him about the latest lion attack. Lion had become the generic word used to mean all of the cats.

"Go interview the mayor instead," said Jackson. "She likes it." He didn't mind answering questions if it helped solve a case, but the media could not help the dead.

"I already tried," Cormac said. "But she prefers the national desk to regional." The reporter paused to see if Jackson objected to her comment. When he didn't, she said, "Just a few questions. And I won't ask for graphic descriptions. But you were there, Chief Hobbs. You discovered the body. Don't you think people should know how dangerous these wild cats really are? Hunters need to be told the truth."

Jackson thought it over. "Okay. A few questions, that's it. And we do it outside."

Jackson donned his gray Riverton hat and blue nylon police jacket. The camera crew was waiting and ready in the parking lot. Cormac began by asking him to confirm Wade's identity, but Jackson refused to do so pending the coroner's report. She asked about the ligers and then moved on to the public hunt in general. Some questions Jackson answered and some he avoided. To end the interview Karen Cormac said, "Chief Hobbs, do you have any advice for the hunters? What can they do to be safe?"

"Stay home," Jackson said.

Iris stormed into Jackson's office a half-hour later. Bobby Grunfield, trailing behind her, gave a helpless and apologetic shrug.

"That's alright, Bobby. I was expecting the mayor. Just close the door and keep everyone out," Jackson said.

As the door shut, Iris yelled, "Stay home! That's your advice to hunters? You want me to fire you, Jackson?"

"How many licenses you sold so far?"

"Close to four hundred. Two hundred or so tomorrow."

"Then whatever I say doesn't matter." Jackson handed Iris an eight-by-ten color photograph.

"What's this?" She looked at the photo. "It's disgusting."

Jackson slid four more color photographs across the desk. "It's Wade Placett."

"That's not funny."

"What the liger left of him," said Jackson. "You can use them for your next TV interview. Show and tell."

Iris looked at another photo and then threw the batch of them at Jackson. "This isn't my fault."

"Whose fault is it, Iris? The lions and tigers?"

"I don't know, Jackson. Maybe it just happened. Like Ed Stevens dying. Or do you blame me for that too?"

"No, I blame myself."

"Well, at least guilt is something you're good at," snapped Iris.

Jackson watched her dark eyes spark and her nostrils flare. He saw her fighting for control. Maybe he wanted her to go ballistic? Maybe he wanted to hurt her? Maybe hell! He knew he did. He removed his shield from his belt and laid it on the desk. "You want to fire me, go ahead."

"We both know this isn't just about Wade or Ed or even Ted and Dolly Cheney," Iris told him. "It never is with you, Jackson. It's always about little Nancy Larsen and how you got her killed."

"You always told me it wasn't my fault."

"I lied. I lied to keep you from sinking any deeper in self-pity. And you know what? It was a waste of time. The man I married was gone by then and not coming back."

"Good to know what you think of me, Iris."

"You know the difference between you and me? I can live with my mistakes. But you need to be so goddamn perfect, Jackson, you can't handle being human."

For a moment Jackson said nothing. Then he picked up the photos and returned them to the manila envelope. "I'm not doing so well at protecting people, Iris. You'd be doing me a favor by finding another chief of police."

"Oh, I get it now. You want out," Iris said. Her anger made her voice shrill. "That's what you do, isn't it? You quit when things get hard."

"Do I?" Jackson stood up. Iris was shorter than him by six inches. "Is that why you tell yourself you left? That why you started fucking Dell the day we hit town? You tell yourself it was me that quit on the marriage?"

Iris laughed. "Jackson, I was fucking Dell before we ever moved here. Haven't you figured that out yet?"

Iris was blind with anger as she ripped through town. She was driving too fast, and the Cadillac CTS fought each turn. She missed the BMW she had driven in Colorado.

Minutes later, she ran a stop sign and was blasted out of her stupor by a car horn customized to sound like a big rig. A black Hummer came straight at her. She swerved, narrowly missing a roadside mailbox, and fishtailed down the street.

Dell heard the car horn and the screech of rubber. While sipping two-inches of Glenfiddich in a cut crystal glass, he moved away from the crackling fire in his den peered out the curtains, and saw the Cadillac CTS pull up.

Iris once described Dell's den as a British club for cowboys: trophy heads lit by green glass lampshades, Native American rugs beneath leather chairs, and a floor-to-ceiling bookcase where numerous family photographs nestled against books. Opposite that wall stood a large fieldstone fireplace. Earlier Dell had been wondering where in the den he would put the liger head or maybe even the whole animal. Now, he knew there would be no liger trophy for the den. The den was his favorite room too.

Dell released the curtain. The phone on his desk rang, and he let it go to voice mail. Then his cell phone rang. His brother again, he figured. Dan was frantic about the potential fallout from Wade's death. How can a man be governor and have no balls? John Tapping, now he had balls, Dell thought, as he examined a tintype photo of his great-grandfather, a robber baron when Idaho was a territory. Next to it were black and white photos of grandfather Daniel, founder of the town bank, and color photos of daddy Abel, also a banker. Other photos featured Dell posing with game he killed or hobnobbing with the rich or powerful; some followed Shane from infant to teenage football player; there also were photos to chronicle Dan's political career, photos of their African safari six years ago; as well as a couple of photos of Iris.

The photo he picked up was none of them. It was a wedding photograph. In it Tilda looked beautiful and fragile, tall for a woman and model thin. Aristocratic, he thought. Iris still believed he had been forced to marry Tilda, but he had married her to elevate the family genes the way wealth had elevated the family stature. Dell wiped an imaginary speck of dust off the glass and returned the photo to the shelf when he heard the front door open.

"Some bastard almost killed me," Iris said as she entered the den. "Some goddamn black Hummer."

Dell grunted. If Iris cursed, she was really pissed. He wondered if she had noticed the license plate. He doubted it. Anyway, nobody could see inside the Hummer, not through the dark glass. "Lots of assholes and idiots."

"I thought maybe the Hummer came from here."

Dell gestured toward a bottle of wine and a wine glass. "I opened an Oregon Pinot for you. The one you like." He moved toward the wine bottle, his face hidden from Iris. "So tell me, did you straighten out Jackson?"

TWENTY-TWO

Dawn was breaching the horizon as Jackson reached town. Hunters already were out in full force, some herding live animals into truck beds, while others loaded slabs of beef and cartons of grocery store chickens. Not all of the hunters planned to lure the cats with bait. Some hunters intended to track them. Some simply hoped to stroll around, stir up a lion or tiger, and shoot them. Rural people were advised not to venture outside without wearing a highly visible orange or fluorescent vest, coat, or cap. Even so, farmers and ranchers that posted 'No Hunting' and 'No Trespassing' signs had covered them over, figuring that lion hunters posed a lesser danger to their animals, and families too, than did the lions and tigers.

Jackson imagined towns during gold rush days had looked the way Buckhorn looked today. Buckhorn even had a tent city now, at least a modern version of one. On the drive to town Jackson had passed the RV's and campers crammed into tiny

Green State Park. Larger, more distant campgrounds were filling up too, according to the radio.

Jackson left downtown and zigzagged his way to the Sportsman Motel. His red Ford was parked outside Katy's room. Last night, after Iris had left his office, he stopped off at the motel but didn't talk to Katy. Instead, he sat alone in the Jeep wondering if the Sportsman Motel was where Iris and Dell had met for sex or if they had gone to Dell's house or out of town somewhere or even used the farmhouse. Afterwards, he had driven home and tossed and turned before finally falling into a restless sleep.

Jackson didn't want to knock on her door this early, so he called Katy from his cell phone. They talked while he drove to the police station. He parked, checked in with Skip Tibbits, and then walked over to the busy town square.

The Split-Rail Café had been open since four-thirty. It was still packed when Jackson arrived. Katy showed up ten minutes later. Janice Beans cleared two places at the counter and motioned for Jackson and Katy to take them. It wasn't their turn, but they took the seats anyway. They had coffee and ordered breakfast.

While they waited, Katy talked about her life in Africa. At one point, she said, "I sometimes help the Maun police when someone goes missing in the bush. Alligators, hyenas, lions, leopards – if I don't find people fast, when I do, it's usually not very pretty." She stopped and sipped her *café au lait*. "You think you can get used to it, but I never do."

Jackson nodded. "If you ever do, quit the job."

"I found cat tracks in the dryer pools of blood. Large tracks. Too large for a lion or a tiger."

"You didn't mention it last night."

166

"I'm going after her today, after Kali."

It took Jackson a moment to remember who Kali was. "After what happened, you want to go liger hunting?"

"It's not a matter of wanting to," Katy said, "I have to. Look, we know a liger probably killed your friend Ed, and Kali certainly killed Wade Placett. The longer she's out there, the more dangerous she is, especially -" she lowered her voice "- once she has cubs."

"All the more reason not to go after her alone."

"You offering to join me?"

"Can't," Jackson told her, shaking his head. "First day of the public hunt and all, I should stick around. Tomorrow maybe I could go. Or I can set up my rotation so that Skip or John can go with you. They're both hunters. But Skip just came on duty, and John's scheduled to work later today." Their food arrived, and the conversation stopped for a few minutes. It continued when Jackson said, "So where do you plan to go?"

"Back to Safari Land, if that's allowed?"

"As long as you don't go in the house."

"I don't expect the cats to be hiding inside."

"Neither did I."

Katy had heard about the Bengal tiger attacking one of Jackson's officers but forgotten it. "Sorry," she said.

"Angie's off today. She might go with you."

"She's the one who was attacked, wasn't she?"

Jackson nodded, his mouth full of dark rye toast. Once he swallowed, he said, "That's why she'll go."

Katy was wrong in thinking that Kali would return to Safari Land. Following her attack on one of the predators that had killed Shaka, Kali returned to Jackson's two-acre plot of prairie.

As she crept through Great Basin Wild Rye grass, much of it four to six feet tall and turning yellow and brown and brittle, Kali sensed that her birthing time was near. The female liger heard occasional gunfire, but it was not close enough to concern her. Safe from any immediate danger, Kali settled in.

Later that morning, Kali gave birth to three cubs. The two females and one male were the size of large house cats. They resembled Shaka more than Kali: their orangey-brown skin had black stripes, and their faces were dark-spotted. Even at birth the liger cubs' sturdy legs and large feet signaled the size they would one day reach. But for now, they were helpless infants, dependent upon Kali. She licked them clean, and they crawled around blindly to find her teats. A young liger can increase its size by a half-pound per day, and to produce the milk to feed them, Kali needed to eat and to eat often. But before she could hunt, she had to find a safer home for the cubs.

Katy loaded the .375 and was examining the Remington 389 pneumatic dart rifle when Angie pulled in. She parked her Outback next to Jackson's pickup outside the Cheney house. It was midmorning now and hot for mid-September. The women exchanged hellos and chatted while Angie removed a backpack and a Browning A-Bolt II Medallion rifle, a .243 caliber. It had a long, 22-inch barrel and was powerful enough to stop deer, elk, or bear.

Upon seeing the weapon, Katy nodded appreciatively. "Jackson said you knew what you're doing."

Angie smiled. "My dad, he wanted a boy."

"Don't they all," Katy said. The pack she slipped on was smaller than Angie's.

"So where we going?" asked Angie.

"The topo map shows water a half-mile south," Katy told her. "We'll head for it. All the animals will."

Angie nodded agreement. "It's near the gravel pits. Fred Bulcher's mined sand and gravel there for years."

They set off, heading south.

"Maybe somebody there spotted Kali?"

"Nobody there now. Ted Cheney booted Fred and his crew off the land a few months ago."

"Why?" said Katy.

Before Angie could respond, they heard a noise that sounded like a door closing. Both women stopped and looked back. Katy quietly moved twenty feet to the left, separating them, and moments later they crept to the house.

Despite the sound that might or might not have been a door, Katy expected to find a lion or tiger or wolf or even scavenger dogs behind the Cheney house. The last thing she expected was a chubby man with a thick, white beard and a flushed, round face shaded by a Tilley hat.

The man carried a daypack and a deer rifle. He wore jeans hooked to red suspenders. His flannel shirt was so new it had folds in it. The moment he saw a pair of rifles pointed at him, he said, "Don't shoot. Don't shoot." He tried to raise his hands above his shoulders, but he was holding the rifle. His belly shook when he moved.

"Nobody's going to shoot you," Angie told him. "Just stay calm. Now what are you doing here?"

"Looking." His eyes bounced from Angie to Katy and back again. "Just looking. I didn't do nothing wrong."

"You mind laying that rifle on the ground while we talk?" Angie said. "Do it real gentle like."

"Okay, sure." The man squatted and laid the deer rifle in the dust. It took effort for him to get back up.

Angie and Katy lowered their rifles but kept them where they could be raised again quickly. Angie then introduced herself as a police officer and told the man to show some identification. When he hesitated, the guns started up again. The trespasser finally took out his driver's license and gave it to Angie. She read it aloud. "Ted Sands from Boise, Idaho." She studied the man for a moment. "How'd you get here?"

"Car." Neither Katy nor Angie had seen a car when they drove up, and they pointed it out to Sands. "Well, I parked a ways back on a side road, off in the woods. Worked my way up here looking for lions and tigers."

"Find any?" Katy asked. She hadn't spoken until now.

Sands shook his head.

"Watch him," Angie said to Katy. She had no radio to use to check his driver's license, so she instead checked the house. After examining the crime scene tape across the back door, she said, "It's been cut and re-taped."

"That could be Jackson," Katy said. "From Monday."

A second later, Angie returned to face Sands. "Did you go inside the house, Mr. Sands?"

"Not me. I looked through the windows, just being curious but … that's it. No reason to go inside." Sands removed his hat and scratched his head. His hair was white and cut short. "You a police officer too?" he asked Katy.

"Professional hunter."

"Oh! Well, how 'bout that. Two girls with guns."

"Women," Angie said. "Where's your hunting license?"

"Hunting license? Didn't know I need one to look."

"I bet you didn't. I should arrest you for corrupting a crime scene, but I'm kind of busy here so ... guess it's your lucky day, mister Sands."

"Well, I appreciate that. That mean I can go now?"

"Yes, I guess it does." Sands reached for his deer rifle, but Angie stopped him. She picked up the gun, a Kimber Classic, and unloaded it before giving the hunting rifle and the bullets to the older man and saying, "Don't load it again until you clear the barnyard."

Sands nodded and walked away without looking back.

"He was lying," Angie said.

"About being in the house?" Katy asked.

"About that and maybe more. That tape on the door is brand new. Now why would Sands have police tape?"

It was a question not meant for Katy to answer so she didn't. They watched Sands disappear from sight. Then they cut across a field behind the house, drawn by the stench of decomposition.

About three hundred feet from the empty animal cages they found a ditch that had been used as a trash dump. Bones were mixed in with household garbage. The bones were mostly large and mostly disconnected from other bones, but a few were clearly identifiable as a horse or cow or even a large cat. Most of the bones had been picked clean.

Katy squatted to examine some tracks near the edge of the trash dump. "Lions," she said. "Most people don't realize it, but lions are scavengers. They'd rather steal food than hunt for it. Lot of wolf tracks here too."

Angie watched Katy's butt, shapely in taut pants, and then caught herself and looked away at the scat. "Some of the wolf scat's fresh. Sands probably scared them off."

"Him or some big cat."

"How exactly are we going to find this liger?"

"Big cats are territorial. I think Kali will return here, especially since she's pregnant." Katy explained about the rarity of ligers mating and the added need to capture Kali quickly now that the male was dead. With nothing further to see at the dump, they soon walked on, and for a while neither of them said anything more. The silence wasn't due to feeling awkward; it came instead from each woman's comfort with not speaking. It was broken when Katy, who had been thinking about Jackson, suddenly said, "You must know Jackson pretty well."

"He's my boss," Angie said with a shrug.

"That scar on his neck, you know how he got it?"

"Did you ask the Chief?"

Katy shook her head no.

"Colorado," Angie said. "A house fire. He doesn't talk about it much." She snorted. "Actually, he's never really talked about it with me. But you hear things."

Katy was watching the ground as they walked. "Stop," she said. She dropped down to look at some tracks.

"These liger tracks?"

"No," Katy said. "Too small. A tiger. A big one."

"Chief Hobbs saved me from a Bengal tiger back there in the house," Angie said. "I'd be dead if it wasn't for him."

"Meaning don't ask anything else about him?"

Angie didn't respond right away. She studied the land as though she was expecting someone to arrive. When she finally did look at Katy again, she said, "Go online and look up the name Nancy Larsen in Fort Collins, Colorado."

"Who's Nancy Larsen?" Katy asked.

"The answer to your question."

TWENTY-THREE

Jackson returned to the Split-Rail Café Wednesday afternoon following a phone call from Sheriff Midden. The sheriff and Major Jessup were in Buckhorn and had asked to meet at the café instead of at the police station.

The café was mostly empty at two o'clock. Jessup and Midden sat in a booth by a big window that overlooked the town square. Jackson greeted the café owners and ordered coffee and cherry pie. Then he pulled a chair up to the booth instead of sitting beside either man.

"So why the secrecy? Why not come to my office?"

"Hell, Jackson, you got something against having coffee with us in public?" Midden said in a deadpan voice.

"Depends I guess on why you fellows are here."

Jessup and Midden chuckled, and Jessup said, "You'll see why once we tell you about -" Jessup paused when Suzy Beans brought Jackson's order and refilled the other cups. "Ronnie Greathouse is why," he added once she had left.

"You found him?"

Major Jessup shook his head. "Not yet. But we know a lot more about him. Pretty interesting stuff too."

"Greathouse is seeing a woman 'round here," Sheriff Midden said. "You know this gal Maryann Fedder?"

"Med and Rhonda's girl. She's in a wheelchair."

"That's the one," Midden said.

"Someone should talk to her," Jessup suggested. "You being local, she might be more comfortable if it was you."

Jackson was surprised by the comment. "Is there a reason she wouldn't be comfortable talking to you?"

"Depends on whether she knows what Ronnie's up to," Major Jessup said. "And if she does, you'll want to know."

Jackson wrinkled his brow in thought. "You think Ronnie has something to do with these cats getting out?"

"I think Ronnie's involved in something he shouldn't be," Major Jessup said.

"Most people are, one way or the other. And you still haven't told me why I should go see Maryann Fedder."

Major Jessup and Sheriff Midden exchanged looks, but neither of them rushed to respond to Jackson.

Jackson cut into his pie. "You know, talking to you fellows is like watching a foreign film with no subtitles," he said. "You got something to say, say it. You don't, let me enjoy my cherry pie in peace." To emphasize his point, Jackson shoveled a bite of pie into his mouth.

"Knights of the Golden Circle," Jessup said.

Jackson chewed and swallowed and then repeated the name and asked what it was.

"From what we can tell, I'd say they're another anti-government militia group," Major Jessup replied. "Neo-Nazis,

Aryan Brotherhood, or whatever, God knows we got enough of them here." The ISP major described the printed material and the notebook written in code that the Roberts twins had found when they searched Ronnie's house.

"Your troopers get a search warrant?"

"We'll deal with that later," Midden said.

"Go on," Jackson said. Major Jessup did, and by the time he finished talking, Jackson had forgotten about the lack of a warrant. "Sounds to me like you've got initials and some dates, but there's no real proof that Ronnie belonged to this group. Maybe he was investigating them."

"If he was," Major Jessup said, "nobody in Meridian knows squat about it. I even contacted the FBI. They played dumb, but they know something. My guess is Ronnie's part of this KGC, and he's probably not the only lawman here involved. That's why we're meeting in the café. The notebook says this group plans to replace you as chief."

Jackson chuckled. "So does my ex-wife." A moment later, he frowned and said, "You saying that some of my officers are part of this anti-government, hate group?"

Jackson was examining the employment files of his blue-pin and reserve officers when Angie entered his office. One of Katy's books was on Jackson's desk. The book jacket was open to her photograph and bio.

"Catching up on your reading?" Angie said.

"Had Sadie order it from Amazon."

"Katy's much prettier in person."

"Never noticed," Jackson said, but the upward turn of his mouth betrayed his words. "Find any ligers?"

She shook her head. "Katy found tracks, but the only thing we captured was a strange old guy nosing around the house," Angie said. "I started wondering if he's a cop, a Fed maybe. Something about the way he handled himself, like he was in control even though we had the guns." She reported the details of the encounter with Ted Sands.

"Probably just being nosy." Jackson then told Angie to close the door and sit down, and once she had, he asked, "What do you know about the Knights of the Golden Circle?"

"That's easy. Nothing."

"Ever hear anyone you work with mention it?"

"No," she said. "What is it? Some kind of club?"

"A white-militia group," Jackson said. "I'd like you to find out about them - why here, why now, what do they want? And see if you can locate the man Pamela and Dolly were both married to, this Edward King Yow."

"So being deputy chief, it's kind of like being your secretary. You forgot to mention that."

Jackson laughed. "Try and get a current phone number for Eddie Yow. I'd like to talk to him."

By the time Jackson greeted Maryann Fedder, afternoon sunlight bathed the three-season porch where she sat reading a book titled *The Girl With The Dragon Tattoo*. He took in immense green fields, the potato plants a week or two from harvest, and beyond them, a thick border of ash, hawthorn, and elder trees. The house was built on a knoll and had a spectacular view.

"Nice place to read," Jackson said.

"I practically live here from spring to fall," Maryann said. "I hate the winters for keeping me inside."

Maryann marked her book and laid it aside as her mother served coffee. Upon arriving Jackson had asked Rhonda about the Placett family. He was not surprised to hear they planned to go away after the memorial service.

Jackson waited until Rhonda left before he pulled a Kennedy rocker up to face Maryann. "Maryann, I need to ask you some questions," he said.

"About Ronnie?"

He nodded. "When did you last talk to him?"

"Sunday. We had a date, but he didn't show up."

"And nothing since then? No phone calls, e-mail?"

"No. Just the package." Maryann moved the newspapers covering the seat of another chair and showed him a box that said Frederick's of Hollywood. "On Monday dad found this beneath the mail box. Wrapped and sent to me." The wrapping paper she pointed to had balloons on it. "But it didn't come through the mail. I mean, there's no postage or address. Just a little card with my name on it."

Jackson wondered if he should tell her who had actually delivered it on Monday. The Roberts twins had admitted to Jessup that they left the box and in their excitement about the lion hunt failed to follow up on it.

"What was in it if you don't mind me asking?"

"Lingerie," she said and blushed.

"Were you expecting a present?"

"No. It's not my birthday or anything."

"Did Ronnie seem worried lately? Or maybe afraid?"

"Nope. Never. I really wish I could help you but -"

"You're doing fine," Jackson told her. "Tell me, did he ever mention The Knights of the Golden Circle?"

She repeated the name and then said, "I'm sure he didn't. Sounds like something out of *The Da Vinci Code*."

"Maybe it is," Jackson said. He finished his coffee and stood. "I'll let you get back to your book."

"That's okay." She picked up her novel anyway.

"So what's it about, your book?"

She thought for a moment. "Deceit and revenge."

Jackson walked to the door, but before opening it he said, "The present you got, could it have been a farewell gift from Ronnie? Maybe he decided to leave town?"

"I don't think so." Maryann blushed again. "You don't give a girl red crotchless panties and leave town."

Jackson had just turned onto the county highway when he met up with Deborah Dawson. Behind her Toyota Tundra she had a horse trailer with two horses. Jackson recognized one of them.

"I see you've got Touie with you."

"Had to let Doc Willis check my mare before he left town, so he asked me to bring Touie home. I told Jesse."

"Need my help?"

"I imagine you've got other things to do. The doc, he has some family emergency in Seattle. A sister."

Jackson nodded and said, "You lose any more sheep?"

"Two more. Armando and me, we take shifts now guarding them at night. The dogs watch over them during the day." Deborah shook her head. "Never thought I'd carry around a rifle to protect myself from lions and tigers in Idaho." Her words spilled out in a rush, a slight accent to them. "I can't believe schools are open and people go to work, carrying on like normal."

"Welcome to the wild west."

"Shouldn't you evacuate the town or something?"

"You're from New York City, right?"

"Upper West Side. Most of my life."

"You live there back in two thousand one?"

Deborah nodded yes.

"When the World Trade Center fell, did you leave?"

"Well, no."

Jackson shrugged.

"Okay, I get it." A smile softened Deborah's boney features, although it exaggerated the crows-feet mapping her eyes. "Speaking of carrying on like normal, Jesse wants to comes back to work."

"As long as she doesn't go out riding, I'm fine with it," Jackson said. "Can't speak for Iris."

Deborah nodded and shifted the Tundra automatic into drive. "You round up your two quarter-horses yet?"

"Haven't been able to even look for them."

"Maybe Armando and me can help. We'll try."

They said goodbye, and Deborah drove off to deliver Touie. Jackson was pretty sure that by now half the town thought of him as 'that negligent rancher'. In Idaho or Wyoming or Montana, you fed your animals first, your kids second, and if your wife only saw you at supper, it simply meant you were a good, hard-working husband.

He pulled away and drove to Safari Land. When he reached the Cheney house, he sat in the Jeep with the windows down and listened to Canadian geese flying south and to the usual buzz and hum and chirps of insects and birds. Nature was never quiet. But Jackson wasn't listening for sounds that should be there; he was listening for sounds that shouldn't. When he heard nothing, he went to the house, opened the screen door, and removed the crime scene tape.

The bullet whistled past him and seared the screenwire a millisecond before he registered the rifle shot. He ducked his head and shouldered the solid wood door as he turned the knob. He heard a second shot and dove to the floor. His only weapon was his Glock 21 semi-automatic. He drew the handgun and crawled behind the couch.

TWENTY-FOUR

One shot could be an accident. Even two shots could mean a careless hunter with bad eyesight and a worse aim. Jackson still wiggled to a window, peeked out, and called for backup. While he waited he tried to think of a reason someone would shoot at him. All he came up with was what Jessup had said about the white-militia group wanting to replace him as Chief of Police. He remained on the floor, his body pressed to the wall, but there were no more shots. John and Brian and Angie showed up within twenty minutes.

If it was not an accident, Jackson knew the shooter would be gone. He sent John and Brian to search the perimeter anyway. If it was an accident, some hunter was in for an unpleasant surprise. After the two men left, Jackson and Angie searched for the bullets. They couldn't find the second one, but the first bullet had passed through the house and broke a window before burrowing in a gnarled Siberian crabapple tree.

Jackson dug out the bullet with a pocketknife and said, "Oh Christ!"

At sundown Jackson entered Benson's Sporting Goods. Buck Benson was an avid hunter and more knowledgeable about guns and ammunition than anyone in the county. If Benson couldn't help him, Jackson would try the state crime lab, although he knew their analysis could take weeks.

He found Benson in his office in the back of the store. Benson had the patrician look that a few lucky aging men get. "Sorry to disturb your supper," Jackson said. He had phoned Benson at home and asked him to return to the store.

Jackson laid the splayed bullet on Benson's desk. Although the bullet was flattened from going through a house and into a tree, it still was larger than an unfired .38 caliber bullet. Benson whistled. "A big boy."

"That much I know already, Buck. But could a gun that fired this thing be used for hunting lions?"

"Not unless you want to blow a hole you can see through," Benson said with a laugh. "Leave it with me for a half-hour; I'll see what I can find out."

"I appreciate it," Jackson said. Benson was already taking measurements as Jackson left. He was halfway to the police station when he got the frantic call from Katy.

The motel parking lot was full when Jackson pulled in. He left his Jeep blocking two cars. A small group of men had gathered, some of them snickering and pointing to a rainbow palette of panties and bras attached to the motel wall like mounted trophies. Jackson suggested the men find better things to do, and they wandered off, grumbling.

"These things all yours?" Jackson asked Katy as he walked up. She was pacing back and forth. Tucker Thule was blocking the doorway to her motel room.

"What do you think?" she snapped.

"Anything else disturbed or missing?"

"I don't know. He won't let me in."

"It's a crime scene," Tucker said. "I told her that."

"Where are your guns, Katy?" Jackson asked.

"In the truck. Your truck. They're safe."

"I need you to talk to the guests here, Tucker," Jackson said. "Somebody must have seen something."

"Roger that." Tucker hesitated. "You mean now?"

"Yes, now," Jackson said. "Start at the far end of the motel." Jackson waited until Tucker was gone. "You can gather up your clothes now, Katy. You want help?"

She shook her head no, her eyes glistening.

Jackson tried to avoid watching Katy remove her lingerie, but he had seen everything already. He was no expert, but he knew granny-panties from thongs – butt floss Sadie Pope called them - and he knew the difference between the plain cotton panties Iris usually had worn in Colorado from the lacy sexy ones she started wearing once they moved to Idaho. Katy seemed to have underwear for all occasions.

Once Katy was done, they checked her motel room to verify nothing had been stolen. After that, they went together to the motel office to talk to the owner.

"Any idea who did this?" Jackson asked Neil Fennis.

"Nope. Kids maybe. But it's more likely somebody who doesn't like her trying to shut down our lion hunt."

"What?" Katy said. "What are you talking about?"

"Same thing I'm wondering," Jackson said.

"On the news a couple hours ago. Some smug, bunny-lover in Colorado said he filed an injunction to stop our lion hunt. He especially mentioned Miss Osborne's name. Said she was a big supporter of what he was doing."

Jackson looked at Katy and frowned. "What's he talking about? What injunction? Who in Colorado?"

"I didn't … I didn't tell Stan to use my name."

"Stan?"

"Stan Ely. We talked about him the other night."

"So you know about this injunction business?"

Katy hesitated before saying, "Sort of."

Jackson continued to frown at Katy, although he spoke to Neil. "How'd they get in, Neil? Lock wasn't jimmied."

"Maybe the door was left open," Neil Fennis said.

"And maybe someone gave them a key," Katy prompted.

"Jackson, I have a motel crammed with hunters. I can't watch them all." To Katy he said, "It'll be better for everyone if you find another place to stay."

"There is no other place," she said. "You know that."

"My new price is triple what she's paying, Jackson." Neil Fennis shook his head. "I gotta hand it to Iris and Dell. This lion safari is just what the town needed."

"Except for people getting killed, you mean," Jackson said. Fennis scowled, but before he could argue, he was called away to handle a check-in, and Jackson told Katy, "I've got an extra bedroom at the house. You can stay there. Should have offered it to you before."

Jackson saw from her expression that she was hesitant about accepting. "Look, you can't stay here and I -" His cell phone rang, and he stopped mid-sentence when he saw the caller ID. "I need to take this," he said. He walked outside into the early darkness. A few minutes later, Jackson left Katy at the motel to pack up, while he returned to Benson's Sporting Goods.

"Elephant gun," Benson said when Jackson entered the office. "The shell is a five-hundred. Big as you can buy without a special permit. I don't sell a single rifle that can fire them things, although I can order the guns and ammo. Can't tell you the exact model and make, but I put together a list of a half-dozen rifles it could be."

He handed a slip of paper to Jackson. A Weatherby Mark V was near the top of the list. That was the rifle Dell had shown Katy and Jackson a couple of days earlier.

"My things were trashed and now I'm being evicted," Katy snapped. She had called Stan Ely as soon as she finished packing to move to Jackson's house.

"F-me," Stan said. "Katy, I'm so sorry."

"Nothing like asking me first, Stan."

"But I did," Stan argued. "You said if the injunction hit a snag, I could use your name as a supporter. Katy, we didn't hit a snag; we hit a brick wall. The good judge I told you about; well, we lost him. He had emergency bypass surgery today. So our hearing got reassigned, and this time we drew some Bush appointee. A black female judge that's so far right she makes Justice Thomas look like Martin Luther King. We don't have a chance in hell."

"You still should have cleared it with me," Katy said, but even as she said it, her words were losing their sting.

"My Hollywood connection says there's no such thing as bad publicity. Controversy will help you sell books."

"Your Hollywood connection probably isn't surrounded by angry hunters with big guns," Katy told him.

* * *

As Shane slid the Toyota to a dusty stop outside the dark house, Jesse turned off the blaring music. At least he was playing Black-Eyed Peas instead of 50 Cent. Jesse's tastes ran to Taylor Swift, Josh Ritter, and the Beatles.

"You don't have to hang around," Jesse said.

"Maybe I want to."

"You don't even like horses."

"But I like you."

She smiled at him but still shook her head. "Touie could be nervous. He doesn't like being away from home."

"Maybe it's you that's nervous?" He ran his hand up the inside of her jeans and kept going until she clamped his hand between warm thighs. "Maybe you're afraid you can't trust yourself in the barn? All that soft hay -"

"You wish!" she said with a giggle. "Okay, but if you're coming in, stay behind me." She squirmed out of the truck and, without looking back at Shane, hurried to the barn in the glow of an outside light.

Jesse slid the barn door open. Even before she turned on the interior lights, she knew something was wrong. Touie was stomping and snorting inside his stall. "Stay back," she told Shane. He was too close behind her.

Jesse spoke softly as she approached the gelding, but he still pawed the straw on the floor, threw his head around, and flared his nostrils. When she reached her horse, she offered him a sugar cube, something she seldom did, since it was unhealthy for Touie. At first Touie ignored her, but as she continued to coo and offer the treat, he finally took it out of her hand. She felt his hard teeth and large, soft lips, the hairs around them tickling her skin, and said, "I'm glad you're home too."

"Do I have to stay out here all night?" Shane said. He didn't wait for an answer before he stepped inside.

Touie immediately pulled away from Jesse and snorted. "Easy, easy, boy," Jesse said. "Shane, I told you –"

"I didn't do nothing," Shane said.

"Easy, easy."

"So what's wrong with him?" Shane asked.

"I don't know. Something's got him -"

Before Jesse could say, "spooked," they heard the growl of a big cat. Touie reared and struck the air with his hooves. Jesse jumped back to avoid being hit and stumbled. With nothing but air to grab onto, she fell and smacked her head against a large, wood support beam. Her face drained of blood, her eyes rolled, and she dropped to the floor.

"Jesse!" Shane ran toward her. "Jesse," he said again as he knelt over her. "Jesse, come on!"

When Shane heard a second growl, he looked up and saw the giant cat in the open doorway. Kali's head was lowered. Her amber eyes swung from the panicked horse in the stall to Jesse and Shane and then back to the horse. Kali showed her teeth and gave a half-growl and half-hiss.

Shane looked around for an escape route or for a weapon. Another door was at the opposite end of the barn, but it was closed. There were stairs going up to the loft, but they were too far away. Closer, he saw a ladder to the same loft. Maybe he could carry Jesse over his shoulder like a fireman and climb the ladder. Maybe. He said her name again, and this time she moaned. Shane glimpsed something metal and a second later realized it was a pitchfork. He looked back at Kali; she had crept closer.

Shane got up slowly and inched his way toward Touie's stall. Shane's eyes never left the liger, and Kali's eyes never left the horse and the boy. Touie was banging and kicking against his stall. A wooden slat splintered.

In slow motion Shane picked up the pitchfork. With his other hand, he nudged open the gate to the stall. At first Touie didn't react to the offered escape. He continued to rear up and snort, his eyes wild with fear.

By the time Shane returned to Jesse, Kali was seconds away from reaching them. Shane felt his body react to the fear. He fought against it. No way he was going to let this become the aspen grove all over again. "Jesse, wake up," Shane pleaded. "Please. You gotta wake up."

Kali unleashed a louder growl and dropped into a crouch as Touie bolted from the stall, racing toward the open barn door. Kali sprang at the gelding, but the liger was positioned to spring forward, not sideways, and there was little thrust to her attack. Touie easily avoided Kali and disappeared into the night. In a flash Kali recovered and went after the horse. Kali had failed once to kill the prey; she didn't intend to fail again.

Shane wobbled on weak legs to the barn door and shut it with a bang. He then slid to the ground, leaned back against the door, and sucked in his first deep breath in minutes. A moment later Jesse opened her eyes and moaned.

TWENTY-FIVE

Angie parked her Subaru behind the Methodist Church, three blocks from Sharon's bungalow on Grouse Road. She had her police uniform in a garment bag and other items in the Buckhorn Bank gifted carryall slung over her shoulder. There was no traffic, and in most houses the curtains were drawn. She was a block from Sharon's house when she saw the truck. The lights switched from low to high blinding her, and she shielded her eyes until the pickup sped past, its radio spewing country music. She turned and watched the truck speed off. The rear of the truck was crusted with mud. In the dark and with the truck moving, she could not read the license plate number. It was an Idaho tag. The pickup left her feeling uneasy, and when she arrived at Sharon's house, she did not mention her encounter. She simply listened to Sharon prattle on and on about school.

When the phone rang, they were on the couch, with candles their only light, and neither of them interested in talking except to say, "yes, yes," or "do that," or "don't stop." The machine picked up the call. Seconds later, they heard heavy, sexual panting and faint country music.

"What the hell's that?" Angie asked. She lifted her head off Sharon's stomach and eyed the answering machine.

"Kids from school, I guess."

"Doesn't sound like kids to me," Angie said.

Sharon turned away. "It's not the first time."

"First time?" Angie said. "Why didn't you tell me?"

"He never speaks. Just breathes like that."

Angie sat up. "You said he."

"So?"

"How do you know it's a man?"

Sharon shrugged. "I'm just guessing."

"Well, he's not guessing. He knows about us."

"Let him. I don't care."

"Yes, you do," Angie said. "You'll lose your job."

"Then I'll do something else."

"Well, I don't want to do something else. I'm a cop and –" Angie stopped. "Damnit! Why's this happening?"

"You're not the one he's bothering, Ang."

Angie went to her carryall and took out the rubber dildo that she had cut off her locker door. "This was super-glued inside my locker at the station."

Sharon made a noise much like a puppy dog whine.

The phone rang again. Before Sharon could stop her, Angie jumped up, grabbed the receiver, and said, "I'll find you, asshole. Just wait. I'll find you."

The Knights of the Golden Circle had never met twice in one week until Wednesday night. This time there was no pretense of a card game. Each man made his own excuse to his wife or girlfriend or made none at all. The meeting was again held at the Umfleet's log house. It sat a half-mile off the blacktop on a dirt and gravel road that was a dead end. By nine-thirty six vehicles had traveled down the road. The last person to arrive was Tucker Thule.

"Nice of you to come," Fred Bulcher quipped as Tucker set down a twelve-pack of Miller cans.

"Had something to do," Tucker said. "And I had to help with the big panty investigation." To everyone's delight, Tucker shared the details of Katy's lingerie spectacle. Besides Fred and Jerry, tonight's group included a corrections officer, a middle-school teacher, and a sawmill worker. "So what's going on here?" Tucker asked as the laughter subsided.

"We'll tell you," Jerry said, "while you hand out them beers." Marcy, Jerry's wife, unwilling to play hostess again, was in their bedroom watching taped episodes of *American Idol.* "The law find Ronnie yet?"

"Nope. But I think the Big Chief knows something."

Fred snorted. "I'll tell you exactly where Ronnie Greathouse is. He's laying in a ditch somewhere dead."

"Or ratting us out," the schoolteacher said. He wore an outdated crewcut and had a beer belly.

Everybody started talking at once. After five minutes, Fred hushed the bickering by saying, "Bag this shit tonight. The main thing you missed out on," he told Tucker, "is hearing this plan Rip has for us to make money off the Idaho Lion Hunt thing." Rip Baxter was a corrections officer at the Saint Anthony Work Camp.

"Thought we were robbing a bank?" Tucker said.

"Ronnie's big idea?" Fred snorted again. "We're patriots, not bank robbers. Our fight's with baby-killers and the godless politicians in Washington. And we don't need to play Jesse James to get rid of the mud people and wetbacks. Just listen to Rip's plan. And next time we meet, Tucker, get your ass here on time."

"So you in charge now, Fred?" Tucker asked.

Fred laughed. "Hell, I've always been in charge."

Jesse and Katy were snuggled up on the couch drinking hot chocolate and talking about horses when Jackson got home Wednesday night. After saying hello, he locked up his handgun and removed his equipment belt and joined them.

"I see you two have met already."

"Jesse's been the perfect host," Katy said.

"God, Dad, her life is so cool."

Jackson smiled.

Katy quickly said, "Jesse's been telling me about Touie and this race she's training for."

"What'd Doc Willis say? How's Touie?"

"Good, he's good. But really skittish." Jesse did not mention that it had taken Shane and her an hour to locate Touie and return him to the barn. Touie was unhurt, and they did not see the liger again. Nor did she say that she had barely gotten home before Katy arrived. "But I'm going to keep Touie in the barn. Not out in the corral."

Jackson was surprised. "Touie hates being locked up."

"I know but ... it's better than some stupid hunter shooting him."

"Speaking of hunters," Katy said, "how'd it go today?"

Jackson scoffed. "Just one tiger killed. At this rate, we'll be hunting lions and tigers at Thanksgiving."

Jesse yawned and soon went to bed. After Jackson and Katy made plans to go liger hunting on the farm Thursday afternoon, Jackson also said goodnight. In the bedroom his blue uniform was still tossed across a ragged old armchair he was too fond of to throw away. He had left the uniform there after Ed's funeral on Tuesday. He folded the trousers and slid them over a wood hanger, hung the shirt over the pants, saw the black armband, and finally remembered Ed's letter. He had forgotten to go see Eileen Stevens and get the letter. I'm losing it, he thought.

The first thing Katy did when she was alone in the guest room was to take out her 13 inch Macbook Pro. Before Jackson came home, while she was alone with Jesse, she felt chilled and had asked her about lighting a fire. The fireplace was laid with logs but was unusually clean.

"We never use it," Jesse had said. "Well, Mom and me, we used it a few times when Daddy was gone. But he could smell it, so we stopped doing even that."

"Your father doesn't like a fireplace?"

Jesse shook her head no. "Doesn't like fire."

When Jesse didn't say anything more, Katy dropped the matter. Now she *googled* Jackson Hobbs; Fort Collins, Colorado; Nancy Larsen; and methamphetamine bust. By the time she shut down the computer and went to bed, she had a better idea of why Jackson didn't use the fireplace.

On Thursday morning Jesse had her dad drop her at school a half-hour early. "You're not gonna believe this," Jesse said the moment she reached Missy, waiting for her outside the entrance. Jesse dragged her friend off to the side where nobody could hear them. She told Missy about the liger, being knocked out, Touie's escape, and all the rest.

"Shut up!" Missy said when Jesse paused for breath.

"Don't never, ever tell anybody. Not even Buzz."

"Oh my god! You could've been killed."

"I would have if Shane hadn't been there."

"Shane? So what, now you really do like him? But you said - " Jesse's face got red. Missy gasped, her mouth wide. "Oh my god! You're finally going to do him."

Jackson drove from the high school to Reynolds' Auction Barn on Hawk Owl Road. The wood siding was faded, the paint flaking, and the cattle pens needed repair. But none of that mattered today. Today, the auction barn was the center of attention. It was where the killed lions and tigers were weighed, measured, and photographed. Then the animals were picked up by taxidermists or skinned out and the remains destroyed.

Although it was not yet eight o'clock, the barn was crowded with hunters and gawkers. A group stood around the spot where a lion and two tigers were laid out side by side on tarps. The animals looked dirty and their skins dull. Flies swarmed over them. Jackson didn't know if he believed in an afterlife or rebirth or a judgment, but he was certain there was something magical about life, and that whatever is magical was gone out of the cats now.

A large whiteboard was set up. It tallied seven cats already killed. According to the scoreboard, and Jackson's own calculations, six tigers, nine lions, and one liger remained. Jackson knew that at least four people had died. The scoreboard did not keep count of the people.

Jackson left after a few minutes. On his way out he spotted Dell Tapper and Fred Bulcher in the parking lot. He couldn't hear them, but their conversation appeared to be heated. He thought about the gun that Dell owned and the bullet that might have been fired at him, but it wasn't the right time or place to ask about it. He avoided the two men, drove off, and headed to the police station.

It had been five days since Ed was killed and Jesse narrowly escaped with her life; four days since they found the Cheneys and learned how many big cats now were roaming free; three days since he first saw Katy in Utah; two days since Wade died; and one day since somebody shot at him. He couldn't begin to imagine what Thursday would bring.

TWENTY-SIX

Parked along a logging road that skirted the Placett farm, Katy sat in the Ford and drank a thermos of coffee, ate fruit, cheese, and bread, and watched a red smear of light spread pink and then flame yellow. When she set out, she chose a trail that avoided the house. Katy did not want to intrude on the family with their grief. She crossed fields to reach the hunting blind, examined the few remains of the doe left by scavengers, and then scouted the area where Shaka had been shot. She found Kali's tracks in the woods and followed them for an hour. The area was far from Jackson's property, but the female liger was headed in that direction.

At nine o'clock Katy returned to the pickup. She poured the coffee dregs, but it was cold, so she tossed it. She felt restless. Jackson would not return to the ranch for hours. She hoped that his cattle herd had not suffered loss and that they could safely round up his two horses. But mostly she wanted to find

Kali's tracks again. She wanted to locate Kali before some hunter got lucky.

Kali dropped the female cub to the ground. The dirt was hard-packed and dry, and the hole in the side of the hill was dark. The female cub hissed once and then nestled against the male. The new mother had one more cub to move.

Kali did not know that the mounds north of Jackson's house were thought to be Native American graves or that humans tended to avoid the area. She merely sensed that her cubs were safer here than in the tall grass. She also knew that she could not move them far today. In her weakened state, for birth had exhausted her, and she had not eaten in a day, distance mattered. The dirt cave would do. For her good fortune, Kali had Floyd Moonie to thank.

In 1862 Floyd Moonie had built a rough-hewn log cabin that backed against the mounds. His fourteen-year-old wife, Lottie, having come from Missouri, was terrified of thunderstorms and tornadoes and asked her husband for one consideration – a root cellar. Eager to please his bride, twenty years his junior, and already his third wife, the first having died in childbirth and the second lost to the Kiowa, Floyd complied. Since that time the cabin had disappeared, while the cellar had provided shelter to wolves, snakes, and mountain lions, as well as refuge to Indians, missionaries, buffalo hunters, bandits, and one time, to three whores on their way to Montana. Before Iris moved into town, Jackson and his family twice had used the cellar, some two hundred feet from their own house, once during a tornado and once when it appeared that a grassfire might reach them. A thunderstorm had drenched the flames.

Kali cared about none of this as she returned to the prairie. The only thing that mattered was protecting her cubs and finding food. Moving slowly, she trampled the delicate yellow flowers of a patch of Missouri primrose. She was entering a sea of bluebunch wheatgrass when she heard and then smelled the wolves. Kali tore through the wheatgrass and into the taller rye grass at full speed.

When Kali sprang into the clearing where she had given birth, five northern gray wolves awaited her - their mouths dripping saliva, their lips rolling back to bare their teeth, and their growls coming from deep in the throat. A northern gray looks slender but is powerfully built, his neck heavily muscled, his limbs long and robust. The male weighs over one hundred pounds and the female slightly less. They're equipped with heavy, large teeth designed for crushing bone and biting through skin. Like other wolf species, they're highly territorial, and Jackson's ranch was their home.

An adult male attacked Kali's neck, while a female jumped on her back. Other wolves nipped at her legs, drawing blood, trying to hamstring her. This is how wolves often bring down large animals like horses and elk. But the wolf pack had never encountered anything like Kali.

The wolf attempting to rip open Kali's throat was the most threatening so she engulfed his head in massive jaws, bit down, and nearly severed it, letting the carcass drop as her mouth filled with the wolf's arterial blood. A second later, a swipe of Kali's paws flung a female wolf six feet, disemboweling her. The wolf managed to slink off, howling. A third adult fled, but only after Kali bit off one of his legs at the knee joint. The remaining pair of northern grays escaped with minor injuries.

The fight was over quickly, but Kali had been too late. Her third cub, another female, was dead.

Angie entered the police station through the rear door. She stopped in the bathroom to check her makeup and add more *Visine* to her eyes. Then she headed to the coffee area. Sadie Pope was pouring coffee when Angie picked up an empty mug and then said, "Next."

"Didn't think you liked my coffee," Sadie said.

"The stronger the better today," Angie told her.

"Rough night?"

Angie groaned.

"Idaho girls, we like our coffee and our men strong." Sadie chuckled when she said it. "Some of us anyway."

Angie smiled and asked, "Is he in?"

"This here cup's for him."

"I'll take it," Angie said. She tucked a report folder under her arm and carried two coffees to Jackson's office.

"Aren't you on the two P.M. shift today?" Jackson asked when he saw Angie in the doorway.

"Yep. If you don't want my report now, I'll wait."

"Well, I can't wait for my coffee, so now sounds good to me. Just don't claim overtime." Jackson took the mug from her, said thanks, and motioned to a chair.

Angie sat down., "I need some caffeine first."

Jackson was careful not to require or even invite more personal information from his officers than was necessary. Still, Angie looked wrecked today, and he wondered why.

"Okay," she said after a few gulps of coffee that was brown and sweet. "Knights of the Golden Circle. Most of what I have comes from Wikipedia, a couple other Internet sites. So it may not be all that reliable."

"Probably good enough for background."

Angie nodded and opened the folder. "I got two pages I'll leave you, but here's the short and sweet of it. The KGC was a secret society started in Ohio in eighteen fifty-four to promote pro-slavery interests."

"So they're ancient history?"

"Maybe not. They were certainly active in the Civil War, robbing banks and trains for the Confederacy, and they probably were involved with the Bushwhackers and such after the war. John Wilkes Booth and Jesse James may have been members. Maybe President Pierce too." Angie grinned. "Puts the Jesse James myth in a different light."

"Myth being the optimum word."

"Anyway, the KGC joined up with a group called The Order of The Sons of Liberty, and this group is still active. They have the usual agenda: taxes are illegal, home-school kids, pack a gun, keep women barefoot and pregnant, send the blacks back to Africa … you know. But if the Knights of the Golden Circle exist as a separate group, they've been good enough to avoid detection."

"Or they're too small to matter. A few locals."

"Locals?"

Jackson told her about Ronnie Greathouse, but he did not mention the likelihood of more officers being involved.

"I'll be damned," she said. "Who would have thought?"

"Anything else that might be helpful?"

"Only if you want to talk to Eddie Yow." She gave Jackson a paper with Yow's information. "He owns a cowboy bar in Bakersfield, California. Fronts the house band."

"I'll call him," Jackson said. A couple of minutes later, when Angie got up to leave, Jackson said, "When I was deputy-chief, Ed had me do all this research stuff."

"Did it help you become a better cop?"

"I'm the Chief of Police," he said, smiling.

After she left, Jackson phoned the number for Edward King Yow. A man answered in a gruff voice. Despite the hour, Jackson had awakened him. Yow still agreed to talk.

In the end Jackson didn't learn much new information from Edward Yow, aka Eddie Yow, aka King Yow. Mostly, what Yow did was confirm that he had an affair with Dolly while he was married to Pamela. When Pamela found out about it, she divorced Edward King Yow and cut Dolly out of her life.

"Dolly and me got married, but it only lasted a year or so," Yow said. "Then she met that other fellow."

"Ever know Dolly and Pamela to get into it?"

"Oh yeah." He chuckled. "Pam hated her."

"And yet Dolly moved here to Buckhorn. Any idea why?"

"I didn't stay in touch with Dolly. Tried to keep up with Pam, but she don't like me talking to Missy, so ...."

The phone went dead quiet. Jackson waited. "This isn't court, Mr. Yow. Proof isn't required."

"Dolly's next husband ... Ted. He had friends around there. Ruby Ridge militia types. What I heard anyhow."

The moment Katy climbed out of the pickup, she heard Touie. Because she had ridden all her life and had four horses at Skorokoro, she knew what the sounds meant. The gelding was frightened, maybe even in distress. Katy got the .375, loaded it, and hurried into the barn.

She searched the interior but found no wild cats, snakes, or other creatures that might threaten Touie. She put down the rifle but kept it close and calmed the gelding. Once he had settled, Katy picked up the .375 and secured the door, searched the outside of the barn, and then the corral. The dirt in the corral was hard and trampled. Had she not been looking for signs of a predator she would not have seen the perfect paw print behind a water trough where a spill had softened the earth. From the size Katy knew the track belonged to a liger. No lion or tiger was ever that large in North America, even in ancient times.

Oddly, few Americans realized that lions had roamed the western United States until about 11,000 years ago or that they were twenty-five percent larger than today's African lion. Remains of them had been found in Idaho. The era of the big lion also was the time of the Sabertooth tiger, and Katy often imagined seeing a battle on the western plains between *Panthera Atrox* and the Sabertooth. As ferocious as these two were, Katy knew that neither cat would stand a chance against a liger, the biggest feline ever and one that was alive now, alive and close by.

Katy strapped the dart rifle to her back, carried the .375 across her chest, and headed to the restored prairie. She knew going there alone was dangerous. It also was the most likely place to find Kali and any liger cubs. The two acre plot Katy entered was home to princes plume, oakleaf sumac, goldenrod, Missouri primrose, buffalo berry, silver sagebrush, ninebark, syringa, yarrow, wheatgrass, Indian rice grass, and the thick Great Basin wild rye grass, plus a dozen other native plants and trees. Some of the plants were confined to one area, while other plants grew wildly throughout. Some were thriving and some clinging to life. For a moment, Katy relaxed enough to appreciate the wonder of it all, and then she refocused on the danger.

Deep into the prarie, as Katy parted rye grass that was as tall as she was, she heard a noise off to her left. She wheeled and shouldered the .375 smoothly and quickly. If a lion or tiger was charging, and in here it likely would be a lion, the motion would be toward her. The grass instead was rippling away from her. She watched it, and before long, she spotted a large wolf crawling away. The wolf appeared to be badly injured.

Katy left the wolf alone and continued until she reached an opening in the rye grass. Here she found blood, fur, and parts of a wolf that had been ripped to pieces. Wet blood colored the ground and clung to clumps of grass. Katy also found cat hairs. She methodically searched the grassy area, keeping the .375 in front of her, the barrel pointed down and her finger on the trigger. It took only a few minutes before she found the remains of the liger cub.

Katy squatted beside the female cub and touched her head. It was still warm. Now she knew for certain that Kali had given birth, but she did not know the number of cubs born or if other baby ligers were alive. A litter of two to four was typical with big cats so Katy was hopeful. A tear rolled down her cheek. Katy wiped her face with her hands, got up, and searched the surrounding area for the injured gray wolf and shot it.

TWENTY-SEVEN

Jackson was outlining what he wanted Angie to do while he was away that afternoon when a call came in reporting a fight at Green State Park campground.

"I'll handle it," Angie said. "You go on."

Jackson's impulse was to respond to the call, but Angie was right. If he did not leave soon, he would not have time to see Buck Benson before going home to meet Katy. Benson had come up with new information about the bullet Jackson had given him. Jackson sent Angie to the campground, called in a reserve officer to help at the police station, and twenty minutes later walked the few blocks to the downtown square. As he passed the Split-Rail Café, Iris stepped outside. Jackson and Iris barely had spoken since the argument Tuesday night.

They exchanged guarded hellos before Iris said, "I hear the lion hunter's staying with you."

"At the house you mean?"

"I'm surprised she hasn't been run out of town."

"She said she isn't part of this injunction."

"Well then, it must be true."

Jackson sighed. "We need her help, Iris."

"I don't want Jesse staying out there with her."

"Jesse likes Katy. And before you ask, I did talk to Jesse, so you can relax. The condoms aren't hers."

"That's even worse if she is having sex."

"She says she's not." When Iris asked for details of the talk, Jackson refused to tell her. "I promised Jesse."

"Well, whoop-de-do. I still want her to come home."

"She is home."

Iris glared at Jackson, but before she could fashion a retort, a police cruiser squealed around a corner and slammed to a stop beside them. Angie bailed out of it. "It's not a fight," she said breathlessly. "It's their boy."

"Slow down," Jackson said. "What boy? What's wrong?"

"This family camped at Green State Park. Their little boy is missing. They're afraid the lions got him."

Idaho's twenty-six state parks and 2.5 million acres of protected wilderness range from rocky moonscapes to verdant forests and from the massive Frank Church-River Of No Return Wilderness to postage-stamp-size Green State Park. Located on Highway 62, barely outside Buckhorn's town line, Green State Park contained a mere dozen campsites.

Rodney Stutz, a fifty-year-old welder from Kremmling, Colorado, had arrived Monday night with his wife, Rene, and their five-year-old son. They got there early enough to grab a coveted spot in the tiny park.

Both Rodney and Rene were outside an older travel trailer when Jackson and Angie arrived. Rodney was talking to a knot of three men wearing orange-accented hunting gear and carrying large caliber rifles, while Rene wept on the shoulder of a woman padded like a down ski-jacket.

Jackson introduced himself and then steered Rodney and Rene Stutz into a Thor Wanderer Toy Hauler. Rodney was a beefy guy with arm tats. Stubbles of dark hair covered his head. Rene was a short, chunky bottle-blond with a big chest. Stutz had four other kids, some of them grown now, from two earlier marriages, but Eric was Rene's only child. Rene was sixteen years younger than her husband.

Once they were seated around the fold-down dining table, Jackson got their names, address, phone numbers, employment, and such, and said, "Tell me what happened."

"That's just it; we don't know," Rodney said. "We left real early, me and Rene, and Eric was still sleeping. And when we got back from hunting, an hour or two ago, he was gone. We looked everywhere, but he ain't here."

"You mean he was alone all day?" Angie asked.

"Of course not," Rene snapped.

"The woman outside." Rodney jerked his head toward the door. "Old Much-Butt out there watches him."

"Rod!" Rene scolded. She then explained, "Her name's Ester Faye, and she's been real nice to us."

Jackson asked for a photo of Eric, and Rene, who had six of them in her wallet, gave him one. The sight of her son's smiling face started her crying again. Jackson looked at the photo and then passed it to Angie. He said, "Anything of Eric's missing, like toys or clothes?"

Rodney glanced at his wife beside him. "Batman."

"Eric's little backpack," Rene managed to say.

Jackson scrutinized both parents. "You having any problems at home? Problems with Eric?"

The air in the camper suddenly felt electrified. "You saying we're bad parents?" Rodney snarled.

"No sir," Jackson said. "I'm not. It's just sometimes kids can take family troubles to heart."

Rodney and Rene insisted their marriage was fine, Eric was fine, and except for money everything was fine.

"What kind of dog is Eric holding?" Angie asked, pointing to another photo of Eric in Rene's open wallet.

"That's Panchutz." Rodney grimaced when Rene said it. "Eric's little chiweenie. A dachshund-chihauhau mix."

Jackson nodded and said, "The dog with you?"

"Who gives a damn about the dog?" Rodney said.

"Don't mind him," Rene said. "We're just both so scared. Panchutz is sick, so we left him in Colorado."

"Mind if I take that photo too?" Jackson said. "I'll return them." While Rene removed the photograph of Eric and his dog from the plastic sleeve in her wallet, Jackson asked, "What day did you say you left home?"

Rene flicked a look at her husband. "Monday."

"The minute we heard about the prize," Rodney said, "we was packed up and gone inside an hour."

"You were lucky to hear about it so fast."

Rodney shrugged. "Friend of a friend, you know."

Jackson nodded and waited, but they said nothing more. A few minutes later, Jackson sent Angie off to interview the baby-sitter and any other people in the campground.

When he got to the police car, he radioed Sadie and told her to gather the full-time officers, on duty or off, and as many reserve officers as she could locate. He then remembered that

Katy was waiting for him. He called her and explained that he wouldn't be checking on his stock today after all or looking for horses. When Jackson finished telling her about the missing boy, Katy said, "I can help."

"You need to find your liger. We can handle it."

"What kind of shoes is the little boy wearing?"

Jackson remained silent.

"If you're going to track him, you need to know what shoes he's wearing," Katy said. "Probably trainers. Sneakers. It'll be easier if you know the tread pattern."

"How soon can you get here?" Jackson asked.

It took nearly thirty minutes for the blue-pins – Angie, Tucker, John, Brian, and Skip – and three reserve officers to gather at the police station. The phone in the station was ringing incessantly, and Sadie answered it as fast as she could, saying, "Hold please."

Jackson was about to join his officers when Iris rushed in. "You find the boy yet?"

"We're organizing a search now, Iris."

"Good. Then you'll need a staging area for everyone. I'll get the Elks Club opened and set up for you." She paused. "You are asking the public for help?"

Jackson had been going over the pros and cons of using only his officers versus public assistance. If he limited the search to police officers and Katy, he could reduce the risk and likelihood of error. But the lion hunt had his crew stretched thin. Plus, time and climate were against them. They only had a few hours of daylight. Around sunset, lions and tigers would prowl for food, and once the sun went down, the temperature would drop. "People will search for the boy no matter what we say," he told Iris, "so I'm going to try to organize them."

"Go find him, Jackson. Before something bad happens."

"Something bad may already have happened."

Iris frowned. "Meaning what?"

"Ever hear of Susan Smith?" Jackson knew that parents were always the prime suspects when a child goes missing.

"His DC Radar sneakers," Rene told Katy. "He won't wear nothing else now." Rene was still sniffling and patting away tears. She described the boy's new multi-colored shoes while she dug out a pair of old Nikes. The Nikes provided Katy with the size, a boy's 7, but not the DC Radar tread pattern.

Katy bagged the shoes, saying, "You told Jackson, Chief Hobbs, you were hunting all afternoon. Most people stop mid-morning and start again before dusk."

Rodney glared at Katy. "Then most people don't need the prize money bad as we do."

Eastern Idaho radio and TV stations broadcast an Amber Alert for Eric Stutz and asked for volunteers. Phones and word-of-mouth worked even better. An hour later Jackson met his officers and fifty-nine volunteers at the Elk's Club. Those who could not join the search due to age or physical limitations were busy preparing the Elk's Club to serve as search headquarters.

Jackson knew many of the volunteers - Dell and Fred and Neil, the Baileys, Deborah and Armando, Stilts and Eagle, the Umfleets, the Fedders, old Buck Benson and so on. He did not know the twenty tourists who showed up.

Over half the people were assigned to six teams that would search the campground. Each team was led by a police officer equipped with a radio. The remaining teams, led by reserve officers, would search outlying areas. Deborah and Armando and four other riders would patrol the road near the campground on horseback. Due to threat of a lion attack, all of the officers and most all of the searchers were armed.

Jackson gathered everyone for a briefing, directed primarily at the volunteers, although his officers were not highly trained in search and rescues either. He explained how to go about conducting a search, what to look for, and what to do if they found something. He ended by saying, "Make sure you're back here by dark. Everyone."

Katy was waiting for the aptly named Green Team when they arrived at Green State Park campground. As soon as she could, she drew Jackson aside. "I want to show you something," she said. She gestured toward a cinderblock cube of restrooms and showers. "I found cat tracks back there. A big cat, but it's not a liger. And it's only using three legs."

"Three legs?" Jackson had shot the leg off a Bengal tiger. He figured it had died. "The Bengal I shot?"

"Maybe. A cat hurt that badly can only kill the easiest prey. He'd be drawn to a campground like this."

Jackson growled, "Let's get going then."

Katy took the lead while Jackson and five others formed a chorus line behind her. They searched the wooded areas and open meadows within the Green Team's grid.

Three hours later darkness fell, and failure to find the boy lay heavy on them. They were on their way back to the campground when a young stay-at-home mom from Sandy Point, Idaho stumbled over a small Batman backpack.

TWENTY-EIGHT

Stan Ely was on the phone trying to talk an aging Hollywood actress into donating money when a young woman with boyish hair and body appeared in his office doorway. Stan motioned for her to go away, but Nancy Punter didn't budge. "You will? Great," Stan said. "The baby ligers thank you and I - Huh? Yeah. I did. You were great." When Stan signed off, he told Nancy who he had been talking to and said, "She's still making movies? Really?"

Nancy ignored him and waved a sheaf of papers. "The judge is ruling tomorrow. Want to know what she'll say?"

Nancy Punter had a small trust fund and an older sister who worked at the courthouse. Both things made her valuable to Stan and ARK. She gave the papers to Stan and continued talking until he shushed her so he could read.

A few minutes later, Stan said, "Holy shit!"

"You can thank me with an ounce of your stash."

"Half ounce. And get everybody in gear. Tell them I wanna roll out of here tonight. We're going to Idaho."

When the searchers returned to the campground, they were met by microphones and bright television lights. Jackson halted everyone out of sight. He watched the interview spectacle unfold, and moments later, he sent the search team back to town after telling them not to mention the backpack. Jackson had examined the bag but found nothing inside it. In the woods they had marked the site where it was found so the police could return in daylight.

Jackson remained behind the corner of an RV while Rene Stutz delivered a tearful plea for the safe return of her son. Neither Rene nor Rodney did or said anything other than what Jackson would expect from grief-stricken parents, and yet something about the interview struck him as wrong. A policeman learns to read people. It's how he knows the teenager pulled over on the highway isn't just nervous about getting a ticket or that the wife-beater is about to escalate the violence or that the gun-totting robber is armed for show and not for shooting.

Once the TV interview finished, the media people packed up, and Rodney and Rene returned to their trailer. Jackson snuck to the door unnoticed. Both parents identified the Batman backpack as Eric's, but neither of them knew what the little boy might have taken.

By the time Jackson reached the Elk's Club, the parking lot overflowed with media trucks. He passed a gauntlet of reporters on his way in. His only reply to the barrage of questions was to say that he would have a statement shortly.

Sheriff Paul Midden was waiting inside. Jackson had phoned Midden earlier and asked to see him before Midden went home to St. Anthony. First, Jackson gathered the search teams and heard their reports – nobody but the Green Team had found anything helpful. He then told the searchers to meet again at 6 A.M. Friday.

When he finished, peopled crowded around Jackson, full of questions and ideas. Jesse eventually pushed her way through them to hug her dad. Jackson had seen her serving food when he entered. The crowd then drifted away and Jesse said, "It's so awful, Daddy. That little boy must be scared to death. When I was chased, I, I -"

"I know. I know," Jackson said while stroking her hair. "We'll find him," he said and hoped it was true.

Paul Midden sidled quietly to a side exit, and catching Jackson's eye, nodded to him. For the past hour Jackson had thought about the best way to approach the sheriff. Unless a better idea came along fast, he would go with what he had – a little honesty, a little flattery, and a lot left unsaid. He asked Jesse to fix a plate of food for Katy, who had remained at Green State Park, and then followed Midden outside.

Jackson began by detailing the interview with Rodney and Rene Stutz, moved on to the search, and ended with the discovery of little Eric's backpack in Green State Park.

After that, Jackson told Midden what he had in mind. He did not mention knowing that the media would feed on the story of a little boy lost in a woods full of monster cats like sharks in a frenzy. Midden would know that already. Jackson also did not mention that he knew the limelight would appeal to Paul Midden, an elected official. Nor did he say that relinquishing the search to Midden would leave him free to pursue a different angle. "I know you'd never take the search away from me, Paul, even though you could, but I'm asking you to. I've got sixteen killer cats out here and five hundred hunters and more unsolved mysteries than a Sherlock Holmes' book. You'd be doing me a big favor."

As Jackson expected, Midden acted hesitant, but then agreed that the Fremont County Sheriff's Department would head up the search. Ten minutes later, Jackson and Midden faced the reporters in the Elk's Club parking lot and announced the change. Once they had finished, Jackson ate dinner and then returned to Green State Park.

He found Katy at the campground talking to Ester Faye and her husband, a tall, skinny, bald man. She joined him, and they sat in a pair of borrowed lawn chairs. Katy picked at her food, and Jackson drank coffee. She said little. After a while Jackson asked her if something was wrong, and she lied to him and said, "No. Nothing."

Katy knew she should tell Jackson that she had found Kali's track by his corral. She should tell him about the dead liger cub in the tall grass. She also knew that if she told him, and Jackson sent in an army of hunters, she would lose her chance to save Kali and her cubs. So instead of alerting Jackson to Kali's presence, she said, "Kids are the hardest for me. And half of the time when I help the police in Afica, it's to search for children."

"Do you find them? Alive?"

"Usually." But that also was lie. She mostly found nothing more than a piece of bone or chewed up belt or tuft of scalp. Katy sat the food plate aside, gathered up her .375, and said, "I'm going to search the perimeter for the three-legged cat again before I leave for the night."

* * *

Two trucks and a van left Boulder Thursday evening. One truck, a Peterbilt 379 outfitted to haul large animals, came from a bankrupt Florida circus. It required a special license to drive. The other truck was a twenty-foot U-Haul purchased at auction. The name and the Dreamsicle color were gone, but the pedigree of the truck was as evident as a bad facelift. All three vehicles were dark green now with Animal Rescue Kingdom, a web address, phone number, and a mural of animals entering Noah's Ark painted on the sides. The U-haul held portable cages and equipment, while the 18-wheeler had permanent cages and carried more equipment.

The caravan took Interstate 25 north out of Boulder, picked up Interstate 80 in Cheyenne, and drove west across the moonscape of southern Wyoming. They were headed to U.S. 30. From there they would zigzag north into Idaho.

Stan started off in the twenty-footer but switched to the van after Cheyenne. Because she was sweet on him, Nancy also changed to the Ford. For a while they stayed with the trucks, but after a food and rest stop, Stan sped on ahead. Nancy was a chatterbox, and it was not until Stan shared some some kick-ass marijuana with her that she dropped off to sleep, allowing Stan time to think.

So much had happened since he first heard about the baby ligers. Had it not been for Eagle Cassel, employed by the Fish and Game Department in Idaho, Stan still wouldn't know about the liger cubs. He had met the puffed-up Native American at a sweat-lodge encampment in Colorado six months earlier and hadn't particularly liked him. Stan only reluctantly had taken Cassel's phone call, but the man's information was invaluable. Not only had he learned that Katy was playing him, keeping the baby ligers a secret, but Cassel's information also unlocked the donor's checkbooks. With the survival of rare, purebred baby ligers at stake, Stan quickly raised the funds to mount a rescue operation.

A second big break had come when he read the judge's ruling. He had known ARK would lose, but what he hadn't expected was the way the judge would support her ruling. All he had to do now was use the ruling to his advantage.

Jackson arrived home shortly before midnight and found Katy sprawled on the couch. Her hair was damp and her face freshly scrubbed. She had on white pajamas with black leopard spots, all of it with a light rose wash that made the pajamas look sexy instead of silly. The body beneath them looks fine too, he thought. Katy had opened a bottle of red wine and poured him a glass.

For a while they talked about the search for Eric, but tiredness soon sent Jackson and his wine glass upstairs. He looked in Jesse's room before recalling that she had stayed in town at her mom's house. He then changed into sweatpants and an old sweatshirt that said *Grand Canyon,* sat on the edge of the bed, and thought about the way Katy's breasts moved beneath the faux leopard pajamas.

The next thing Jackson knew it was Friday morning. The wine glass was gone. The lamp had been turned off. He looked out a front facing window of his bedroom. His Ford pickup was gone too. He wondered where Katy was off too so early. In the bathroom he peered in the mirror and saw a man who looked ten years older than a week ago.

Jackson showered and shaved and while he did he thought about the dream that had awakened him. He had dreamed about a battle between the Creator and the Destroyer. According to the Bible, God created the world and then rested. Jackson thought maybe this difference explained why things so often went wrong. The Creator takes a day off, while the Destroyer never rests.

He had just finished shaving when his cell phone rang. Moments later, Jackson was in the Jeep speeding to town.

Jackson found the downtown square jammed with vehicles and people. Two of his officers were trying unsuccessfully to unclog traffic. He saw trucks from the network news agencies, from CNN, and from other television outlets. There was even a media truck from Canada. But none of these held his attention as much as a green semi and a twenty-footer belonging to ANIMAL RESCUE KINGDOM.

Jackson skirted wide of Iris, surrounded by microphones, and headed toward a portable stage bearing the CNN logo, where Katy was arguing with a man. The man was average size, mid-thirties, and wearing jeans and a jean jacket over a T-shirt that mimicked the logo on the green trucks. Katy introduced the man as Stan Ely.

As he shook hands with Stan, Jackson said, "Katy didn't mention you were coming, Mr. Ely."

"Because Katy didn't know," she said.

Stan grinned. "I wanted to surprise her."

"Mind if I ask why you're here?" Jackson indicated the truck with the animal cages. "And what these are for?"

As though she overheard Jackson's question, a woman seated behind a table on the nearby CNN platform answered it.

She had lacquered blond hair and droopy eyes. Jackson recognized her as a legal shill on CNN, a pretend expert who specialized in tragedies that involved children.

The blond announced that a federal judge in Colorado had issued a ruling declaring that the current public hunt to be illegal. The ruling stated that - and here the woman began to read directly from the court papers - "neither the town of Buckhorn nor the county of Fremont nor the State of Idaho has the authority to sell licenses and limit the public's right to bear arms and to hunt if to do so threatens public safety."

They blond woman milked the next moment, playing to her TV audience. "The Idaho Lion Hunt is free, America," her shrill voice announced. "The first lion and tiger safari ever held in the United States, and all you need is a gun." A few seconds later the woman said, "By tomorrow night at least five thousand people are expected to arrive in the tiny hamlet of Buckhorn, Idaho to hunt down these lions and tigers and monster cats that are killing people while they're out searching for poor little Eric Stutz."

The fact that the information was confused and misleading didn't matter to anyone, not even to Jackson. All hell was about to break loose. That's what mattered.

TWENTY-NINE

Jackson sat in the Jeep staring at the bricks of the old Tapper Elementary School. He had been staring at the red bricks for five minutes while pondering the events of the morning and asking: what now? The bricks still failed to reveal a single answer. He gave up and went inside.

As soon as he entered, Iris began the meeting. All of the town council was present. Everyone looked stressed or angry or both except for Pamela Yow. She looked ill.

Iris was a small woman, but she seemed to Jackson even smaller today, as though her hopes and dreams had been squeezed out of her, leaving her deflated. Jackson felt sad for her. Iris began by reviewing the federal judge's ruling. After she had deciphered the legal language for them, Dell, Neil, and Fred took turns raging against the federal government. As usual, Clancy didn't say much. He didn't even ask Jackson where his police uniform was. If he had done so, Jackson would have told him that it was in the Grand Cherokee, along with a dark blue suit and black dress shoes. Wade's memorial service was Friday afternoon.

An hour later, after reviewing all the options, the town council concluded the obvious: if the lion hunt was free and the money the town had received selling hunting licenses returned, Buckhorn was broke. The town had used the little cash it once had to promote the event.

A public gathering was scheduled for Friday evening in the high school gym to explain the return of license fees and the status of the prizes offered. The announcement was fed to radio and television stations, and hundreds of printed flyers were posted around town. Jackson spent the next two hours trying to calm the irate hunters and locals who came to the police station. Some of them demanded that he arrest Iris. Others called for Dan Tapper's scalp. One woman, wearing a Tea Party button, blamed President Obama and demanded he be impeached. From there it got worse.

On Friday afternoon Wade Placett's memorial service was held in All Souls Unity Church on Antler Street in a building that previously housed a hardware store. All Souls was the most liberal church in Buckhorn where, like most of eastern Idaho, the Latter Day Saints dominated religion. Both Wade and Mandy were raised Mormon but had chosen not to yoke their children with its conservative dogma. All in all, Mandy thought Wade would have approved.

Jackson arrived late and slipped into the rear pew. Sadie Pope and most police officers attended with their families. Tucker was there with Eileen Stevens. Jackson spotted Iris and Dell, Stilts and his wife, and all of the town council except for Pamela. He did not see Jesse and Shane seated with Katy in a middle pew until much later. Most of the locals out looking for Eric Stutz had taken time away from the search to pay their respects. Mandy, her children, and assorted relatives sat up front, facing a photograph of Wade instead of a casket.

Jackson had worn his navy-blue suit today. His shield was in his pocket, and an ankle holster held the snub-nose .38. Before Tuesday, he couldn't recall the last time he had worn the ankle rig.

Mandy Placett cried throughout the service. She wasn't alone, but her tears mattered the most. When the closing prayer began, Jackson slipped out of the church. On his way to the Jeep, parked in the very rear, he heard someone behind him. He looked back and saw Eileen Stevens.

He backtracked to her, and when they met, they hugged, and she said, "Thanks. I was trying to catch up, but you walk fast." Eileen then wagged a head of thick, gray hair and added, "That poor, poor family in there."

Jackson agreed with the wrongness of Wade's death and said, "I'm sorry I haven't come by to see you."

Eileen made a sound that might have been a laugh a week ago. "Jackson, I was a cop's wife for forty-two years. With what's going on, don't even think about it."

Jackson mumbled a "thank you," while Eileen reached into her pocketbook, brought out a letter, and gave it to him. He tucked it away in his suit coat without looking at it. A few minutes later Eileen left to join the mourners.

People had crept from the church while Jackson and Eileen were talking. He had glimpsed Katy among them but then lost sight of her. As Jackson weaved through cars and pickups, he wondered again about her role in Stan Ely's sudden appearance. Katy was waiting for him at the Jeep Grand Cherokee. She was wearing a black dress too nice for Buckhorn, where black was worn for funerals rather than for style. "I didn't know if you'd come," he said to her.

"Of course I came. I've been to their house and gotten to know Mandy and her children, and I feel -" Katy stopped as suddenly as if she had used up her word allotment for the day. Her eyes dampened. "I just spoke to Mandy. She invited me to this – this whatever it is."

Without an actual body, no procession to the cemetery was planned. Wade's remains would be buried quietly and privately. Instead, people would gather at the grieving widow's house to eat, drink, and offer condolences. "It's a country thing," Jackson said. "Sort of like a wake."

"In Botswana they don't say a person is dead. They say someone is 'late'. I know it refers to the departed, the late so-and-so, but I think of it meaning that the person will show up any moment but just hasn't arrived."

"Never though of that. But like you said, things work differently in Africa. Good and bad, truth and -"

"Ask me, Jackson. You want to." Katy paused, but Jackson said nothing. "Okay then, I'll just tell you. I did not know about the court ruling or ARK coming here today."

Jackson studied her face and her body posture.

"Stan didn't tell me about it, because I didn't tell him about Kali being pregnant." Katy shuffled her feet as she spoke. She had on black spike heels. "I knew if I told him, he'd rush up here to capture Kali and the cubs. And I was right. When he found out, he came running."

"And how'd he find out if you didn't tell him?"

"A man named Eagle Cassel."

Oh hell! Jackson had told Stilts Venable about Kali, and Stilts must have told Eagle. "Eagle Cassel?"

"He's letting ARK set up their cages on his land. I guess he found them motel rooms somewhere too."

Jackson nodded. He knew that one of Eagle's cousin's owned a little motel on the highway about twenty miles north. "So now you and Stan can team up to find Kali."

"Stan's mad at me," Katy said. "Besides, he told me he already had some big plan, and it didn't include me."

"What plan?"

She shrugged. "Some way to get the baby ligers."

"Which nobody has even seen yet."

That's not true, she thought. She had found a dead cub, and she knew Kali likely gave birth to more than one. Whatever she told him now about Kali, Jackson might not believe her; even if he did, he wouldn't forgive her. But if she didn't say anything …. "Jackson," she said, "I –"

"Great! You're still here." Jesse appeared from behind a pickup. She had on a black pencil skirt, charcoal gray sweater, and pumps that had a reputation. Jackson thought she looked fifteen going on twenty-five.

She smiled and Jackson said "Wow!" and then Jesse said, "Daddy, Shane won't go to Mandy's house so can I ride with you?" Jesse had babysat the Placett kids for the past few years, whenever Wade and Mandy had a night out.

"Your mother's not going?"

"With Dell." She screwed up her face to let the world know what she thought of riding with them.

"I have to stop by the police station first, Jesse."

"Ride with me," Katy said. "I'd like the company."

Jesse smiled and said, "Sure. Great. Just say when."

The police radio in Jackson's Grand Cherokee squawked.

"How about now?" Katy said, and then looked at Jackson and added, "We'll finish talking later, okay?"

Jackson watched them walk off together. Did he believe Katy? He wanted to. That was the problem.

There were two-dozen vehicles including his Ford 350 parked along the road leading to the Placett farmhouse. Jackson got lucky and found a spot close in when a big Dodge Ram pulled out. He noticed Dell's Escalade parked next to the house, one tire in a flowerbed.

Jackson exchanged hellos with a group of men standing around smoking, saw Jesse and Katy talking together beside the house, and then he heard yelling from inside.

As he climbed the steps, he heard Mandy saying, "I can't handle seeing either of you right now."

Dell said, "We're both so sorry, Mandy."

Nobody paid attention to Jackson as he eased inside.

"Everybody's sorry today, Dell." Mandy looked daggers at Iris. "Sorry comes cheap at funerals."

"Mandy," Jackson said, drawing closer. "This isn't going to help you or your children." He caught Dell's eyes and tilted his head toward the door.

"What's wrong, mommy?" Josh said, coming up to her. Josh tried to wrap his short arms around Mandy's hips but settled for what he could grab onto. "What's wrong?"

"Everything," Mandy said. She rubbed her son's head, but she looked at Jackson. "I never expected much from those two." She snorted something between a laugh and a scoff as Dell nudged Iris out the door. "But you should have stopped them. Stopped this crazy lion hunt plan."

"I know," Jackson said.

"You told me we'd be safe."

"I know." He reached out and touched her arm.

"Leave me alone!" she shrieked.

Josh burst into tears and flung himself at Jackson, his small fists pummeling Jackson's thighs and belly and even his groin. "Leave mommy alone! Leave mommy alone!"

"What do we do now?" she said, peeling her son off Jackson and pressing him against her. "What do we do now?"

A few minutes later Jackson walked out of the house, stood on the porch beside Jesse and Katy, and watched Dell and Iris maneuver through traffic and drive off.

"Why is she being so mean to you and mom?" Jesse asked.

"Because she hurts more than she can endure," Jackson said. He peered off in the distance at a cloud of dust moving rapidly toward them. Through the dust he could make out the swirling lights of a Buckhorn police car. Jackson felt like the man in this movie he once had seen where the same things happen to him over and over, the day repeating.

What now? Oh Christ! What now?

When the Dodge was close enough, he saw Tucker Thule behind the wheel. Tucker killed the swirling lights and slammed the cruiser to a stop. Jackson hurried to the car as Tucker climbed out, saying, "Chief, they found him."

Jackson felt his stomach drop. "Little Eric?"

"No, no. Ronnie. They found Ronnie Greathouse."

THIRTY

Vehicles lined the county road near Brown's Creek. Fewer than half were police cars. Skip Tibbits was the first officer Jackson saw when he arrived. He was clearing a spot for an ambulance, while Deborah Dawson and Armando Diaz wrangled eight skittish pintos out of the way. Skip's team, the group using Deborah's horses to search the area for little Eric Stutz, had found the body. Jackson left his Jeep at the end of the line and walked back to where people were gathered below the two-lane asphalt.

On the hillside three men wrestled a mangled Harley-Davidson half-buried in dirt and weeds. Some thirty feet away, other people surrounded a body. In addition to Skip and Tucker and search volunteers, Jackson spotted two state troopers and the state police detective Jessup had sent to town a day earlier. Judy Gatwick was mid-thirties and built like a fireplug. Jackson had met her briefly and arranged for her to talk to Tucker. Gatwick and everyone else wore surgical masks or some other facial covering to lessen the smell. Despite the strong odor, there wasn't enough body left to fill a baby's casket. Jackson wouldn't have known he was looking at the body of Ronnie Greathouse if Gatwick hadn't shown him the driver's license and State Trooper identification that had been found nearby.

"Judging from the skid marks," Gatwick told Jackson and Sheriff Midden, who arrived a moment after Jackson, "he lost control of his bike, and the crash either killed him or he laid out here until some animals did the job."

Gatwick took photos and measurements, and after the coroner officially pronounced the obvious, the body was removed. Tucker Thule watched the removal and wept. Earlier, Jackson had seen him off in the bushes vomiting. He spoke with Tucker now and sent him back to town. Then he saw the country sheriff beckoning him and joined him.

Paul Midden was leaning against his white Chevy SUV. It had a big county sheriff's star on both front doors. Midden informed Jackson that he had brought in a team of search dogs and their handler from Atomic City, but the dogs didn't picked up any scent of Eric Stutz except in the campground. He asked, "Now, what's that suggest to you?"

Jackson thought about it for a moment. "That Eric left there in a vehicle that was parked close by."

Midden bobbed his head. "We've broadened the Amber Alert. Checking motels and convenience stores in a fifty-mile radius. If that doesn't work, I don't know what to do."

"Not much else to do," Jackson said, "except start looking for a fresh grave."

"There's a lot of woods to cover 'round here."

"Eric's parents, they were hunting the day he went missing. Might be a good to start wherever they were."

Midden groaned and spat tobacco juice. "Aw, hell."

After Midden left, Jackson called the police station. He told Sadie Pope what he wanted. He waited while the dispatcher/secretary dug around in his desk for an address book and found Gary Peterson's phone number. Jackson's former neighbor in Fort Collins, and the man responsible for Jackson becoming a policeman, was now a homicide detective with the Colorado Bureau of Investigation. He also had become a born again Christian and anytime they talked, he eventually tried to convert Jackson. Still, Gary Peterson was the best contact Jackson had in Colorado.

Peterson was at home when Jackson reached him. Once they caught up on families and careers, Jackson outlined the details of the Eric Stutz case and asked Peterson for his help. "I was thinking I might get in one last fishing trip before snow," Peterson said. "Now you've given me an excuse to go fly fishing in the mountains. There's that butcher shop I like up in Kremmling too."

Iris flagged down Jackson as he circled the downtown square. He pulled over and lowered the window on the driver's side. Iris was too short and the Jeep too high for her to lean in the window, but she did her best.

"I heard that lions killed Ronnie Greathouse."

Jackson nodded. "State boys are handling it."

"This injunction puts all of us in more danger."

Jackson thought, it was really you and Dell who made it more dangerous when you sent the troopers home. But all he said was, "Maybe you can stop it. You're a lawyer."

"And you're Chief of Police, so you could make life inconvenient for these ARK people."

"What exactly should I do, shoot them?" he asked.

"That'll work for me."

"Unless they break the law, I can't bother them."

"Trespassing. Speeding. Unlawful assembly. You can think of something. If you don't, other people will."

"Vigilante justice?" said Jackson. "So we're back to the wild, wild west?"

"We never left it," Iris said and walked off.

Jackson still wore his blue funeral suit when he entered the police station. He planned to change before paying a visit to Stan and his ARK crew, but the moment he saw Major Jessup and Detective Gatwick, his plans changed. Jackson offered them something to drink, since he badly needed a cup of coffee, and then they went into his office.

"Any thoughts about what happened?" Jessup said.

In his mind Jackson ticked off the body count: Ted, Dolly, Ed, Wade, and now Ronnie. "I think if the killing keeps up," he said, "I'm going to wear out my dark suit."

For a while they talked about Ronnie Greathouse. Then they talked about the lion hunt and what the court ruling would mean. Jessup ended a rant against the Colorado judge by saying, "I can send a few troopers to help. Best I can do without going upstairs."

"Thanks. We could use some help." Jackson paused. "But you didn't come here just to offer me troopers."

"Not exactly." Jessup sipped the tea he had made from Sadie's personal stash. "We think we've deciphered some of Greathouse's notebook."

Jackson nodded and waited. A moment later Jessup handed him a slip of paper. A line of initials ran down the left side of the paper. "No names?" Jackson said.

"Thought you might be able to figure out who some of these people are by their initials."

"You're sure the letters refer to people?"

"Nope," Jessup said. "But it seems likely."

Gatwick piped up. "I might know one of them." She said the name of a man she identified as a truck driver in Rexburg. "His name came up in a case I handled."

Jackson stared at the list: F. B. could be Fred Bulcher or Fern Bruce or Frank Brotherton ... and T. T. could be Tim Thunder or Terri Tomms or ... Tucker Thule. Fred, Ronnie, and Tucker. Christ! "I'll check into it," Jackson said. "Let you know if I come up with anything."

The state cops left, and the afternoon faded into sundown by the time Jackson was free of duties and phoned Katy. His call went to voice mail. He left her a message. Then he went into the break room and turned on the TV. He ran through the channels looking for news about the lion hunt or the search for Eric. He knew Sheriff Midden would be talking to the press as soon as he had something.

He didn't find Midden on television, but he did find Eric's parents. Rene wore a nice dress and heavy makeup, and Rodney sported a fresh haircut. They made a tearful plea to the public and offered a $10,000 reward for any information that led to finding their son. They thanked an anonymous donor for the money and provided their contact information for anyone who wanted to send donations so that they could increase the reward. "Sis-boom-bah!" muttered Jackson. He was reminded of a couple of hustlers in the 1990s that used a pulpit to fleece people. It took him a minute to recall the names: Jim and Tammy Baker. He shut off the TV.

That's when the call about the fire came in.

Eagle Cassel's doublewide sat above a dirt road a mile off State Highway 34. Jackson parked behind a lone fire truck and Tucker's cruiser. Half a dozen vehicles were scattered along the road. The ARK trucks were in a field across from Cassel's house trailer on an acre of timberland that Cassel also owned. The smaller of the two trucks, the one that had once had been a U-Haul, looked like a piece of burnt toast. The fire was out but the engine block still gasped with smoke and steam. The larger truck and the ARK van had been moved a safe distance away.

"What've we got here?" Jackson asked the fire chief.

"Arson." Hank Dow was a veteran fireman from Boise.

"Somebody torched it?"

"Yep." The fire chief spat. "Eagle's family was gone and these bunny-lovers, they were in town having a party." Dow grinned. "Careless of them to leave like that."

"Let me guess," Jackson said. "You can tell where the fire started and how it was done, but you can't find a single clue to the identity of the arsonist?"

Dow spat again. "Professional job. Nobody local."

"Thanks, Hank," Jackson said and walked over to Stan Ely and his small band of merrymakers. Stan was livid and demanded police protection. Jackson listened to him patiently and then gave him the name of a private security firm in Idaho Falls. "I can't spare any officers to watch your operation," he told Ely.

Jackson also talked to a small woman that he at first mistook for a boy and large man that he might have mistaken for Jerry Garcia had he not known that the rock idol was dead. The rest of ARK's crew was at the motel.

"I told'em they should've expected trouble," Tucker told Jackson a few minutes later.

Jackson led Tucker away from the others. "How'd you get here so fast?" he asked.

"I don't live but five miles away."

Tucker was off duty. He was dressed in civilian clothes. Jackson thought he smelled gas on Tucker, but he also smelled smoke and other scents he couldn't identify.

"Well, since you're here, get the preliminary report from Hank," Jackson said. "Then I want the truck towed to town and impounded. I'll have somebody else examine it."

"Impounded? But we don't have an impound lot."

"We do now," Jackson said.

THIRTY-ONE

When Stan Ely showed up at her front door, Iris barked, "What the hell do you want?"

"Same thing you want," Stan replied.

"You got a lot of nerve coming here," Iris said, but she stepped aside and let Stan enter. "Anyway, I'm in a hurry. There's a gym full of pissed-off hunters waiting to shoot me if I'm late." While she spoke, Iris walked through the living room and into the dining room where a bottle of tequila and a shot glass were on the table.

"I wouldn't mind a drink," Stan said. He sat down. "Tequila will do fine." Thirty minutes later, Stan left in his dark green Ford van. He followed Iris's sporty Cadillac to the Buckhorn High School gymnasium.

The gym wasn't as packed as on Monday, but even so, a few hundred people had come. None of them looked happy to be there. The moment they saw Stan Ely, the gym filled with boos and shouts. Iris quickly hustled Stan to the stage where Dell and most of the town council were seated.

Iris asked for quiet and repeated her words in the microphone until the crowd settled. Once they did, she said, "Now, I know everyone here is as angry as I am." This time she talked through the groans and jeers. "You all think you've been cheated out of a chance to win the prize money. And I know you want your thousand dollars back." This brought another uproar. "You'll get it too."

The crowd jeered and yelled out "when?", and Iris waited for them to be quiet again before she continued.

"Or you could trade your lion hunting license for a chance to win a new and bigger prize."

Some of the audience cheered. Others shouted out, "How?" Most people remained quiet and looked confused.

Iris nodded to Stan Ely, then stepped aside, and he replaced her at the podium. The floor shook from boos and catcalls and stomps. Stan waited until the noise died down before he said, "The big, new prize mayor Inslay referred to is an offer from Animal Rescue Kingdom." The mention of ARK brought another round of boos and jeers.

"I know all of you have heard about this big female liger. But what you didn't hear is that she's pregnant or has already gave birth to a litter of liger cubs. What you don't know is that these liger cubs are rare. They're so special, in fact, that Animal Rescue Kingdom will pay you good people twenty-five thousand dollars for each and every liger cub that you can capture." This news brought a rippling of applause. Stan talked over it. "And we'll also offer twenty-five thousand dollars to anyone who locates the female liger and guides me to her."

The applause was louder now, but it also was easier for Stan to quiet the crowd. "Now I said capture, not kill. The liger cubs must be alive." Stan glanced back at Iris. She smiled. "One more thing. This offer isn't bound by the court ruling. It's not open to just anybody. To be eligible, you need to trade your hunting license for a prize ticket. Mayor Inslay will explain the details. Just remember, you could go home with twenty-five or fifty thousand or more. Anybody here like a hundred grand?"

The crowd answered with cheers and applause. Iris breathed a sigh of relief. It wasn't her fault if Stan believed she had engineered the fire and that Jackson and the Buckhorn police were responsible. Her smile never left her face, not even as her mind churned out a way to screw over Stan Ely. She watched him hold up his hands, like Moses parting the sea, and yell, "Twenty-five if alive!"

When Jackson arrived, Stan Ely was basking in adulation. Jackson had sent Angie, Brian, and two reserve officers to the assembly to keep order and deal with traffic while he finally changed clothes and ate dinner. Now that he was at the assembly, he at first could not fathom what had happened. Upon hearing about the miraculous turn of events Jackson was happy that the town had escaped disaster. His second thought was that Katy had not been as lucky. Katy only had herself to look for Kali. Stan Ely now had a whole town.

While Stan was turning the hunters in the gym from mob to disciples, Katy was at Green State Park following the trail of the three-legged tiger. She had been following the trail of the cat since leaving the Placett farm, changing clothes, and gearing up. Just as she thought she was closing in, the tracks had ended at an asphalt road. For the past hour she had been trying to find them in the dark using a flashlight.

She shut off the light now and stood in the road and listened. She shivered as the wind rustled the leaves around her. Then she turned and headed back to the camp.

To her surprise Jackson was at the campground talking to two oil workers from Galveston that had been part of his search team the first day. When he saw her, he peeled off from them. "Any luck?" he asked Katy.

She told him what she had been doing. "But I can't find any tracks on the other side of the pavement."

"So the tiger's following the road now."

"Seems like it."

"And that road leads into town," Jackson said. So far there had been no confirmed sightings of big cats in town despite six calls from people in the last day claiming to have seen a lion. "So what now?" he asked Katy.

"I don't know. Talk to Stan, I guess. He left a strange message on my cell phone."

"Oh hell! You don't know what happened, do you?"

"Know what?"

He told Katy about the public assembly and Stan Ely's surprise offer. When he finished, Katy said that she needed to see Stan, jumped in the Ford, and drove off.

On the drive home Jackson tried to think about something other than Katy, so he thought about the coded names Jessup had given him. If any of his officers were part of a militia group, he would put his money on Tucker. But he had no proof. Not yet anyway. Before leaving for the night, Jackson had shared the information and his own suspicions with Angie.

She had offered to investigate Tucker. She seemed delighted by the opportunity.

The farmhouse was lit up when Jackson arrived. Only then did he remember that Jesse was spending the night. The door was unlocked. He entered, called her name, and heard his daughter reply.

"Upstairs," she said. "We'll be right down."

We? That was the other part of the message Jesse had left. Missy Yow was spending the night too. Missy had stayed over many times before, but Jackson hadn't known about the condoms before. He was not happy that Jesse's sleepover friend was a sexually active fifteen-year-old.

After uncapping a beer Jackson plopped down in the recliner in the living room. Jesse and Missy clomped down the steps a few minutes later. Both girls wore floppy lounging pants and oversized t-shirts. His daughter brushed his cheek with a kiss. "You look tired," she said.

"Cause I am." He said hello to Missy. "So how'd you two get here?" he asked Jesse. "Your mom?"

"Mom's busy with Dell," Jesse said sarcastically. "And with celebrating. Shane gave us a ride." Jackson wanted to say something about the need for her to get along better with Iris, but while he was searching for the right words, Jesse said, "Daddy, you find the little boy yet?"

"Not yet," he said. "But I'm hopeful."

Jackson told the girls about the Bengal tiger Katy had followed. Both Jesse and Missy thought the story was deliciously scary. Even so, their conversation soon drifted away from big cats and little Eric to more of the normal stuff that interests teenagers.

Jackson listened to their chatter until he felt his eyes close. He got up, kissed Jesse, and told Missy goodnight. Missy leaned forward offering her cheek for a kiss too. As Jackson hesitated, a necklace popped out of her t-shirt. It was a silver cross on a chain.

"That necklace you're wearing," he said to Missy, "where'd you get it?"

"This old thing?" Missy said, touching the cross and chain. "My mom gave it to me. She has one just like it." Missy wrinkled her brow. "But I think she lost it."

The call came at five-fifteen Saturday morning. By five-twenty Angie was dressed, and five minutes after that, she unlocked her Subaru. She had no police radio with her, since she was off-duty, and when she tried to phone Tucker at the police station, her call was routed to the communication center in the county seat. "Asshole," she said, and quickly added, "No, not you," as soon as she realized the dispatcher in St. Anthony she had talked to earlier was on the line again. "My duty officer's MIA."

Last night, she had instructed the communication center to call her instead of Jackson in case of an emergency. A tiger prowling Martino's Market, a block from downtown, was certainly an emergency. Martino's was a deli and grocery store known for good meats. A frantic Mexican janitor had reported the tiger and then ran off.

Angie hadn't followed Tucker Friday night since he was at work. But she had tailed him the two previous nights, before Jackson made her surveillance official. She didn't know if Tucker belonged to a militia group or not, but she knew that he was the one harassing Sharon and her. On the second night, he had cruised Sharon's bungalow three times. Today, she planned to confront his homophobic ass.

Angie stopped at the police station and swapped her Subaru for the Dodge cruiser. She didn't use the siren, but flashed the lights as she drove to Martino's Market. A few minutes later, she pulled into the parking lot and parked next to another Buckhorn police cruiser. The car was empty.

She popped the trunk on the Dodge and removed her M4 tactical rife and loaded it. Then she jogged to the front of the market and peered through twin glass doors. The lights were dim, but Angie could see shelving was knocked over and food scattered in the aisles. She heard noises inside. A second later Tucker crashed into a shelf. Angie only saw him for a second, long enough the see the blood.

Angie rattled the doors, but they were locked. She ran around the building to a side door near a tumble of milk crates and strewn garbage. The door was open. Angie was about to radio for backup when she heard Tucker scream.

She entered as Tucker scuttled across a meat case, a three-legged Bengal tiger right behind him. Angie was so dumbstruck, she couldn't move. In fact, she didn't move again until after Tucker stumbled, until the tiger pounced on him and knocked him off the case. They thudded against the black and white tile floor behind the meat case. She slid along the wall until she could see them again. The tiger had Tucker's right arm in his mouth.

"Oh god! Oh god! Oh god!" Tucker shrieked. His bowels and bladder had released. Angie could smell him now. When Tucker saw her, he stopped screaming for a second. She would never forget the surprised and fearful look on his face. She really didn't mean to grin.

Angie shot the tiger in the neck, breaking his spine. As the big cat fell, the bones and muscles that attached Tucker's arm to his body snapped and tore, and his right arm was severed. Blood spurted from the stump. Angie grabbed up a pile of towels and called for help.

THIRTY-TWO

By the time Jackson reached the Buckhorn clinic, Tucker had been taken to Rexburg. He phoned Madison Hospital and learned that Tucker was alive and in surgery. Jackson wouldn't be able to see him for hours. He then told Angie to write up a report. She had recapped the events on the phone, but he had to go over everything with her in person. "I'll see you soon as I'm done with Katy and the Fish and Game boys."

"Katy?"

"She wants to cut open the tiger you killed."

Twenty minutes later he watched Katy slide a sharp butcher's knife into the soft belly of the Bengal tiger and slice through skin and fat and muscle tissue. Jackson and Stilts Venable stood a few feet away. The odor wasn't pleasant, but Jackson had smelled worse things recently.

Katy laid the bloody knife on the tile floor of the market. She reached inside the tiger with both hands until she had a firm grip on the gut sack. She piled the entrails and stomach on the floor, and then she sliced and diced the tiger's guts until she dropped the knife and said, "Thank god." Whatever happened to Eric Stutz, the contents meant the Bengal tiger had not eaten him.

By the time Jackson left the market, Angie was out on a call. Jackson phoned the hospital again. There was no update on Tucker. He thought back to his original plans for the morning. A short time later, he was sitting opposite a small ranch house with a half-brick front. The house backed onto the high school football field. A ten-year-old Honda Accord the color of dried blood was parked outside a one-car garage.

Jackson knew Pamela Yow wasn't the only person in town that considered Safari Land a nuisance, although most people in Buckhorn didn't care much what you did as long as you were white, Christian, Republican, and heterosexual. The Cheneys likely scored high on these. Most everyone did in Fremont County. Even so, one question nagged at him – if the goal was to get rid of Safari Land, why not just kill the cats? He got out and walked toward the house.

Pamela was dressed for work when she answered the door. She didn't act surprised to see him. Five minutes later Jackson laid out Dolly's broken necklace on the kitchen table. For a moment he looked at the cross and thought about the different meanings it had: an implement of torture, a religious symbol, and a clue to a crime. Put anything in a new context and it changes meaning.

"You recognize this?" he asked Pamela. They were seated around an antique oak table. Pamela had given him a cup of herbal tea that he hadn't touched.

"Looks like the necklace Missy and me have."

"Could I see your necklace?"

"You could," she said, "if I knew where it was." She fiddled with her herbal tea bag and said, "Sure you don't want coffee? I don't drink it, but I can make it."

He told her no, that he'd had enough coffee already.

"You ever go out to Safari Land to visit your cousin?"

"I told you, we're not ... we weren't close."

"Ever hear of the Knights of the Golden Circle?"

"What's that? Oh, you mean that Catholic group?"

"I believe that's Knights of Columbus." Jackson watched her. She was lying. She wasn't good at it either. "I need to see your necklace, Pamela."

Pamela squirmed in the chair. "Well, I can look for it but ... where'd you get this one?"

"It was in Dolly's hand when we found her."

"Oh."

"You should get yourself a lawyer."

"A lawyer? What do I need a lawyer for?"

Jackson waited, watching her. Did she not understand?

"God will protect me," Pamela said in a near whisper.

"I'd still get a lawyer if I were you," he told her.

When Jackson reached the downtown square, traffic coming into Buckhorn off highway 34 was backed up for a solid mile. On the square itself traffic looked like an Idaho Falls shopping mall parking lot at Christmas time. Even pedestrians were having trouble getting anywhere today. He counted two reserve officers and two blue-pins, nearly half his force, and all of them traffic cops now.

While he inched his way along, trying to get to the Elk's Club, Jackson listened to the local radio station. The woman who read the news had a slight lisp. She said hunters were booking hotel rooms as far away as Idaho Falls. Rexburg, St. Anthony, Ashton – anyplace closer was sold out of rooms. He knew that local people were opening up their homes to rent out the spare bedroom. Jackson hoped that the promised state troopers would arrive soon to help out. Hell, he thought, it still won't be enough.

He reached the Elk's Club and found Sheriff Midden coordinating the search dogs with Deborah's group on horseback. "I'm going to start charging you stable rent," Deborah said to Jackson. She grinned when she said it.

He looked at her curiously.

"Armando found one of your horses. We have Blaze."

"Blaze? My mare's okay? Any sign of Boots?"

She shook her head no. "I'll bring Blaze by later."

"So where's the sheriff sending you off to now?"

"Above the old Newdale farm," she said. "That's where the parents were hunting the day Eric disappeared."

An hour later Jackson was getting ready to leave for the hospital in Rexburg — Tucker was out of surgery now — when he received a phone call and heard, "She's been shot."

"Who's been shot?" Jackson asked. "Who's this?"

"State Trooper Len Grey here, Chief Hobbs," the trooper said. "The horse-lady, Deborah, she got shot."

Since the Fremont County Medical Clinic in Buckhorn was not downtown, it didn't take Jackson more than five minutes to reach it. A short time later, a nurse led him to a curtained cubicle. Deborah was lying on her side, her eyelids closed, and Jackson asked the RN, "She asleep?"

Deborah's eyelids flickered. "No, she's not asleep. She's thinking she should go visit friends in New York while she's shot and can be the queen of dinner parties."

Two off-duty State Police troopers helping in the search had given Jackson the details when he arrived at the clinic. A large caliber bullet had nicked Deborah's ass cheeks as she stood in the stirrups to look around. "Way I figure it," trooper Grey explained, "some dumbass hunter mistook her pinto for this big liger and shot at it."

"They say I'll need surgery if I want a perfect ass," Deborah said, laughing. Her words and laugh were slurry. "Told'em I never had one to start with." High on pain drugs, Deborah prattled on about her failed marriage and 'the other woman's' perfect ass, and Jackson, knowing that she'd regret her words later, quickly left.

Angie Kuka was waiting for him outside the clinic. "You've been avoiding me all morning," Jackson said.

"Are you going to fire me 'cause of Tucker?"

"Should I?"

Angie hesitated. "Tucker's been harassing me and my ... my girlfriend. So I was already watching him, even before you asked me to. I had to be sure it was him."

"You still saved his life."

"I just told you I'm a lesbian."

"Well, guess that explains why you never hit on me. Anything else? If not, get back to work."

Angie smiled, got in her car, and drove off. Jackson was still standing outside the clinic when his cell phone rang. He looked at the caller I.D. and saw the Colorado area code. "Gary," he said, "how's the fishing?"

"The Lord giveth and the Lord taketh away, Jackson, and yesterday he took the trout somewhere else."

Jackson forced out a laugh.

"So listen. I talked to the Stutz's closest neighbor, a woman named Marge Merkle-Jones." Jackson asked Peterson to spell the name. He did, and Jackson wrote it down. "Anyway, this neighbor woman, she sometimes watches their dog for them if they go away. She's pretty sure they had the little dog with them when they left for Idaho."

"Maybe they took him to a vet if he's sick."

"Thought of that too," Gary Peterson said, "so I called every animal hospital and vet in Grand County and even checked in Summit County. Nobody has Poncho."

"Panchutz," Jackson said.

"Whatever. Ugliest little dog picture I've ever seen." Jackson thanked him and started to hang up, but Gary Peterson wasn't done. "That brother of Rene Stutz, I checked him out while I was at it. He's still locked up in Buena Vista, five big ones to go. He's definitely Aryan Brotherhood or something like it. But his wife, she packed up and moved to your neck of the woods two years ago."

"Idaho?"

"Somewhere around Rexburg is what I was told."

They chatted a few more minutes, and then Jackson tried to get off the phone before Gary could ask him if he had found Jesus yet, and he almost made it but not quite.

"Gary," Jackson replied, after the inevitable question, "I can't even find Eric Stutz."

The next time Jackson phoned the hospital in Rexburg he spoke to Eileen Stevens, Tucker's aunt. Eileen and Tucker's wife were waiting for him to be moved from recovery to a private room. Jackson provided Eileen with an edited version of the events in the market that led to Tucker's injuries. "I need to see him soon as possible."

"As a friend or the Chief of Police?" Eileen asked.

"Tucker's in trouble," Jackson said. "But that's all I can tell you right now."

There was a long pause. Jackson could hear her breath over the phone. "Tomorrow is what the doctor recommends," Eileen finally said. "Give him until tomorrow. Please?"

Jackson delayed his plans to visit Tucker until the next morning. With his trip to Rexburg on hold, he then contacted the county prosecutor, Bud Spiegel.

After talking to Spiegal Jackson arranged for Missy to stay overnight or even longer with Jesse and Iris. Then he took Angie with him to make the arrest. Pamela had finished her shift at the town library, and they arrested her as soon as she returned home. Jackson did not cuff her, although he did read Pamela her rights.

"What'll happen to Missy?" Pamela said on the way to Jackson's SUV. Her lips quivered and her eyes were wet.

Jackson told her what he had arranged, and Pamela thanked him. For a moment he thought she was going to hug him. It was the strangest arrest he ever had made.

"Can I see Missy? What do I tell her?" Pamela said.

"The truth, I guess." He nodded at her Bible. She had a white-knuckle hold on a worn Bible with black, fake-leather bindings. "The truth will set you free, right?" At the police station Pamela was given of choice of being locked in the storage room or handcuffed to a desk. She chose the storage room. After she was locked up, Jackson retreated to his office to wait. The only reason he had arrested Pamela was to make her talk. She knew something about Safari Land; he needed to know what it was. Even so, there were times when he hated his job, and right now was one of them.

Four Idaho State Troopers arrived around 3 P.M., and Jackson turned over crowd and traffic control to them. He then sent as many of his people home as he could spare. Everybody needed rest. Angie refused to leave. Then he phoned Major Jessup. When Jackson didn't reach him in the office, he tried Jessup's cell phone. Jessup answered after one ring, although he was changing a dirty diaper. "You have a kid, right?"

"A daughter," Jackson said. "She's fifteen now."

"Diapers or teenagers, tough choice," Jessup said.

Jackson chuckled and thanked him for the troopers.

"I tried to get you more help. The problem is our acting-governor now wants troopers patrolling a hundred miles in every direction up your way. He's scared shitless that some of those cats will get out of Fremont County."

"With all the people here," Jackson said, "he could be right. The hubbub could cause the lions to scatter."

"Oh shit," Jessup said, "hold on while I clean up the mess." Jackson did and listened to Jessup talking to the baby the way adults always seem to talk to babies. He had done the same with Jesse. When Jessup finished his clean up task, Jackson explained what he wanted to do.

THIRTY-THREE

Jackson knew he should leave. Three times he had promised Katy to explore his land with her, and three times he had cancelled. He needed to check on his Black Angus cattle. He had seen the carrion birds circling their field for two days. He was hopeful that Boots, his quarter horse still out in pasture, had avoided the wild cats. He needed to get Boots into the barn. Even so, when Pamela asked to talk to him, Jackson had Angie bring her to his office.

"Before you say anything, Pamela, I want to remind you that you have a right to an attorney."

"I told you, I don't want a lawyer," Pamela said.

"You change your mind, you tell me." He turned on a miniature tape recorder and said, "Do you understand you don't have to talk to me without an attorney present, and if you do, anything you say can be used against you?"

"It's God's punishment I fear, not the court's."

"I need you to answer yes or no."

"Yes, I understand. I don't want a lawyer."

"Okay. Then let's talk." He removed the necklace found in Dolly's fist and asked, "Is this your necklace?"

She nodded her head.

"Could you reply verbally, Pamela?" he said.

"I gave it to Dolly. It's mine."

"Can you tell me when and why?"

"Dolly came to the library about two weeks ago," Pamela said. "I hadn't spoken to her in months. If we saw each other in town, one of us would always go the other way. But that day, she wouldn't leave without talking to me." Pamela hesitated, her eyes damp. "She told me she was dying, that she had cervical cancer. She said she wanted to make peace with me, that she'd do anything to make amends for the wrong she had caused me with King."

"Do you recall the exact day?"

Pamela shook her head. "But I remember Dolly saying Ted got in a big argument that day."

"With?"

"Fred. Fred Bulcher. Some lawman was there too."

"A lawman? I don't suppose she said who?"

Pamela shrugged. "I didn't ask."

"Go on."

"There's not much more to tell," Pamela said.

"How do these wild cats figure into all this?"

"Dolly wanted to make things right, so I told her to get rid of those cats and stop what they were doing."

"So she helped you set them free?"

"It doesn't matter whether I opened the cages or told somebody else to do it. I'm still the one that let them out. The ligers are an abomination, a sin."

250

Jackson was stumped for a moment, and then it fell into place. "Dolly freed them?"

"I don't know." Pamela began to cry. "She said if she poisoned the cats, Ted'd know it was her. So I told her somebody would have to shoot them if they got out." Pamela stopped and blew her nose and wiped her eyes. "I told her I'd open the cages, but she said the cats were used to her feeding them and wouldn't bother her. I never meant for Dolly or anyone – oh, dear God! – all these people are dead because of me."

Jackson gave her a minute to compose herself before saying, "So how'd she get your necklace?"

"I gave it to her in the library that day," Pamela said. "To show her I forgave her for taking King away from me. And to comfort her."

Christ! Jackson thought, all this over a man.

Jackson returned Pamela to the storage room. He was still deciding whether to jail her in Rexburg or what to do with her when Angie walked in. "Somebody here to see you." She stepped to one side, and Jackson saw an older man who looked like a department store Santa Claus in the doorway. "Chief, this is the guy I told you about," Angie said. "The one snooping around the Cheney house that day."

The man held out his hand. "Agent Ted Sands." Jackson stood and shook hands. "FBI," sands added.

Jackson looked at Angie who mouthed "told you," and before Jackson could ask, Sand's showed his credentials.

Jackson motioned Sands to a chair. "What can we do for you, agent Sands?" Jackson said.

The three of them sat as Sands said, "I see you arrested Dolly's cousin, this Pamela Yow."

"I did. But why's the FBI care about that?"

"We don't." Sands paused and waited for a reaction and when none came, he said, "Not unless she killed Ted and Dolly Cheney. You see, they were the real targets of this operation. It was never about freeing lions and tigers."

Oh hell, thought Jackson. "How do you know that?"

"Cause Dolly was a CI for us. She was our informant about this group of terrorists you have here."

"Terrorists?" It took Jackson a moment to link the dots. "You mean the Knights of the Golden Circle?"

Sands nodded. "We've had our eye on them for a while. We're sure they burned that women's center in Rexburg."

"The Planned Parenthood clinic?"

"Those two girls that got murdered right after it happened, one of them worked at the clinic."

"The murders were a few months later, weren't they?" asked Jackson.

Sands shrugged. "Dolly got ten thousand dollars. The deal was she'd provide the names of the terrorist cell."

Jackson saw Angie lean forward in her chair. "And did she? Did Dolly give you any names?"

Sands shook his head. "She didn't know their names. So we were working on getting her to turn Ted Cheney. We think the terrorists found out about it and killed them and covered it up by releasing the lions and tigers. Hard to say if a man was shot by the time the lions are finished."

"But Dolly wasn't shot," Angie said.

"No, she wasn't. Maybe somebody let the cats out too soon or – hell, any number of things could have gone wrong," Sands said. "Don't take these terrorists lightly."

"How long had Dolly been your CI?"

"A few months," Sands told Jackson.

Jackson was pissed that the FBI was investigating people in his town and keeping it a secret, but he kept his feeling to himself. Sands stayed another twenty minutes, revealing just enough that Jackson and Angie could fill in the rest for themselves: Dolly was afraid the members of the anti-government group would harm Ted for leaving them, and since Ted was desperate for money to keep Safari Land going, she had turned informant. Sands' information didn't tell Jackson who set the cats free, but it did clear Pamela Yow. Jackson released her once Sands left and drove her home. When they got there, Pamela hugged him.

Katy was wearing her safari gear. A small daypack and the two gun cases were spread on the floor. "You made it," she said to Jackson as he entered the living room.

"I'll hurry and get ready before anything happens."

Jackson went upstairs to change while Katy prepared her rifles. She felt guilty that she was not out looking for Eric Stutz. Truth is, she didn't know where to look. She also knew that her chance of finding Kali and her cubs was disappearing. She would search for Eric again tonight.

When Jackson returned, outfitted in jeans, flannel shirt, and hiking boots, Katy was loading the .375 with 300- grain Winchester Silvertips, three in the magazine and one up the spout. Then she fed the Model 389 dart rifle a 10 CC Type "C" cartridge-fired dart with a gel collar.

"The darts contain succinylcholine, a muscle relaxant," she explained. "A small amount usually works, but then nobody usually tries to tranquillize a nine hundred pound cat. Some people prefer etorphone hydrochloride, but if you prink yourself, it kills you." She examined the dart gun. "The stuff I use is safe."

Katy added water bottles and protein bars to her pack, and since she was carrying two rifles, she gave the pack to Jackson. He had his M4 today, loaded with a full clip of .223s designed to penetrate. He also wore his Glock 21 handgun. After a final equipment check, they set off in toward the field where Jackson had his cattle herd. Halfway there, Katy stopped to examine some lion excrement. "A female lion," she said.

"How do you know that?" Jackson asked.

"A female lion spore is different from a male's."

Jackson smiled. "I'm not even going to ask."

"I'm not an expert tracker," Katy said, "but I'd say there are three, maybe four lions. But they're not going toward the cattle." She pointed east. "What's out there?"

Jackson thought for a minute and then said, "Aw, hell! That's where my two horses were grazing."

They looked at each other.

"Boots is still out there," Jackson said.

They headed east at a brisk pace. Katy's eyes followed the ground, but just as often she looked up and around. When Jackson asked her why, she said, "Animals will tell you whether a predator is close. You see a group of impala all looking the same direction, something's got them worried."

"Not many impala out here."

"Deer, elk, wolves, antelope, whatever. Anything out here will run from lions except maybe Kali."

When they stopped to rest, Jackson leaned the M4 against a dogwood tree and removed the daypack from his back. "You don't mind me asking," he said, "what made you become a big-game hunter in the first place?"

"Took you long enough." Katy laughed, drank some water, and passed the bottle to Jackson. "You ever wonder why our eyes face forward? Not just human eyes either, but the eyes on every land predator. But the herbivores like deer or cattle, they have side-facing defensive eyes. Fact is, we humans are born hunters. It's in our genes."

"Never cared much for hunting. Faulty genes I guess."

"No, they're not. You're just a different type of hunter. What you and I both do really is hunt danger."

Jackson thought about her words as they set off again. He was still thinking about them when they crested a rise ten minutes later and spotted a herd of white—tailed deer running away. Katy took out her binoculars.

THIRTY-FOUR

Kali flicked her long tail at the bothersome Blue Bottle flies swarming around her and licked her muzzle. She could see the prey on the rim of a gully. Unlike the big gray prey she had chased, this prey was smaller and reddish brown. This prey wasn't running away either. This prey already was dead. Kali had no qualms about stealing another predator's kill if she could do it safely.

Predators usually return to feed on a kill until it's all gone, so Kali inspected a stand of locust trees and the spotty patches of gray rabbit brush and silver sagebrush that grew alongside them. She was looking for movement – a twitch of tail or the flutter of ears - but mostly she listened. Sound carries at 1100 feet per second. The forest slows it down some, but the ears tell most animals a predator is close long before the eyes do.

When she saw nothing and heard nothing, Kali moved out from behind the bitterbrush where she was hiding. If she used the gully and approached from below, she could be out of sight until she reached the prey. Even then, she would not eat in the open. She would tear off a portion of meat and drag it away. Only when she was safe would she satisfy her hunger.

"The land drops away sharply" Katy said, rotating her Leupold Camo binoculars from left to right. The Pocatello gun dealer had provided the expensive binoculars.

"It's a creek bed. Dry this time of year," Jackson told her. "Never runs much water now anyway. There's a gully. Pretty steep in places, but not everywhere."

"I see something on the edge of the gully, maybe six hundred feet northeast. If it's what I think it is, you're not going to like it. But I can't be certain from here." There was a knoll with western red cedars between them and the gully, and the viewing angle was poor.

Katy gave her binoculars to Jackson. He adjusted them for his vision and found the gully and traveled along it until he could glimpse the downed animal. After a second, he said, "Oh hell! It looks like Boots."

Seconds later, Kali leaped over the edge of the gully and pounced on the mare. It was Jackson's first sighting of the female liger. He saw the giant maneless head and huge body and uttered, "Christ Almighty!"

Kali clamped her jaws on the mare's foreleg where the humerus attaches to the shoulder. She ripped away twenty pounds of horsemeat. She slowly looked around, and then tore off a smaller piece of horsemeat and ate it. Her hunger had overwhelmed her caution.

Katy reclaimed the binoculars and located the giant cat. It was her first sighting of the liger as well. Katy's pulse raced.

After a second, she said, "She'll settle in to feed for a while. If we get the wind in our face, I might get close enough to dart her."

"How close is close enough?" Jackson asked.

"Under a hundred yards, but the closer the better. Kali's a big cat. The dosage could be tricky."

Katy strapped the dart rifle across her back and picked up the .375. She waited for Jackson to gear up, and then without speaking, they set off. Although he was not a skilled hunter, Jackson still realized that Katy possessed a set of trail skills unlike anything he had seen before. Not a twig snapped or a dry leaf crackled when she walked.

When they were a hundred and fifty yards out, Katy ceased even whispering and resorted to hand signals. In this way she told Jackson to stop and sit. He quietly lowered to the ground. She sat beside him, their thighs touching, placed her lips against his ear, and whispered instructions. Her warm breath caressed his skin and made his groin ache.

Katy noticed that Jackson was distracted, and she waited until he nodded yes. Then she handed him the .375 and checked the load in the dart rifle. Satisfied, she pocketed a second dart, nodded to indicate it was time to go, secured the .375 to her back, cradled the dart rifle with both hands, and crawled forward on her elbows and knees. Jackson followed her.

For twenty minutes they crept toward the red cedars on the knoll. When they arrived, Katy unharnessed the .375 and gave it to Jackson. He already had set his M4 aside. She shouldered the dart rifle now and calibrated the scope.

Kali suddenly lifted her head and licked her bloody muzzle. The liger looked straight at Jackson and Katy and held the look for a long time. Then suddenly whipping her head around, Kali sprang to her feet. Katy's finger was on the trigger housing when Jackson tapped her and pointed toward two female lions bolting from the brush.

In the lion kingdom females do most of the hunting, although males help with large prey, but the main role of the male, other than to procreate, is to protect the pride. The male learns to fight, while the female learns to hunt for food. Even so, the female lions charged Kali. Most prey will flee upon seeing a lion's flash of teeth, the low tail, and the fast charge. Not Kali. She dropped the horsemeat she was eating and sprinted toward her attackers.

The three large cats met up ninety feet from the horse. It seemed to Jackson that they would crash into one another, but at the last second the two lionesses veered off and attacked Kali from the side.

Lions mostly kill smaller prey by slapping them or hooking them with their claws and then biting the back of the neck or throat. Sometimes a lion will place its mouth over the animal to suffocate it. Larger prey is pulled down. The lion either punctures the throat or strangles the animal, although the kill often requires a group effort.

Since the two female lions lacked the power to pull down Kali, they attacked her neck. A lion's canine teeth are shorter and his bite less powerful than Kali's, but a single bite from either lioness still could be fatal. While Kali fended off one attack, the other lioness managed to sink her front canines into Kali's throat. Fortunately for Kali, the greatest bite pressure is in back near the jaw, and the bite didn't kill her. Before the lioness could bite again, Kali ripped off part of the attacker's left ear. In doing so she also left herself vulnerable.

The second lioness swiped at Kali's face, her sharp claws extended. A lion paw moves as fast as eighteen feet per second, and Kali's large head was an easy target. Had Kali not twitched, the lion's claws could have torn off her nose instead of merely shredding her face.

Kali nipped the leg of the new attacker and drove the lioness back six feet. She then shook off the one-eared lioness as the injured cat tried to jump on her back. Kali forced her to retreat as well. The three animals stood eye-to-eye like boxers psyching out their opponent. All three emitted a deep guttural sound. Blood dripped from Kali's muzzle; she wiped it with her tongue. The two lionesses sensed that Kali was weakening and charged her. There was a tangled blur of cats rolling and biting and snarling and clawing and springing up.

"Shouldn't we do something?" Jackson asked as they watched from afar.

"If I dart Kali now, the lions will kill her."

"And if you don't –"

"They may kill her anyway," Katy said.

"Or maybe they'll kill each other," Jackson said.

Katy shook her head, rejecting the idea. "I can't risk that." A second later, she said, "We can do it, but we'll have to work together. And it'll happen fast, with no margin for error. Okay? So when I say I'm ready, you shoot the two lions while I dart Kali. Don't hesitate. Shoot one, then the other. Got it?" She paused and studied Jackson. He seemed calm. "Can you hit them from here?"

"Guess we're about to find out," Jackson said.

Before Jackson could raise the .375, Kali grabbed a lioness by her throat and bit deeply, shaking the five-hundred-pound cat like she was a ragdoll. While Kali was killing the one lioness, the second cat clamped her teeth onto Kali's rear leg. Legs are vulnerable. Sever a tendon and the liger could not escape or defend herself. Kali released the dead lioness as her injured leg buckled.

"She's down," Katy said. "Hurry!"

Jackson had the remaining lioness in his crosshairs and told Katy he was ready. As she was counting down from three, they heard a roar off to their left. They both looked up to see a large male lion and a much smaller adolescent racing toward Kali in a second attack.

"Give me the rifle," Katy shouted.

Instead, Jackson swiveled the .375 away from the lioness and toward the new attackers. The big-game rifle roared and bucked. The male's front legs folded. His shaggy head hit the ground a second before the rest of his body. The shot sent the adolescent lion sprinting for cover. Jackson swiveled the rifle back toward the lioness, but she was gone already, and Kali was limping away too.

Katy swung up the dart rifle and, seemingly without taking aim, fired. Kali flinched and kept moving.

Jackson drew a bead on the liger. "Got her." As he fired, Katy smacked the gun barrel. The shot sailed high, and Kali disappeared. "What the hell are you doing?"

"What I came out here to do," Katy said. "Save her."

"The deal is we stop her, one way or another."

"You kill her and I lose her and the cubs."

"Christ, Katy! You don't even know there are cubs."

"You're wrong. I do know. I've seen them, one of them anyway. I found a dead cub out on your prairie. But if you shoot Kali, I'll never find any others."

"You found a liger cub by my house? When?"

Katy confessed to finding the female cub in the tall rye grass. She also told Jackson about finding the liger track by the corral. He was furious at her secrecy. But even as Jackson chastised her, he remembered how Stan had learned about the liger cubs. It was him; he had caused it. Jackson stopped yelling and silently walked away.

Five minutes later he returned and told Katy what he had said to Stilts and how his words made their way to Stan Ely. "But that still doesn't mean I forgive you."

"And I don't expect you to."

"Oh, damnit to hell anyway." He gestured toward the dead lions and Boots. "Let's just deal with all this." Jackson started toward the animals.

"Wait," Katy said. She hurried to catch up with him. "We want to come at the lions from the rear," she told Jackson as they neared the large male. Once they did she shot the cat in the heart. "In Africa they say, 'It's the dead ones that get up and kill you.' " She then walked over to the female lion that Kali had killed and shot her too.

Certain the lions were dead, Jackson left them and went to look at his bay mare. She had four white stockings that accounted for her name. The sight turned his stomach.

While Jackson mourned the loss of his horse, Katy examined the creek bed. It was mostly sand and gravel, but it was dotted with rocks that had been rounded by water and wind until they looked like the eggs of some prehistoric animal. Katy located the spent dart, climbed down the three feet high bank, and reclaimed it. The tip of the dart was not broken or bent and the chamber was empty.

"The dose was too weak or the drug was bad," Katy said. Jackson didn't respond, and she called out to him.

"I can't leave these animals out here like this."

"We'll bury them," Katy said.

Jackson shook his head. "Wolves or mountain lions or coyotes, they'll dig them up." Jackson stared off into the distance toward Colorado. "I'll have to burn them."

THIRTY-FIVE

Jackson and Katy hiked to the house, loaded an old tractor with the supplies they would need, and returned to the gully on the John Deere. They used a logging chain to bind Boots' legs like a bulldogged rodeo steer and then used the tractor to drag the horse into the gully. After that, they dragged the two lions to the edge and rolled them down the shallow bank next to Boots.

With the wind light and the creek bed wide, there was little chance of a fire spreading, but they cleared the dry grass and brush growing along the top anyway. When they finished, Jackson walked back to the tractor, and Katy climbed into the gully with a gas can. He had asked Katy to handle the burning, telling her that the fumes made him ill. With his back to the gully, he watched darkness douse the daylight while she doused the animals with gasoline.

Katy finished and climbed out again and stood on the edge of the bank while she lit a road-flair and tossed it on the animals. The flair landed, and there was a WHOOSH. Even from where he stood, Jackson felt the burst of heat. "Thanks," he said solemnly when Katy reached him a minute later. He was ashamed that he had not done the job himself and trying to justify it wouldn't change the shame.

They stood in silence for a minute before Katy said, "Remember telling me you had somebody research me?" It wasn't a question meant for an answer, so she didn't wait for one. "I did the same thing. I know about Colorado."

Jackson didn't say anything.

Katy said, "The Internet says –"

"I know." He turned to look at her.

"I understand."

"Do you?" Jackson touched the scar on his neck. It not only itched, it burned. "Do you understand that I was a real supercop back then? That I made detective faster than anybody on the Fort Collins police force ever had? Or that in a small city a detective does whatever comes across his desk, including the takedown of a meth-cooking house?

"None of the stories tell what it was really like that day - how we stormed the house, seven of us wearing body armor and heavily armed, even though we didn't expect trouble. Nobody told about how fast your heart beats when you ram through the door and rush in shouting. Busts are really more about shock and awe than shootouts. Except this time there were two guys inside, and one of them did shoot at us. Then all hell broke loose."

Jackson flinched as the fat behind them popped and sizzled. Then he said, "We took cover and returned fire. Then the house started burning. I don't know why. But there was smoke everywhere, and we couldn't see, and we were pinned down.

We're worried the house will blow. Methamphetamine cooking is highly explosive. So we got the order to lay down a barrage - handguns, shotguns, tactical rifles. We killed one man and wounded the other. We dragged them out and called an ambulance, but the wounded guy kept babbling about his little girl inside. By then the old wood house was ready to collapse. We can't wait for help, so I went back. He told me her name was Nancy Larsen. I called and called for her, and finally, I heard something – a moan, a cry. I found the girl and carried her out. She'd been shot in the neck. I had her in my arms when she died."

"Sounds to me like you're a hero."

"She'd been hit by a stray," Jackson said. "The bullet came from my gun. She was seven years old."

"Oh god," Katy said. "I'm … I'm so sorry."

They remained with the burning carcasses for another two hours without mentioning Colorado again. When the fire was out they buried the bones. Then they returned to the farmhouse on the tractor.

They entered without talking and went into the kitchen. Each of them got something to drink. There was awkwardness and wariness between them now. The silence built until it was more uncomfortable than words could be.

"Look, I know what I did was wrong," Katy said.

"You put my daughter at risk," Jackson blurted.

"I know."

"I won't let anybody endanger Jesse."

"You shouldn't. And my being here did that." Katy started toward the stairs. "I'll go pack. I'll leave."

"No!" Jackson said. He crossed the distance between them in a few strides. He grabbed her and kissed her hard. For a second Katy resisted, and then she responded. When Jackson's cell phone rang, he ignored it. He ignored his home phone when it rang too. The kisses didn't stop until they heard Major Jessup's voice leave an urgent message.

Jackson took ten minutes to shower and change clothes, and then he jumped in the Jeep and drove south. An hour later he found Major Jessup at the McDonald's on Valley River Drive in Rexburg. Jessup was eating a cone of fries. "My weakness," he said as Jackson slid into the booth opposite him. "Forget about their burgers, but Mickey D fries, um-uh."

"I have no jurisdiction here," Jackson said.

Jessup ate the last fry. "Then don't shoot anyone."

They left Jackson's car at the fast food joint and rode together in Jessup's Lexus ES. Twenty minutes later, Jessup turned onto a street of ranch houses and bungalows.

The house they approached on foot had pale yellow aluminum siding and a small front yard. Jessup covered the front while Jackson hurried around to the rear. As soon as they were in place, he heard Jessup bang on the door and identify himself as the State Police. Then Jackson heard a small dog yapping inside the house. After that he heard someone running. Then the back door crashed opened. A woman spilled out, pulling a little boy behind her. The boy was carrying a dog.

When Rene's ex-sister-in-law saw Jackson she screamed. The dog continued to bark. The only one quiet was Eric.

"Back here," Jackson yelled to Major Jessup.

Seconds later, Jessup handcuffed Sue Dodd, placed her under arrest, and read her rights to her. Jackson squatted to Eric's height and petted the chiweenie he cradled.

"Is this Panchutz?" Jackson asked.

The boy nodded.

"And I bet you're Eric?"

Eric nodded again. "I was on TV."

"I know. I saw your picture."

"I'm playing hide-and-seek with my mom and dad."

"Well, son, I think you just won," Jackson told him.

Eric Stutz was placed in the care of state social service until his maternal grandmother could arrive from Arizona the following morning. Once the boy was safe and secure for the night, Jackson headed back to Buckhorn. He made two phone calls as he was leaving Rexburg.

The town had a rowdy, Saturday night buzz on when Jackson arrived. After one circle of the downtown square, he had seen enough alcohol and motor vehicle violations to keep him busy for an hour, and that was only if he ignored the couple having sex in a car parked behind The Bar-J. He ignored them all and continued on to the police station.

Brian Patterson and reserve officer Bobby Grunfield were on duty until 2 P.M. when Skip took over. Jackson left Grunfield at the station and took Brian with him. When they reached the Green State Park campground, Sheriff Midden and four deputies were already there. They wore body armor and carried shotguns and tactical rifles.

"We expecting trouble, Chief?" Brian asked.

"No," Jackson said, "just television."

As Jackson and Brian suited up, Karen Cormac and her news-crew arrived. Midden spat tobacco juice. "Hell, Jackson, didn't know you had media savvy in you."

Sheriff Midden and his deputies took the lead while Jackson and Brian covered the rear. Midden pounded on the camper door. The second it opened, all seven officers stormed inside. Five minutes later they brought out Rodney and Rene Stutz in handcuffs. Midden did not cover their heads or let them avoid the TV lights and camera.

Eric's parents were taken to the St. Anthony jail where they were booked and interviewed. They admitted to running a scam as a way of gaining notoriety and money, but Rodney denied being involved with the Knights of the Golden Circle. Sue Dodd, Rodney's sister-in-law, had already told them that the militia group was the mastermind. When Rodney and Rene learned of this, they asked for a lawyer.

Afterward, Midden, Jackson, and Bud Spiegel, the county prosecutor, faced the media outside the Fremont County Sheriff Department. Midden announced the safe return of Eric and the arrest of his parents. It was a good story for everyone, but only Karen Cormac got a scoop.

It was eleven o'clock when Jackson got away and returned home. Katy's bedroom light was on, but Jackson didn't bother her. He knew what would happen if he did. He didn't think it was a good idea to let it happen tonight or maybe any night despite what his heart told him.

He climbed the stairs to his bedroom and started to drop into the raggedy easy chair when he noticed his blue suit draped over the back of it. Instead of hanging it up, he left it there and plopped down in the chair anyway.

So much had happened in one day that his head was spinning just thinking about it all: Tucker was maimed, a tiger was killed and gutted, Pamela Yow was arrested and then set free, his hunch about Colorado had paid off thanks to Gary Peterson, the FBI had come calling, Eric Stutz had been found, he had shot his first and only lion, Katy had almost captured Kali, animals had been burned down to the bone, Rodney and Rene had been arrested and charged with a smorgasbord of crimes, Katy had confessed to lying to him about Kali, by omission if not by commission, he had let shame overpower him, and then he had kissed Katy and –

He fell asleep sitting in the chair. When he awakened, it was after one o'clock. He went to bed.

THIRTY-SIX

On Sunday morning Jackson awoke at dawn. The house was quiet. He looked out and saw the Ford parked below next to his Jeep. Then he looked down the hall and saw Katy's bedroom door open. His first thought was that she had left. His breath caught in his throat until he peeked in the room and saw that her clothes and luggage were there. Wherever she was, she was on foot and would return.

He did not know that Katy had left at first light to return to the dry creek bed. Nor did he know that while he made coffee and a sandwich of fried eggs and ham, Katy was following the liger's trail from the gully back toward the farmhouse. The trail was easy for Katy to follow; Kali was dragging her injured rear leg.

Jackson ate his breakfast while driving to the Rexburg hospital. Tucker's wife and Eileen Stevens were there. He did not talk to Tucker about the incident until the two women left to get coffee. Tucker was drugged, but he assured Jackson that he understood well enough. Even if Tucker still had two arms, his days as a cop were over. Jackson told him that. Once Tucker improved, Jackson intended to grill him about the Knights of the Golden Circle. He let Tucker know that too. "I'm sorry this is the way it has to be," he added.

By the time Jackson returned to Buckhorn, Katy had reached the Indian mounds north of his house. She easily found the old root cellar burrowed in the earth. She got a flashlight from the house, fought off a sense of unease, and entered the cellar. She carried the .375 but not the dart rifle. She couldn't risk using darts in a confined space. She didn't want to kill Kali, but she would if she had to. Katy hoped to at least save any cubs she found.

The old cellar was empty. Based on the scat and hairs she examined, Katy guessed at least two and maybe three cubs had been there with Kali. "So where did you go?" she said aloud as she stepped out into the light again.

Kali's wounds from the two recent attacks, first by wolves and then by lions, were plentiful and limited her ability to defend her cubs and herself from further attacks, especially in close confines. So despite her injuries, long before dawn broke, Kali moved her cubs.

In Africa the territory of a lion pride ranges to forty miles or more, while the distance between the root cellar and the Placett barn was less than a mile through fields and woodlands. With Kali carrying the cubs one-by-one in her mouth, it still took her two hours to move them. Kali then explored all the buildings from the outside, and some from the inside as well. She found no predators and no danger. She found only food and safety.

*   *   *

Cindy Phelps rousted her son, Buzz, out of bed at 7 A.M. Sunday morning and told him to go to the Placett farm to feed the chickens. Mandy and her children were visiting Mandy's sister in northern Utah. Buzz's mom believed it was their Christian duty to help the family despite the dangerous wild cats. Cindy prayed about the dilemma, and God had assured her that Buzz would be safe. Still, Cindy instructed him on exactly what to do and where to go.

By the time Buzz reached the farm, the dozen chickens he was to feed had been reduced to feathers, beaks, and feet. The wire coop looked like it had been bulldozed.

Buzz texted Missy that something had killed and eaten the chickens. Then he headed home to tell his mom. As he was driving off he spotted Kali, although Buzz did not know her name, crossing a barley field. The shorn field had a dilapidated log cabin in the middle of it. Wade had planned to tear the ruin down until Mandy intervened. "People's hopes and dreams went into building it," she said upon visiting the log shell for the first time. "We owe it to them to let it be." Wade let it be.

Buzz didn't mention seeing the liger until after church. Once he told Missy, she phoned Jesse, who called Shane, who contacted some football buddies. The message that Buzz had seen the monster cat, worth twenty-five thousand dollars, was passed around until ten teenagers gathered outside Buckhorn High School at one o'clock.

The teens brought an odd and mostly inappropriate assortment of weapons. Shane commandeered his father's .375, for Dell was with Iris that day, and Shane knew the combination to his dad's gun case. Will Ohly had a Remington

.30-30 but only two cartridges. Piper Bowersill added a 20-guage Rossi. The other guns ranged from a .22 to a .45 Colt pistol to a flare gun.

"Nobody's going to shoot anything anyway," Jesse said.

"She's right, twenty-five if alive," Shane echoed.

After Randy Foyle arrived with some beer, two trucks, an old SUV, and a car set off for the Placett farm. For thirty minutes the teens scoured the road, the yard, and barn area, but they failed to see a liger, big or small. Jesse was relieved, and when she suggested that they quit and return home, nobody argued much. That would have been the end of the foolish adventure had Shane not encountered a large lion with a red mane crossing the road in front the field where the old cabin stood.

Startled, the lion sprinted off, jumped a fence, and crashed through the barley stubble. Although the grain had been harvested, the straw had not been cut and bailed, so the field was covered with dry, golden stalks. Everyone was so shocked to see the big animal that by the time the first gun appeared, the red-haired lion had disappeared.

"That's not the liger," Jesse said.

"So? It's still a lion," Buzz said. "And it's huge."

"I bet it killed somebody already," Missy said.

"And now we're going to kill it," Shane announced.

The teens argued about what to do next. In the end they left the SUV and the car parked on the road and piled into the two pickups. They opened a gate and drove across the field looking for the lion.

The trucks drove back and forth, ruining much of the barley straw, but they did not see the lion again. When the trucks stopped side-by-side near the cabin, Shane pumped two shots into the logs. The shots caused the lion to move around enough that they knew he was hiding there.

Though no one later would admit to suggesting it, they began to empty beer bottles and refill them with gasoline from a five-gallon can. Then they flung the bottles at the dry logs. Most of the bottles hit and burst. Not everyone liked the plan to burn the cabin, especially Jesse.

"It's stupid and dangerous," she said.

One or two others backed Jesse. Even so, Piper Bowersill fired off the flare gun to ignite the gasoline. The flare fizzled out and died short. The boys, for it was mostly boys wanting to torch the cabin, disagreed about what to do next until Shane volunteered to get close enough to toss a match. After the liger hunt fiasco with his dad, Shane wanted to show his bravery.

"Stop showing off," Jesse told him.

"You didn't mind it when I saved your ass."

"Which is why you don't have to prove anything to these guys."

While Jesse and Shane argued, Brett Cowel made a Molotov Cocktail. He had learned how to do it on Google.

Brett finished the bomb as someone shot into the cabin. The lion bolted. Maybe he was trying to flee, although the teens later insisted the lion attacked them. Piper quickly lit the rag fuse, and Brett threw the bottle at the charging lion. His skin was spotted with gasoline from the earlier shattered bottles. When the bottle hit him there was a WHOOSH as the lion burst into flame. He ran in circles, then rolled in the dry barley stalks, and then got up and ran around more. The field caught on fire.

Some of the teens laughed and some were now quiet. Brigit Buhler started crying. Shane simply watched. Jesse ripped the

Weatherby from his hands and shot at the lion. She missed. Shane took the big-game rifle from her and shot the tormented lion three times. Others shot the cat as well. After that, they put out the grass fire, although they left the lion carcass smoldering.

The caravan was speeding back to town when they met Mandy's silver Chrysler minivan on the county blacktop. Nobody had expected her back for days. Her return was bad news for them. Mandy would see the burned field and the lion and call the police to investigate.

Jesse, who had said nothing since the killing except, "Take me to my dad's," climbed out of the Toyota the second they arrived at the farm. She did not look at her friends and barely glanced at Shane. He called after her, but Jesse did not slow or turn back. She was done with him.

The red Ford 350 was there, but nobody was home. Jesse was relieved to be alone. She needed to figure out what to do. She knew she would be grounded when her dad and mom discovered what she had done at Mandy's. She knew if she were grounded, she couldn't train Touie. If she couldn't train Touie, she knew she couldn't race in the Tevis Cup. She had to fix things, so she decided to return to the field to bury the lion and camouflage the burned stubble.

Jesse then hurried to the barn and saddled Touie. She was tying a shovel to the equipment rings when she heard Katy say, "What're you doing?" Jesse yelped.

Katy's shirt was damp from sweat, and her khaki pants were smeared with dirt. She had spent all morning looking for signs of Kali and her cubs. She either found too many or none at all and finally had given up.

"It's too dangerous for you to go riding." Katy eyed the shovel. "Jesse? What's going on here?"

It took prompting from Katy, but eventually Jesse told her about the chicken coop, the lion, and the fire. Jesse cried the whole time.

Katy hugged her and murmured words of comfort, but even while she attended to Jesse, she phoned Jackson and said, "I know where Kali is."

THIRTY-SEVEN

"Tammy, come put your stuff away like I told you." Mandy was unpacking her own suitcase while she yelled at her daughter. Although the bag held a week's worth of clothing and toiletries, they only stayed two nights with Mandy's older sister. Soon after Cindy Phelps phoned to tell her about the chickens, Mandy started home. "Tammy Jane Placett! You hear me?" shouted Mandy.

"She's on the back porch, Mom," Josh said from the doorway of Mandy's upstairs bedroom. Unlike his sister, Josh already had unpacked.

"What's she doing out there?"

"Looking at the chicken coop."

"Again?" Mandy's expression was equal parts concern and anger.

"She's weird."

"Get her, Josh. Tell her to get her butt up here and unpack her suitcase or no pizza and movie tonight."

"Mom!" Josh stretched the word into two syllables. After a deep sigh, he went off in a huff.

Mandy smiled for the first time in days. Josh was a miniature version of Wade, despite what Wade had thought.

"Mom wants you," Josh told his younger sister a minute later. He found her with her nose pressed against a windowpane staring at the ruined chicken coop.

Tammy didn't budge. "You think it hurts?"

"What hurts?"

"To get eaten," said Tammy.

Although Katy spent ten minutes arguing with Jesse before she left, she still got to the Placett farm before Jackson. In the end Katy had decided it was safer to bring Jesse with her than to risk having her ride off on Touie. "Remember, you stay in the house," Katy said as she shut off the engine. Jesse's groan conveyed how much adults exasperated her, even a cool adult like Katy.

Katy got out and looked in every direction. Both her .375 and the dart rifle were within easy reach. When she saw nothing to alarm her, she motioned to Jesse.

Mandy's bedroom had windows on two sides, and when she heard knocking, she looked out and saw Jackson's red Ford. "Oh Lord." She had shed her wrinkled travel clothes and was in her underwear. She hurried away from the window, went to the doorway, and yelled, "Josh, answer the door. I'm not dressed." Someone knocked again. "Josh!"

Josh ran to the door, but Tammy remained glued to the window. A few second later, she saw the baby liger in the barn entrance, although she did not recognize the cat for what it was. "Kitty," she said. She turned around to tell her brother about the kitty. "Oh!" she said to the empty space. When she looked out the window again, the new kitty was gone. Tammy opened the door, jumped from step to step, and ran toward the barn, calling, "Kitty, here kitty."

Minutes later, Jackson parked beside his pickup, removed his M4, and slammed in the clip. He then laid the tactical rifle across the back seat and locked the Jeep.

Katy, Jesse, and Mandy were in the living room when Jackson tapped on the door, called "hello", and then entered. The others were seated, but Mandy was pacing. "Is it true, Jackson? The monster cat's back here again?"

"Probably" Jackson said, while looking at Jesse.

Jesse met her father's eyes. "Daddy, I know I –"

"Not now, Jesse. We'll talk later." Jackson's voice was flat. "Right now, I need to -" Jackson stopped when he heard the loud slap of sneakers against linoleum.

"Mom! Mom!" Josh ran into the living room and grabbed Mandy by the hand. He pulled her in the direction of the back porch. "I can't find her. Tammy's gone."

Mandy shook her son loose and dashed to the back of the house. When Josh started to follow, Jackson grabbed him and said, "Stay here with Jesse." Katy already had sprinted after Mandy. Jackson looked back at his daughter as he too ran out of the room.

As Jackson banged through the back screen door, he could hear Josh crying and Jesse trying to comfort the boy. Jackson jumped the steps and hit the ground running. Fifty feet ahead, Katy had caught up with Mandy. She was trying to hold onto her, but Mandy was struggling.

Jackson called out, "Mandy, wait." Then they heard Tammy scream. Mandy went berserk. She punched Katy on the side of the head, broke free, and scrambled toward the barn. "Get the rifles," Jackson yelled to a stunned Katy as he ran past her. He didn't need to tell her to hurry.

Jackson finally grabbed Mandy a few feet from the barn door and wrapped her in a bear hug. She kicked and screamed and clawed at his arms. "Let me go! Let me go! Damn you, let me go!"

Her nails were not long but when Mandy raked them down Jackson's cheek, she drew blood. He flung her away and sent her sprawling to the ground. Jackson thought about handcuffing her. But he instead removed his Glock pistol and rushed into the barn. "Stay back, Mandy," he yelled as he ran. "Goddamnit! Stay back!" He knew his handgun would be next to useless when confronting a lion or tiger, let alone a giant liger, but he could not wait for Katy.

"Tammy," Jackson yelled from the doorway. The interior of the barn was dark and shadowy even in daylight. He didn't see Tammy or the liger. Then he located the light switch, flicked it on, and saw them.

Kali had Tammy's right leg in her mouth and was dragging her away. The girl's arms trailed limply. Her body bounced against the ground like she was a rag doll.

Mandy screamed, and Jackson knew she was right behind him. "Stay back!" he shouted, but even as he said it, he knew Mandy wouldn't listen. He spun around, grabbed her arm, dragged her to the doorway, and shoved her outside. He closed the barn door and used a two-by-four to bar it.

The liger had not moved much in the seconds he was away. In fact, Kali didn't seem to be in a hurry. Jackson had no way of knowing yet if the girl was dead or alive. Oh Christ Almighty!Not again, he thought. Not again!

"Let me in!" Mandy cried as she pounded on the door. "Let me in you sonofabitch." She kept pounding the door.

Jackson raised the Glock. What if he hit Nancy? Did he just call her Nancy? He meant Tammy. Of course he did.

"Oh God, oh God. Please God, save her!" Mandy cried. She said it over and over, and as she did, the pounding got weaker and her tears and her wails stronger. "Please save her…"

Jackson squeezed the trigger. The Glock 21 sounded like a bark as it echoed through the barn. As Jackson walked toward Kali, he fired again and again. The shots from the handgun didn't bring down the liger, but Jackson now saw that Kali was limping. He also saw dried blood on her and a nasty face wound that still was oozing. Jackson stopped, used the two-handed stance taught to police, and shot the liger in the lower neck.

Kali finally released Tammy and turned her full attention to Jackson. There was blood on Tammy's leg, but Jackson could not tell if the blood came from the liger's teeth clamping her leg firm enough to hold her or if the blood meant something worse. Kali roared and flashed her teeth. Jackson knew the charge was coming.

How many bullets were left, and where was Katy? Then he remembered; he had locked her out. It was just him now, and he had a good idea of how things would end. Well, if he was going to die, he thought, he would die saving the girl. He would save Tammy. This time he'd get it right. Jackson opened his arms wide and motioned to Kali to come for him.

"Come on! Come on!" he said.

As Kali began to lope toward him, Jackson heard a loud crash. The wooden barn door splintered. He also heard the sound that sheetmetal makes when it crunches. Jackson glanced away long enough to see the nose of his red Ford punch through the barn door. Just as quickly as he had looked away, he looked back. Kali was coming faster now. The Glock spit bullets, but they didn't slow the liger. Kali covered the distance in seconds and leaped. She extended her claws, flashed her teeth, and growled.

Jackson tucked his head into the curl of his arms a second before Kali hit him. He flew backward ten feet before he slammed against the floor. The last thing he heard before all the breath left his body and he blacked out was the sharp explosion of a big-game rifle.

Katy stood in the doorwell of the Ford, the .375 resting against the frame. Her first shot took out a long incisor and pierced Kali's throat. Her second shot destroyed Kali's lungs. Even that didn't stop the liger. As she wheezed for breath, Kali crawled toward Jackson. Kali had nine bullets in her - Jackson had missed a few shots, but she still was intent on protecting her cubs from the predators. Katy fired again. When Kali finally collapsed, Katy climbed down from the pickup, cautiously approached her, and placed the rifle barrel against the liger she had tried to save and blew her heart to pieces.

Nobody would ever know why Kali did not kill Tammy right off. Perhaps the small girl was not viewed as a threat by the giant cat. Nobody would ever know.

In fact, Tammy was not seriously injured, although she would have tiny scars on her leg from the liger's teeth. When she was told about this, Tammy replied, "Cool."

Jackson had a numerous cuts and bruises, two busted ribs, nail marks on one cheek, and claw marks on the other. The claw marks made by Kali required thirty-four stitches from the doctor at the medical center in Buckhorn.

Before long, Jackson's face was half numb, and he was high on some drug that made him feel far better than he had a right to feel. Iris and Jesse came to see him as soon as the doctor allowed it. He assured his daughter and his ex-wife that he would be fine and then fell asleep. It was left to Katy to tell Iris all that had happened.

Once Jackson was released, Katy drove him home in the Jeep. For a while they rode in silence, although Katy kept glancing over at Jackson. Suddenly, she gasped.

"What?"

"Did you notice anything different about Iris?"

Jackson slumped against the door. "She was nice?"

Katy grinned but said nothing more. At the farm Jackson changed into a t-shirt and sweatpants and went to bed. After he was asleep, Katy poured a glass of red wine and took it with her to the bathroom. Alone at last, she cried for Kali.

THIRTY-EIGHT

Jackson awakened to the sound of the bathtub draining. He got up and padded out to the hallway. The earlier pain medication had worn off. His body hurt in more places than he could have imagined. He had pain pills, but he hadn't taken them yet. The door to the bathroom was open. Steam billowed out like evening fog. The light was switched off.

He started into the bathroom as Katy stepped out. She was wrapped in a large white bath towel that barely covered the parts she intended to cover. She was carrying a glass of wine, still half-full.

Startled by Jackson, she jumped back, causing her towel to slip, and when she tried to stop it from falling, she dropped the wine glass. Jackson stabbed at the glass and miraculously caught it, although the wine spilled out. The towel puddled at Katy's feet. She shrieked and grabbed it off the floor and covered her front. The white towel had soaked up wine, leaving behind a pink Rorschach test.

They stood in silence looking at each other, Katy hugging the towel against her body. "Katy," he said. Jackson said her name like it was the only word he knew. "Katy," he repeated.

She dropped the towel and walked into his arms. They kissed and pressed their bodies together. This time the kisses were softer but more urgent. This time Jackson felt the softness and warmth of her body, her skin pink and damp from the hot water. This time he knew that Katy felt his desire for her. She ran her hands up under his t-shirt and tugged it off him. Skin-to-skin from the waist up and pressed together, they tumbled into Jackson's bedroom.

When he was naked as well, they eased themselves onto the bed and explored each other's body like cartographers mapping a new land, and only then, after becoming familiar with the new smells and tastes, did Katy roll on top of Jackson and take him inside her. The furious pace of their lovemaking left them both limp and damp. Then they rested, and while they rested, Katy outlined her plan to Jackson. Then they made love again, this time slowly.

Jackson didn't remember falling asleep, but when he awakened, he was alone. Katy had left a note on his nightstand. He read it, and then he got up and put on the same t-shirt and sweatpants that he had discarded a couple of hours earlier. He went downstairs, gulped a glass of water, and swallowed a pain pill.

He returned to the bedroom and started to sit in the easy chair. His blue suit still was draped across the back. What has it been, he thought, two days? Three? He hung up the pants and then the coat. That's when he found Ed's letter. Christ! He had forgotten all about it.

He read the letter while sitting in the old chair and afterward read it a second time. Then he got dressed. He clipped the gun holster to his belt, loaded the Glock 21, and went outside. His wrecked Ford pickup was gone. Angie and Brian must have dropped it off while he and Katy were making love, he thought. The pickup would need extensive bodywork. He hoped it was safe for Katy to drive. He got into the black Jeep Grand Cherokee and drove to town.

"Jackson," Dell said, surprised to find him at his door. Dell had a highball glass in his hand. He was dressed as though he had recently come from a nice dinner.

"We need to talk," Jackson said.

"Well, sure. How are you? Come on in, come in. Iris told me what happened out at the Placett farm. My god!"

"Jackson, is that you?" Iris said. She walked into view. "What are you doing out of bed?"

Jackson looked at her. Something different? He didn't see it if there was. "I have to talk to Dell."

"Tonight?" she asked. "Kind of late, isn't it?"

"Yes, tonight." His body felt better, but he tried not to move suddenly. His head was clear enough so far.

"Then I'll leave the two of you alone." Iris took three steps away before she said to Jackson, "But you can congratulate me first if you'd like to." She held up her left hand and flashed her engagement ring.

For the longest time Jackson was speechless. The silence began to weigh on everyone until he laughed and then congratulated Iris and Dell. Ten minutes later, after a celebratory drink, Iris left them alone to talk.

"Freshen up your drink?" Dell asked.

Jackson had barely sipped the Black Bush in his glass. He shook his head no. "Pain pills."

Dell was seated on the couch. Jackson sat in one of the leather club chairs. He removed Ed's letter from his jacket and laid in on the coffee table between them.

"What's this?" Dell asked.

"The truth, I think. You tell me."

As Dell read the letter, his expression changed a dozen times. "This doesn't prove anything."

"Not in court. In public, at election time, with your brother running for governor ...." Jackson shrugged.

"Sonofabitch!" Dell said. "Is this payback for Iris?"

"Iris?" Jackson laughed. "Dell, I'm happy about it." And he was too, for it meant the end of Jesse and Shane. Jesse had told him she was over Shane, but he knew what a teenage girl was done with on Friday, she would die for on Saturday. Iris marrying Dell made it permanent.

Dell scowled. "So what do you want then?"

"To know who's involved in this KGC group and who let all these cats loose and got so many people killed."

Dell forced a laugh. "And you think I know?"

Jackson crossed his arms and said nothing.

Dell got up, went to the wet bar, and refilled his glass with scotch. "Ed didn't have all his details right," Dell said. "But then Ed never did."

"Which detail is that? You didn't shoot your wife?"

"I did. Technically. It happened like the letter says. I was putting a new scope on my deer rifle, and she grabbed the gun during an argument. It shouldn't have been loaded. I never leave my guns loaded here in the house. I imagine Shane and his friends got into my gun case and one of them loaded it playing around. I didn't know for sure, probably didn't want to know." Dell sipped his drink. "Anyway, neither Ed nor I wanted to lay that guilt on a ten-year-old. It was a horrible, unbelievable accident."

Jackson didn't say anything.

"Suppose I do know something?" Dell asked. "What happens then?"

"Depends. Depends on whether you point me to someone I can arrest. Tucker and Ronnie and this KGC group, I already know about. What I don't know is who let the lions and tigers out and why?"

"I wasn't there," Dell said. He drifted back to Jackson and sat on the couch again. "But Fred would be my guess. Bulcher's a hothead. Always has been. And he was really pissed at Ted. I figured it was because their sand and gravel deal went sour but maybe not."

"Like maybe he didn't want Ted talking to the Feds."

Dell arched his eyebrows and sipped his drink.

Jackson picked up the letter. "Somebody shot at me. They used a gun like the one you own, that elephant gun."

"I have no reason to shoot at you."

"Know anybody else with a gun like that?"

Dell shook his head. He didn't mention his brother, although Dan had a matching elephant rifle.

"Somebody's going down, Dell," Jackson said. "You want it to be you, that's fine with me." He stood.

"Now just hold on a second!" Dell waited until Jackson sat again. "Fred borrowed my Mark Five, okay. He said it was for a friend of his. Two, three days later, he brought it back. It'd been fired. He cleaned it, but I could tell. I knew it'd been fired."

"So it's all on Fred; that's your story?"

"You asked what I think, and I'm telling you."

"Why'd Fred or his friend shoot at me?" Jackson asked.

"You might be surprised, Jackson, but some people around here consider you a big pain-in-the-ass."

"So was somebody trying to scare me or kill me?"

"I don't know." Dell chuckled. "But if I wanted to kill you, you'd be dead. I don't miss what I shoot at." Jackson didn't say anything else, and Dell nodded toward the letter. "So what are you going to do?"

"With Ed's letter? I haven't decided yet."

"That detail that Ed has wrong," Dell said, "it involves the Knights of the Golden Circle."

Jackson nodded. His head was fuzzy. "I'm listening."

"It wasn't me that was involved with them. It was my brother. Tilda found out that Dan was part of the KGC militia and threw a fit. Her father was bankrolling Dan's political career back then. It was Dan we were arguing about. Tilda wanted to expose him. But he's my brother."

"Christ!" Jackson said. "He's going to be Governor."

"Yes, he is. And he left that group six years ago."

Jackson stared at Dell for a long time. Then he tore up the letter, dropped it on the floor, and left.

When Jackson got home Katy met him at the door. She kissed him. "What're you doing up and about?"

"Looking for answers."

"You find them?"

"Maybe," he said. Jackson wasn't convinced Dell was telling the truth. He doubted if he would ever know the whole truth.

Does anyone ever know the truth, he wondered? "How about you?" he asked Katy. "You locate the cubs?"

Katy's note had told him she was returning to the Placett farm to look for Kali's liger cubs. She pulled a check out of her jean pocket. It was made out to Mandy Placett for seventy-five thousand dollars.

"Wow!" Jackson said. "Where'd you get this?"

"I found two cubs in the barn. Feisty little cats. I don't know if I'd have caught them without Josh's help. Anyway, we got them in a portable cage and I took them to Stan. Two baby ligers, a male and a female, at twenty-five thousand each. I told him if for twenty-five more, I'd help him capture the remaining lions and tigers."

"You must be very persuasive," Jackson said.

Katy kissed him again. "I hope so."

Katy stayed for another three days, the time it took the hunters and Stan's rescue group to kill or capture the remaining lions and tigers. Katy shot one tiger and helped capture another, along with a pair of Barbary lions. A day after the last of the exotic cats was accounted for Jackson drove Katy to the Pocatello airport.

"I wish you'd stay longer," he told her. "I was just starting to get used to having you around."

Katy laughed. "Used to having me, you mean."

"That too."

"My god, you're blushing," Katy teased. She touched his cheek with her fingers. "I wish I could, but I really do have to get back to the ranch in Africa."

They both tried to hide the sadness they felt at saying goodbye. Neither of them did a good job of it.

"I have a surprise," Katy said when they reached the security station. It was as far as Jackson could accompany her. She gave him an envelope. When he opened it, he saw two tickets to Botswana. "They're booked for Christmas, while Jesse's on school break," Katy explained, "but they're changeable."

When Jackson saw the cost of them, his eyes widened.

Katy laughed. "The publisher paid for them, a bonus for signing a new book deal." Her new book deal to write about the Idaho Lion Hunt also meant that she could keep Skorokoro. Only now she wasn't sure that she wanted to.

EPILOGUE

Iris filed an injunction to keep the baby ligers from leaving Idaho. She argued that the two cubs, the only purebred ligers in the world, belonged to the heirs of Ted and Dolly Cheney. Since Ted had no heirs, it meant that Pamela Yow, Dolly's cousin, owned them. Stan was furious at her betrayal. Nevertheless, he had to leave the ligers in Buckhorn until the courts resolved the ownership.

The baby ligers were housed at Reynolds' Auction Barn while awaiting removal to their temporary home at the zoo in Pocatello. They were kept in cages that Stan and ARK provided. On the same Thursday night that Jackson took Katy to the airport, someone broke into the barn, opened the cages, and released the cubs. They were never found.

A year later an elk hunter from the tiny village of West Yellowstone, Idaho's lone gateway to the famed national park, claimed to have seen giant cats prowling the woods there. He described the cats as monsters.

CPSIA information can be obtained at www.ICGtesting.com
Printed in the USA
BVOW011003140213

313257BV00001B/6/P